For my parents

Tuona e fulmina il Ciel

The heavens are full of thunder and lightning

from
L'Estate, Summer
Le Quattro Stagioni, The Four Seasons

Il Cimento dell'Armonia e dell'Inventione
The Trial of Harmony & Invention
—Vivaldi

So, it's as if I never left. I can barely believe the summer storms we've been having. They've been raging now for over a week. Mad stampeding night-time storms striding off the Irish Sea like Colossus – something weird is going on, unusual masses of air are colliding in the darkness. I came running out to the garden last night. I swear to God, in the middle of the night I blundered out in my nightdress to check on the stable and almost got blown away. I'd drifted into a troubled sleep but then bang, I was awake again and sitting bolt upright on the bed. Something had slammed against the house.

An anguished cry arose in the lull of the wind – a fox screaming? Was it the right time of year? The howl of a neighbour's dog? (Who could leave an animal out in this?) A screech of hinges and another crash – it was the door of the stable, swinging in the wind. I'd been so careful about locking it only a few hours earlier. Had the padlock split off? Had someone split it off? How did they know to look there? Someone was watching the house.

The torch and key were still on my dressing table. I grabbed them and rushed downstairs. I slotted my feet into the shoes by the door – why were my father's shoes set by the door? – and out I hurried. The shoes were as big as boats, and I clattered down the side path in a sort of stunted gallop, a child again in my father's house, though there were no storms like this when I was small. Wet leaves blew into my face, the lighthouse beam blinded me, the wind shrieked wildly in the telephone wires. I rounded the corner and stopped dead in surprise. The stable door was shut. The bolt was drawn across, the heavy steel padlock was in place. I ran up and gave the padlock a good rattle, but still I wasn't satisfied. I was positive I'd heard that door slam.

I undid the padlock and switched on the torch. The stable is stacked with manifestations of my father's eclectic mind. An astrolabe, antiquarian books, 1916 memorabilia, a creaky telescope. Rare coins, early cameras, taxidermied animals, the works. I swept the torch over things; nothing was missing, nothing had been touched. The stuffed animals were aghast at my intrusion – two visits in a twenty-four hour period? Something, they twigged, was up.

They stared down at me in silence; the stoat with its glassy eye, the fox with its bared teeth. I burst into tears. That was unexpected. I was not crying for my father, but for Daniel. It is easy to feel defeated at that hour of the night, particularly when the thin wet fabric clinging to your skin is turning cold. I stood there shuddering and shivering, monitored by the fixed eyes, dripping a circle of rain onto the floor. That's when it sunk in about the shoes. The shoes on my feet were new. My father has been gone these past eight years. He has no need of new shoes. This pair belonged to another man.

Something scuttled across the corrugated roof and I froze: I was not alone. I'd been pursued all the way across the Atlantic. I ran out of the stable and bolted the door up, rammed the padlock on. Dashed back through the storm and blockaded myself into the house, leaving the new shoes exactly as I'd found them. I sat tight on my bed until dawn.

The shoes were gone when I woke again at noon. That scared me even more. There has been no male presence in Sandpiper for years. There's just me, my mother, and a battalion of empty rooms. And yet there is clearly a male presence in Sandpiper once more; the whole place is resounding with it, the entire house is up in arms. I haven't encountered him yet, have only found traces, traces which are as quickly removed. I have chosen to say nothing to my mother for fear of alarming her. Two women alone in an old house are not safe, not with an intruder on the loose. Something is going on when my back is turned. Someone is up to no good.

Quest' è 'l verno, mà tal, che gioia apporte

This is winter, but such are the joys it brings

from
L'Inverno, Winter
Le Quattro Stagioni, The Four Seasons
—Vivaldi

In an Upper East Side neighbourhood marked by a preponderance of specialist dry-cleaners, after a full nineteen years of preparation with one outcome in mind, I made my concert debut as violin soloist. When we took our places on the waxed golden stage, the members of the month-old New Amsterdam Chamber Orchestra, we could have been in a cornfield in July. It did not matter that it was the first week of January, that ice had paralysed the city like snakebite. It was summer under the hot lights. We had effected a better season. Outside, there could have been murders in the snow. There could've been lung-choking fogs. There could have been wild dogs on the loose. We were immune to it. The New York winter couldn't touch us. It couldn't get past the cloakroom door, though it lurked in the folds of our coats for our return.

The dress rehearsal finished at five o'clock. I had been aware of the pinch in my guts since that morning but had ignored it, there being no time to do anything but ignore it. I went along to the pre-concert dinner and smiled through the thank you speeches delivered to mark the orchestra's inaugural night.

The pain intensified sometime around seven. At first I had dismissed it as nerves – my debut was looming after all. But at five minutes to eight, just before we were due onstage, it stabbed me so hard that I buckled. I slithered down the wall and placed my violin on the dressing-room floor. 'Valentina?'

She looked around and then down. 'Oh my God, Eva,' she exclaimed in her lovely precise English, and reached for my inhaler.

'V, it's not asthma.'

'I'll get Zach.'

'No, lock the door.'

7

She locked the door and hunkered down beside me. 'Oh Jesus, what's wrong? Are you okay?'

Someone knocked politely. 'Eva?' It was Zach.

'Don't answer,' I warned her. Another knife of pain and I clenched my teeth, the halogen lights suddenly blindingly sharp. Zach knocked again, loudly this time, his tension seeping under the door and infecting the room. I grabbed Valentina's wrist. 'Something's happening.'

'Can you stand up?'

I shook my head.

'Eva? You in there?' Zach cursed when the handle wouldn't yield to him. 'Why is this door locked?' His voice was now addressed to someone behind him. 'Where's Valentina? Jesus Christ, it's almost time.' He took off down the corridor.

'Valentina, I can't go out there.'

She blanched. 'Show me where it hurts.'

I showed her where the pain was. 'I think my appendix is about to burst or something.'

'That's not your appendix.'

Thump thump thump on the door. Zach was back. 'Open the fucking door, Eva, it's practically eight.'

The pain eased. I released Valentina's wrist and told her to let him in. She rearranged my skirts for modesty and unlocked the door.

'I can't go onstage,' I said when Zach blustered in, unwelcome as a wasp.

'What? Why not?'

'I'm sick.'

'You're not sick. It's stage fright. Get up.'

'She *is* sick,' Valentina insisted.

Konrad stuck his head into the room. 'Eight o'clock,' he reminded us, then spotted me in a heap on the floor. 'Superb.'

Zach shut the door on him and turned the key in the lock. 'I'm not cancelling the concert, so I don't care if you can't play, Eva, you fucking *have* to.'

Alarm was rising in the corridor like the water level in a

sinking ship. I waited for another wave of pain, but none came. Strange. As if it had been listening. As if it cared about me and said, Okay, I can wait, but not for too long, mind. I lifted my face. 'It seems to have stopped,' I said cautiously. Zach helped me to my feet before I could change my mind. 'Valentina, go organize the others.' She grabbed her violin and left. The ache was still there, but now the fear was more immediate. Fear conquered pain. Applause down the corridor as the others filed onstage. Zach put his hands on my shoulders and chanted words of encouragement. The usual stuff about my gift, his faith in me. He armed me with my violin and bow.

Panic surged as I stood in the darkness behind the stage door – a few seconds of my heart pumping so hard and so fast that I thought I might collapse. I watched the group onstage through the glass panel. Valentina sounded the clarion call, concert pitch A. The note swelled as each instrument joined it, then it died away. The audience coughed and settled. Zach pointed his baton at me.

'Don't leave me standing out there like a fuck, Eva.'

'I won't.'

'I mean it. Don't do that to me.'

'I won't.' He didn't look reassured. 'I won't,' I said again.

The door guy pulled the door back and Zach strode out. He gestured at the orchestra it had taken him three years of begging letters to found, and this newborn orchestra of his rose to its feet for a maiden bow. There was something marvellous about it.

Zach stepped onto the podium, took his bow, then turned my way.

'Go for it,' the door guy said.

The first drink after a performance goes straight to your head. I raised my glass to my lips, but my glass was empty. I didn't recall emptying it; not a problem. I held it out and Zach refilled it. We toasted ourselves. Though, apart from my dear friend Valentina, I barely knew the names of the members of this new orchestra, I loved them all. This was no overstatement. I felt a very real love for each and every one of them right then, and I believed that they loved me back. It was not a love characterized by its longevity – we'd be sick of one another again in an hour or so – but it was love nonetheless.

I knew, somewhere in the back of my head, that I was wheezing, but it didn't matter. Our reception mattered. The Board of Directors and their words of appreciation mattered. The crystal chandelier and ornate plasterwork mattered. It was important to make note of them and shore them up for later. During the long hours of solitary practice ahead, such memories would sustain me. We toasted ourselves once more.

I felt warm. In fact, I was a little hot, and then I was as quickly cold. I looked up at the domed glass ceiling and saw that it had begun snowing again. The snow collected at the apex and slid down the curved glass in segments. I shivered.

'Ms Tyne?'

'Yes?' I turned around, smiling. It was the theatre operations manager. The sight of him was disheartening; he had the manner of a funeral director. Although he'd known me on and off for several years now in various incarnations, all of them more humble than that of soloist, he always used a title when addressing me, and he always used it mournfully, as if it grieved him. Ms Tyne. It was an apology, a signal that something unpleasant was about to occur. How quickly the anticlimax had set in.

The room flickered. I glanced up at the chandelier in time to see a bulb fizzle and expire. The jaundiced light drained the colour out of things. The floor lurched and began to descend, as if we were in a huge elevator. I steadied myself against a chair.

'Ms Tyne?' the manager repeated, this time touching my arm. 'Are you sure you're feeling all right?' I shook my head. No, I wasn't at all sure. The pain in my gut was back.

'Could you please take this?' I handed him my glass. 'I'll be fine in a moment. I just need some air.'

I pushed through the room, excusing myself and apologizing. 'Ms Tyne, Ms Tyne,' the guests muttered in my wake, and some of them were saying 'Eva Tyne,' which was worse. I plunged through the double doors and hurried downstairs to the restroom, shutting myself into a cubicle. Over and over I vomited into the toilet, getting it on my hands, my hair, my dress.

The door to the restroom opened. Two women came in, no, three, discussing the performance. I retched again and the voices fell silent. 'Please,' I implored the partition, 'whoever is out there, can you find me Valentina, the concertmaster?'

'Someone's had a bit too much to drink,' commented one of the voices.

'I'm not drunk. Go back upstairs and get Valentina. Blonde hair, very pretty.' Not a sound out of them. 'Hurry,' I begged, and threw up again. The last of the champagne. Fizzy vomit.

There was a stupefied silence, then the doors clattered shut. I sat back against the cubicle wall in unbelievable pain. Blood. I moaned at the ceiling. I couldn't look at the blood, couldn't climb off the ground to escape it. The restroom doors opened again.

'Eva?' Valentina.

'Get me an ambulance.'

There was another blast of pain, and as I cried she ran out of the place. God bless my fleet handmaiden, my Monégasque angel – she did exactly as asked. Within minutes we were out on the side lane with the rats. The icy air against my bare skin was a shock, like being hurled overboard. I was bundled into the back of the ambulance that would take me the few blocks to the hospital.

The medics didn't shout at each other as I'd imagined they might. They were efficient, kind. Valentina stood by, the blue light of the ambulance flashing across her stricken features. She looked Edwardian in her black satin, she looked spectral. I didn't want to let go of her hand. 'Tell them I had a headache,' I said, and she nodded vigorously. Tears were streaming down her cheeks too. The worst of it was almost over, though I didn't know it then.

The stretcher was locked into place and we raced off. I was still wearing my red silk evening dress. I kept my eyes on the dress. It was important to concentrate on it, on how well it suited me, how pretty I felt in it. The stains on the silk, had the people upstairs glimpsed them, could easily have passed for splashes of champagne.

They discharged me from the hospital the next evening. I signed my name across their forms and pocketed their ziplock bag of painkillers. An uppercase command warned me not to mix them with alcohol. I wished I hadn't slept through the daylight hours.

Valentina had been by at some stage and dropped off a bag of stuff. A pair of her pyjamas, her jeans, a T-shirt and jumper – we took the same dress size. She must've swung by the concert hall en route, because my coat was hanging in the small hospital wardrobe, the New York winter still lurking in the folds of it. My bag and inhaler were on the nightstand. She'd tucked a fifty-dollar bill into my empty wallet. The red silk dress was gone.

I shivered along with the smokers beneath the hospital canopy and watched the traffic creep by, the taillights flowing along Madison Avenue like lava. The honey-roasted nuts guy was packing up his stall. The T-shirt and baseball-cap hawker had already left, which was too bad because Valentina hadn't brought me a hat. The wind was icy on the back of my head. It felt as if I'd a bald patch, a tonsure.

The neon thermometer across the street read 22°F. That city was always issuing its inhabitants with status reports. It liked to keep you informed of how it was getting on, to make you feel part of the whole thing, make you feel like a New Yorker. The success of the endeavour depended on participation. If you didn't feel part of it, you couldn't tolerate it anymore.

I was neither ready nor able to go home, not in that sorry state, and not with Kryštof still out of town. The prospect of unlocking the door to an empty apartment was too grim. The act of switching on the lights and pulling down the blinds would be too bleak. I simply couldn't face it right then.

The traffic was headed uptown, so I went with it. I didn't intend to do anything more than wander for a while. The idea, inasmuch as there was one, was not to go far, seeing as I was in such poor shape and wearing last night's heels. Last night's glittering heels with Valentina's pink socks sticking out through the open toes. She had forgotten to bring along boots.

I'd have strayed into a cinema, or a nice shop had I passed one – somewhere that sold hats would be good. But I didn't pass a cinema, or a nice shop, or anywhere that sold hats. I passed a Blimpie, a Western Union, a surgical supplies pharmacy, a six-foot heap of garbage sacks. I crossed the street and passed an empty schoolyard, a jammed parking lot, a podiatric clinic, a dental hygienist. Next block: a barbershop, an Irish bar, another Irish bar, and a sign saying NO LOITERING LITTERING STANDING RADIO PLAYING. Then I passed the hotel.

The Madera, it was called. I followed the three marble steps which went down instead of up. Not initially to check in. All I wanted was to sit in a place where I would meet no one, or more precisely, no one I knew. I could've chosen one of the Irish bars. You never meet Irish people in Irish bars that aren't in Ireland. I'd have been anonymous in there, but an undertow had deposited me another block along. I was perished, I ached, my legs were weak. The wrong two words and I could've been made to cry. The doorman wore a skinny maroon suit, black shirt and tie. Opaque sunglasses, patent leather shoes, seventies Afro. The way he raised his face at my approach suggested blindness. He appeared to gauge me with his ears, his sense of smell. I liked the way he made me feel: unobserved. He leaned forward and pulled open the door.

Inside, it was designer seedy. Light fittings that glowed but illuminated nothing. The same three colours were everywhere: olive, mustard and chestnut-brown. Ambient trance was playing on the sound system. It wasn't offensive at first, but after a while, after it had insinuated itself into my head, I came to see how hollow it was, how empty and cynical. It was the opposite of music.

14

The hostess greeted me. 'Table for one, madam?' She had the impassive eyes of an Egyptian pharaoh. She led me along a corridor, down a flight of stairs. The hotel was larger than the entrance had suggested. It was divided into chambers on either side of the corridor, long narrow chambers that daylight would never reach. The black and tan geometry of the carpet made it difficult to gauge my step. I kept thinking I was losing my footing, that I was about to fall. Should have gone to the Irish bar, I thought. Should have gone home.

The hostess gestured at a table and I sat with my back to the wall. A waiter approached.

'Would you like to see the menu, madam?' He proffered a maroon leather booklet.

'No, I can't eat.'

This didn't faze him, a woman in his restaurant who says she can't eat. He removed my napkin and cutlery.

'Would you like to see our drinks menu?'

I would. It was extensive. I ordered a Madera, the house cocktail. It was the colour of claret, but cloudy and served with ice. I drank it steadily through the twin black straws.

Most of the tables appeared to be occupied, but it was impossible to tell for sure. Vertical spotlights shone down on the tabletops, highlighting what people were consuming, but not the people themselves. I took out my ziplock bag. DO NOT MIX WITH ALCOHOL. I popped a capsule out of the blister pack and swallowed it. It inched its way down my oesophagus like a small dry maggot. I hadn't eaten that day, bar a few spoonfuls of ice cream at the hospital. Americans cured everything with ice cream. My internal organs felt engorged and tender, like they'd been taken out, pummelled, then stuffed back in the wrong way around. I put my elbows on the table and massaged my temples.

'Bad day?'

I'd been vaguely aware of the presence at the next table. I turned to examine the darkness. A man. We were seated on the same velvet banquette, which ran the perimeter of the room.

There was no drink on his table, nor cutlery either. He seemed to be wearing an overcoat.

His hand appeared in the spotlight as he beckoned the waiter. When the waiter approached, the man leaned towards me. 'Can I get you another drink?'

'Yes,' I said without smile or hesitation, resealing the ziplock bag. 'I'll have another one of these.'

'So will I,' said the man, and ordered two.

The Maderas arrived. We clinked glasses, drank, and then sat in silence. Not an awkward silence. I didn't particularly want to talk to the man, but I didn't particularly want to be alone either. It was my assessment that he felt the same. The little dry maggot found its way into my stomach and dissolved in a warm swell of alcohol. My body stopped feeling like my body.

The man removed his coat. I shuffled out of mine. 'Cold out there,' he observed, and I told him he had a point. He guessed straight off that I was Irish. He said he'd known by looking at me that I wasn't American. He'd thought I was French until he'd heard me order the drink. Then he knew. He just, like, knew. He was good with accents, he said.

'Really?'

'Yes, I have a gift.'

He said that the liberator of Chile was Irish too. 'Bernardo O'Higgins was the name,' he told me, and I said, 'Pleased to meet you, Bernardo, I'm Eva Tyne.' The man said that no, *he* wasn't Bernardo O'Higgins, that Bernardo O'Higgins was the Irishman who'd liberated Chile. 'Okay,' I said. I wasn't going to argue about it. Nobody could be called Bernardo O'Higgins.

'No really,' the man insisted, 'I'm not making this up.'

He asked me whether I was a Catholic, and I said I'd been reared one. This seemed to count as a mark in my favour. 'Me too,' he proclaimed, and I shut my eyes. He went on to state that his spiritual beliefs were of the utmost importance to him. He embarked on a long-winded description of some sacred place he'd visited in Brazil. A plateau, I think he said. A plateau is what I saw in my mind. A wide-open space. Barren, rocky, empty vault of a sky. No evidence of the modern age for miles around. Only the sound of the rainforest a thousand feet down. I knew I'd never go there. It didn't matter that it existed.

The man must have sensed that he was losing me because, apropos of nothing, he grabbed my hand and smiled. 'Hey, what do Irish girls want?' I wondered if the answer was going to offend me. I hadn't the energy to stalk off.

'I don't know,' I said warily. 'What do Irish girls want?'

'More alcohol.'

He ordered two more Maderas. I felt a rush of fondness for him then. He had just read my mind, after all. 'Nice socks,' he said. I laughed and pulled off Valentina's pink socks, and inserted my bare feet back into the shoes. 'Nice shoes,' he said. I agreed.

'I debuted in them last night,' I mentioned, but he failed to pick up on it. I was waiting for him to ask what I did for a living. I wanted him to know that I was a classical violinist, not some drunk off the street. I noted that I was now sitting at his table, though I'd no recollection of slithering across. A powerful urge engulfed me to lay my head on his shoulder. I peered at his face. His hair was black, his skin and eyes were darker than mine.

'Are they racist in Ireland?' he asked out of nowhere.

'They are,' I asserted. 'They're savage.'

'Would they kill me for not having freckles?'

'They'd try. But I'd protect you.'

'Would you?'

'Oh yes.'

'That's very considerate.'

I nodded and finished off Madera number three. Number four was already lined up. 'I'm staying here tonight,' I announced, which was news to me.

'Are you here on business, Eva?'

'Uh huh,' I confirmed, 'business.' Escaping reality was a business of sorts.

'Not a very corporate hotel.'

'The Plaza was full.'

'I see.'

He didn't pass comment when, some minutes later in compliance with his request, I handed him a piece of paper on which I'd scribbled out my cell phone number and he saw that it was a local one, a nine one seven. Nor did I mention that I lived a mere twenty minutes away. He started telling me, as he gazed at my unsteadily scrawled digits – the tip of the pen pierced right through the paper at one point, that he'd, recently broken up with his long-term girlfriend. 'Shocking,' I said, frowning at my fingernails. I didn't want to hear it. And I certainly didn't want to get around to the topic of my own relationship status. I didn't ask for his cell number, but he gave it to me all the same. He wrote it out on the back of his business card and I slotted it into my pocket.

At some stage during the proceedings, I know I attempted to explain the mess I was in. It was a roundabout way, I think, of excusing my present drunken state, a bid to establish that I didn't normally chat up strange men in strange bars. 'Not that you're strange,' I assured him, 'just, you know what I mean.' He seemed to.

I found myself trotting out a list of mitigating circumstances, citing the hospital, the ambulance, the puke on the dress. 'That's okay,' he said, looking around the room. I decided I mustn't be telling it right, so I kept raking over it, trying to hit on a detail that would make him understand. 'I was bent over double with the pain.' 'I thought I would die.' 'They had to carry me out on a stretcher.' 'That's okay,' he kept repeating, 'that's okay, that's okay,' so I eventually gave up. In the silence that ensued, I saw that the man was right not to want to hear it. I was sick of it myself.

I got up to visit the restroom and tripped on the carpet. When I returned, I was surprised to find him still there.

Surprised and pathetically grateful. I'd have bolted, were I he. We celebrated our reunion with another Madera. I clapped my palm to my forehead.

'Mad era – I just got that.'

'Yeah,' he told me, 'it's a place in California.'

'No, mad era. Mad. Era. Crazy time.'

'Yeah, do you want to go? We'd have a crazy time, all right.'

The glasses in which the Maderas arrived were getting progressively smaller. Either that, or my hands were getting progressively bigger. To my very minor credit, I had the decency to remember Ming, to realize that no one had filled her dinner bowl since yesterday morning. I got upset, and informed my new friend that I had to leave immediately, right this second, that it was an emergency. I stood up and he helped me into my coat, but then I couldn't remember why I had to rush off, and so sat back down again, defeated. I found myself close to tears.

'Ever kissed a Latin man?' he wanted to know.

I popped another painkiller out of the blister pack. 'Allergies,' I muttered when he squinted at the label. My coat came off again. I shed my clothes piece-by-piece, unaware that I was doing so until I saw their cumulative effect strewn about me. The coat, the scarf, the heavy woollen jumper, Valentina's pink balled-up socks. Like clothes abandoned on the beach before a swim. I thought of drowning, and got tearful again. 'My big night was fucked,' I said, staring at the palms of my hands. 'It was fucked, fucked utterly, and after so much work.'

The man touched my face and the world instantly brightened. We took to the floor to dance, and it must've been then that my handbag was stolen from under our table. Later, I couldn't give the manager a description of anyone suspicious in the room. I couldn't give her a description of anyone at all in the room. There was only this man. He smiled as he gently swung me to the music, which was not music. We danced well together, surprisingly enough. It was slow and intimate and very natural. I thought of this small child from home. He couldn't have been more than one and a half or two. When his big sisters clapped, he sprang into motion like a clockwork toy. I don't know why this man made me recall that baby. I was in thrall to him already, I suppose, in a way.

Once we established that my bag was gone, and with it my wallet and credit cards – though not, thank God, my painkillers, which were still in my coat pocket – the man said he'd pay for my room, and he signed for the drinks too, a sum which was outrageous and to which he added a sizeable tip. I wasn't especially upset about the loss of the bag, as it happened. It meant that I didn't have to ring home. And home couldn't ring me, seeing as my cell phone was in the bag. I was off the hook. I had been ignoring my cell all night because, yes, I had indeed been able to hear it ring. Over and over it had pleaded for my attention. My new friend was well aware of it too, of that I was certain, but he didn't allude to it either. Maybe because his phone had also been dialling out.

He held me in his arms on the way up in the elevator. The moment we were inside the bedroom, he pressed himself against me with an ardour that was out of keeping with the languor of downstairs, but when I spread my hands out flat on his chest – at which point, they alarmingly didn't look like my hands at all – and told him that I couldn't do this, that I didn't even know his name, he said, for the millionth time, 'That's okay.' He backed off immediately, showing no sign of pique.

He swung himself onto the bed and fell asleep on his back, fully clothed but for his coat and shoes. That's when I got to inspect him. Turned out I'd been way off in my estimation of his years. Not forties, as I had thought, but mid-twenties. In fact, he could've gotten away with nineteen, he was that boyish, but his driver's licence, which I located in his breast pocket, confirmed him as my age, though you'd never have known it to look at us, the state I was in that night.

I stroked his jet-black hair, which was thick and straight and nothing like mine. He was Latin all right, though he shared a surname with the kid I'd sat beside in second class. Jackson. From Lima originally, he'd mentioned downstairs, but resident in the States since the age of five. A pinch of Scots on the paternal side accounted for the green eyes which gave me such a surprise the next morning. I was one hundred per cent certain they'd be brown. Sometimes I try to convince myself that he was a common specimen, but I know in my heart he was not.

'My name, by the way,' he said when I finally turned out the lights, thus indicating that he hadn't slept through this preliminary appraisal, 'is Daniel.'

Daniel. I had read it on his driver's licence, but it sounded unexpectedly melodic when spoken aloud. He didn't want to fall asleep beside a woman who didn't know his name, he added. I liked him for that. 'Daniel,' I repeated. It was a musical word.

There was too much alcohol in my system to allow proper sleep. Pain and nightmares reduced me at some point to tears. When I awoke the next morning, way too early, I was encircled by Daniel. He was terribly affectionate, right from the start. Like a puppy, I thought, gazing at his sleeping face on the pillow. Like a silky puppy who needed my love and care, and who would've wagged his tail, had he had one. But then he opened his eyes and became a man again, and I felt foolish for having thought these things. I never quite figured that bit out, how he managed to change so effortlessly. I didn't stick around to contemplate it, though. It was time, at last, to go home.

We embraced before we left the hotel room, and we embraced the whole way down in the elevator. We held hands as we walked through the foyer, and Daniel carried what was left of my stuff. Seven o'clock on a Sunday morning. There had been a fresh fall of snow overnight. The light of the sunrise was flamingo-pink. I could've done with my sunglasses, but they too were in the stolen bag.

The concierge hailed a taxi and the two of us climbed into it, seeing as we were both headed downtown. No comment from Daniel on the fact that I'd stayed in a hotel when my apartment was a short journey away. We passed the hospital, and I nudged him.

'Look, that's where they brought me.'

Daniel glanced up vaguely and nodded. He reached for my hand, gave it a brisk rub. 'Cold, isn't it?' he remarked.

We pulled up outside my apartment and I stepped onto the snow. There was already a set of footprints exiting my building. I'd make the first set going in.

Daniel told me that he'd call in a few days. The taxi driver snorted. It was a deflating noise. Daniel knew that my phone had been stolen along with my bag. There would be no phone call. I didn't need the taxi driver to alert me to that.

I shuffled my feet about in the snow, which was seeping into my socks. It was difficult to know how to conclude our encounter. It seemed we should shake hands, or exchange business cards, or something. I told Daniel that I'd had a very pleasant evening. Daniel said that he'd had a very pleasant evening too, and he raised his gloved hand in farewell. My cue. I closed the door carefully on him. The taxi pulled out onto the empty street. It was over. I was back.

I stood on the kerb and watched the cab recede. Daniel didn't look around for a final goodbye. I would have preferred it had he done so. I'd have felt better. Don't know why. It wasn't like I was ever going to see him again.

I glanced up at my building to check if anyone was watching. Anyone in particular. The blinds to my apartment were shut.

Estelle was in the hallway when I reached the top of the stairs, dressed in a pair of her eighties baggy pants. These ones were purple and jade paisley. Either the pants had stretched over the years, or she had shrunk. Folds of jersey pooled about her ankles, so that she appeared to melt into the floor.

'Hello, Estelle,' I said. It wasn't a greeting, more an observation that she was there. Here's the rain. Traffic's bad. Hello, Estelle. She was not a benign presence.

'You been gone a while, Eva,' she informed me.

'I was just out of town for the night, Estelle.'

'Oh yeah?'

'Yeah.'

'Friday night too?'

Christ. 'Yeah.'

'Thought so. I'm a real light sleeper. If you ever need me to feed your cat, you just let me know.'

'Thanks, Estelle.'

'Yeah, you just bring over that funny little cat of yours and I'll take care of it in here. Okay, Eva?'

'Okay, Estelle. That's very kind of you.'

'No problem, Eva. I like cats.' Estelle had come with the apartment. The clanging radiator, the jammed kitchen window, and the light-sleeping neighbour across the hall. I didn't have to tell her my name; she'd already read it off the intercom. It was the first thing we did when we moved in, Kryštof and I: We proudly slotted our names into our new buzzer. Kryštof Král and Eva Tyne, living together in New York City. We stood back on the stoop to admire our handiwork, arms wrapped around each other, expansive with happiness. Kryštof gave me a squeeze. It was a momentous achievement.

Two people in love. We'd cracked it.

We went back upstairs and celebrated with a bottle of screw-top wine. Estelle must've scuttled down and read our proclamation. When I opened the door, maybe ten minutes later, she was standing right in front of me, one eye shut. She'd been trying to catch a glimpse of us through the peephole, I think.

'So, you must be Eva,' she'd said in this ravaged voice, as if she'd been smoking roll-ups since birth. She opened the other eye, the better to size me up. Which she did, without shame or hurry, starting with my feet. Spent a lot of time on my feet. Took an instant dislike to my shoes. She was totally unselfconscious that way. You had to admire her. Entirely oblivious to how her behaviour might offend others. I assumed, because of her proprietorial air, that she must be the landlady, or the owner of the whole building, and I proffered my hand.

'Pleased to meet you.'

She bristled. 'What are you, British?' said the scary voice. It was an accusation.

'Actually,' I told her, 'I'm Irish.' I waited for her to soften. She didn't.

'Hmm,' she growled sceptically, as if I couldn't fool her. She sized up my shoes again and snorted through her nose: Irish, hmm, a likely story. 'Yeah well,' she concluded, 'I'm Estelle, and I live over here.' Hee-yah. She was one of the few people I'd encountered in New York who had a genuine New York accent. 'And I'm a real light sleeper, Eva Tyne.' She stumped back to her apartment and slammed the door.

This time, however, Estelle wasn't snarling. She reached a hand out to my elbow.

'You look pale, honey,' she said.

'Just a little tired, Estelle.'

'You all right, honey?'

She'd never called me honey before, now twice in a row. I must've looked bad. 'I'll be fine thanks, Estelle. I just need to get some rest.'

'Yeah, you get some rest, Eva.' She looked concerned. She actually looked concerned. Which made me concerned. She nodded at my door. 'My best friend used to live in there, you know?' This, out of nowhere. Information she'd sat on for two full years.
'No, I didn't know, Estelle. You never told me that.'
'Yeah. My best friend lived in there for fifty years, right before you. I lived here, she lived there, but we were always in each other's places. I still think when your door opens it might be her.'
'I'm sorry to hear that. I had no idea.'
'Yeah well, what can you do?' She raised her shoulders to her ears and kept them there for too long, crazy old East Village lady. 'You remind me of her sometimes.' She relaxed her shoulders and looked down the stairs. 'Her name was Eva too. She didn't play the violin, though. I mean, she did, but not professionally. She worked in the Garden Cafeteria, but it's gone now. You probably haven't even heard of it.' I hadn't.
Estelle pulled a crooked face and melted another couple of inches into the floor. Then she re-inflated and tipped my elbow again. 'Hey, you wanna come in for coffee? Got a babka inside.'
'Oh Estelle, I'm so sorry, but coffee's the last thing I need right now.'
She looked crestfallen. 'Of course, honey, I wasn't thinking. You get some rest. I'll see ya later, I guess.' She shuffled back into her apartment and was about to close the door when her face lit up. 'Oh yeah,' she said, sticking her head back out, 'your boyfriend was around here looking for you last night. Seemed a little upset. Asked me if I'd seen you coming and going. Coming and going! *Whaddaya think I am?* I said to him, *a goddamned spy?* Yeesh.' She threw an invisible ball over her shoulder and swung the door shut. I faltered in the slammed silence. I'd have run back down the stairs only for Estelle watching me through the peephole. Now I had it coming. Kryštof was back.

I wheezed on my inhaler, then unlocked the door.

Somewhere along the hundred-block trip from the concert hall to the hospital to the Madera to my apartment, the notion of home had withered up and expired, like something left to die in the snow. I might as well have wandered into the apartment next door, that's how blank it was. I'd only been away for two days.

A man's black overcoat was slung over the sofa. At least, not so much slung over as thrown at it, indicating that the owner felt equally ill-used. Because Kryštof always hung up his coat. First thing he did when he returned home in the evening. Hung up his coat, placed his keys by the lamp, turned the lamp on, kissed Ming on the head. A creature of habit and a great man for order. He treated his every possession with care. It would have been a struggle for him, leaving his coat thus, sprawled in such a way it would certainly crease. The arms were outstretched as if shielding a blow. I picked it up and shook it out and hung it in the closet. The living room immediately looked better.

I regarded the bedroom door. It still wasn't too late to go in and tell my angel how much I'd missed him. I hadn't touched the man in the Madera, after all. I'd slept beside him, nothing more. We hadn't so much as kissed.

I crept up to the bedroom door, and that's where the idea to confide in Kryštof failed. It wasn't strong enough to penetrate wood. The room on the other side was wounded and volatile, and my guilt made me evasive and weak. I went back to the closet and pulled down the spare blanket.

I dreamt of household objects. Our nailbrush, the chequered tea towel, the canister in which we kept the tea. I dreamt that the bathroom scales were built for two. We could've weighed ourselves together, Kryštof and I, standing before the medicine cabinet, holding hands. I dreamt about our pots and pans, the cups we'd bought, our wooden spoon. I browsed through the day-glo bottles of cleaning products that had accumulated beneath the kitchen sink. The names on the labels were unfamiliar because we were in America, we were far from home. Those products would never do as good a job as the ones we grew up with, the ones by which our mothers swore. The dream was peaceful. It was like wandering through a museum. Exhibits from a dead civilization. Kryštof was in the armchair when I woke up. I wanted to go back into the dream.

'Hi,' I said.

'Hi.'

My head pounded and the January sun was stark. I shielded my eyes with my hand. Kryštof came over and kissed my forehead, and for a moment I thought he was going to take me into his arms. I think he thought he might too, because he vacillated for a second, but then turned away in a manner that was shocking to us both. He re-alighted on the armchair, fixing his eyes on me like knives.

I pulled myself into a seated position. 'What time is it?'

'Ten past two.' He didn't have to check the clock.

'Ten past two?'

'Ten past two,' he repeated, his initial irresolution now mastered. His stare was unrelenting, his jaw was set. Questions were jostling for order in his head. He'd been thinking them through for hours with that scrupulous mind of his. A solid bar of fear formed in my chest. Why fear, I don't know. I was not, and never could be, afraid of Kryštof.

'Why are you sleeping on the couch, Eva?'

'I didn't want to wake you when I came in.'

This was met with silence. It was horseshit, he knew.

'Where've you been these past two nights?'

'My bag was stolen.'

I issued this statement as if it explained everything. Kryštof didn't move. Nor did I. So he repeated the question in the exact same tone of voice.

'Where've you been these past two nights?'

'I was just hanging out. Didn't want to be in the apartment on my own.'

'That's not what Valentina said.'

Christ, he'd been on to Valentina. Of course he'd been on to her. He'd come home early from Boston to discover my absence, then gone wild with worry. That was what the coat was about, the abandoned overcoat. Not a protest, but a mark of his distraction. He'd probably called my mother.

'Valentina told me that you'd been taken to the hospital. She said you'd been rushed there in an ambulance, and that you'd instructed her to tell everyone you had a headache.'

'The Board of Directors and the sponsors were upstairs. It would've ruined the group's reception.'

'So you've been in the hospital these past two nights?'

'Yes.'

'And they discharged you this morning?'

'Yes.'

His head fell back and he looked at the ceiling. I was confronted with his Adam's apple, a little nut of bone. Hadn't ever considered it in isolation to the rest of him before.

'Are you okay now?'

'Pretty much.'

He lifted his head. 'Did they give you the injection?'

Asthma, I realized. He thinks I've had another asthma attack. 'No, just the nebulizer this time.'

'Why didn't you call me?'

I shrugged. 'It wasn't that bad an attack.'

'You always call me, Eva. I always come get you. Why didn't you call me this time around?'

'I don't know. You were in Boston.'

I stared at his long fingers. In the old days, Kryštof's fingers hypnotized me by forming shapes to illustrate words, as if language was another musical instrument you could play. This was his response to living in a country in which his native tongue was not spoken. He had a vast vocabulary of signs, not like teachers or politicians who repeated the same dogmatic gesture over and over to drive their point home. It was a trait I loved in him, but on which I'd never commented, lest in being made conscious of it, he changed it in any way.

But this wasn't Kryštof's usual display of curlicues and flight. This display was jagged and blunt, his poor face contorted with emotion. I hoped he wouldn't cry. His hands formed claws. 'Do you have any idea of how worried I was?' I didn't know what to say, so I kept my eyes on his clawed hands. 'What's wrong with you, Eva? How can you just sit there without even looking at me?' His mother, I thought out of nowhere, is going to kill me. She will never forgive me. Nor will mine.

He cleared his throat. 'Eva, I know you didn't spend last night in the hospital. I went with Valentina to visit you, but you were already gone.' He said this apologetically – he didn't want me to think he'd been checking up on me. 'Tell me his name.' I glanced up at his face. Tears were rolling down his cheeks.

'What?'

'Tell me his name, Eva.'

'Whose name?'

'The man you were with last night.'

'Oh.' I looked at his fingers again. 'Daniel.' The fingers twitched.

'Don't lie to me.'

A beat then, as Kryštof realized that I hadn't lied. He sat back winded and embedded his fingernails into the armrests. 'Daniel,' he hissed, as if it were a curse, not melodic. I caught my breath, as panicked as he.

The phone started ringing and he jumped up and swooped on it. 'She's back, she's fine, yes yes no. Sorry for the confusion, thanks for all your help.' He hung up and circled the room, telling me over and over that he didn't understand how I could do this to him. He didn't understand, he didn't understand, and I couldn't help him because I didn't understand either. 'You're better off without me,' was the best I could manage. We were in agreement there. Kryštof and I had been together for more than two years, and now it was over, just like that, because something had fallen out and died in the snow. 'I thought you loved me,' he said in disbelief.

He wanted details after that. He sat down and took a deep breath, then said that he needed to know everything, every last thing that I'd done with this man. This information, he told me, was essential for his sanity. The not-knowing was driving him mad.

His questions were vulgar and revealed the extent of his disgust. 'Nothing happened,' I protested, but this only enraged him. 'Don't keep lying to me, Eva, it's too late for that. You spent the night in bed with a strange man while I waited for you here.' He screamed at the thought of it. I pressed my face into the couch to drown out his voice. The phone rang again and he got up and yanked the flex out of the wall. He overturned the telephone seat and kicked it across the room.

He left the apartment once he'd worn himself out, forgetting to take his coat. He slammed the door and took off down the stairs before Estelle got a chance to detain him. Her door opened and closed. Ming crept out from wherever she'd been hiding, her belly skimming the floor. I got up and pushed the telephone seat back against the wall, then filled myself a hot-water bottle. I shut the blinds against the watery winter light, and Ming and I huddled together on the couch. All I felt was relief that he'd finally gone away.

Estelle observed me the next morning for a long time without speaking. I'd resolved not to say hello unless she said hello first. It heartened me that she was there all the same. Her presence took the edge off the awfulness. There is gratification to be derived from ignoring someone, so I was grateful to Estelle for granting me that opportunity. The silence, I think, was her idea of being considerate. Her raddled old head projected between the door and the doorframe, a turtle with a white wooden shell. She watched me carting boxes out of the apartment, making gluey noises with her dentures.

'You guys have an argument?' she finally asked on my third or fourth trip. It was a rhetorical question. Estelle knew all about our argument. She'd listened to every word, and taken sides.

'Something like that.'

'Hmm.' She watched me drag out a sports bag. 'You moving out, Eva?'

'Looks like it, Estelle.'

'Hmm.' She stepped into the hallway. She was wearing the baggy pants again, even droopier than the day before. The crotch swung around her knees. She put her hands on her hips and contemplated the sports bag, as if my broken relationship were inside. She shook her head and her glasses slid down her nose. 'Leave me your new address and I'll forward your mail.'

'That's okay, Estelle. Kryštof is staying. I can collect my mail from him.'

'Kryštof is staying?'

'That's right.'

'He's not going with you?'

'Nope. He's staying.'

'You leaving him, honey?'

'Sort of.'

'I'm real sorry to hear that. Always thought he was too good for you anyway.'

Her tone of voice was sympathetic, so there was a possibility she'd gotten it the wrong way around. Unlikely, though. I knew not to take it personally. It wasn't calculated to hurt. Kryštof had two things going for him which automatically distinguished him as my superior in Estelle's book; firstly, that he was male, and secondly, that his name had a háček in it. This made him her grandson, or something. Kryštof's háček made it Estelle's duty to welcome him to America, which was immensely irritating since Kryštof had lived in the States a decade longer than I. His family had emigrated to Brooklyn when he was fourteen.

We'd return to the apartment together and she'd be waiting at the top of the stairs, arms outstretched in one of her batwing tops. Jesus, I'd whisper under my breath, but Kryštof would step forward and present her with a kiss on the cheek, at which she'd squirm with glee. Then she'd throw a triumphant glance in my direction. Her displays of affection, I became convinced, were in no small way targeted at me. Look how you should be treated, she was telling him, and yet you put up with that bitch. And now I'd only gone and proved her right. To her credit, however, she wasn't taking pleasure in it.

'Yep,' she concluded, 'you're too reckless for him, honey. Kryštof is a fragile boy who needs a settling type, and you're no settler, Eva. You're like me that way. You make things hard on people, and you make things hard on yourself. I'll miss you, I guess.'

'Will you, Estelle?'

She nodded. Her glasses slipped. She pushed them back up her nose and clomped back into her apartment. The dead bolt slid across, which meant that she was gone for a bit. I picked up the sports bag and hoisted it onto my shoulder.

Estelle didn't bother opening the door when I made my final

trip, which was with Ming in her carry-case, beside herself with dismay. Down I went, like a convict, determined not to cry.

I opened the carry-case in Valentina's apartment, but Ming wouldn't be coaxed out. I filed Daniel's business card in the trash. My red silk dress was hanging in dry-cleaner's cellophane on the back of Valentina's closet door. The stains were gone, as if nothing had happened. I picked up the phone.

'Hi, Mum, I'm just ringing to give you my new number.'

'Why? Have you moved?'

'I'm staying with Valentina for a bit.'

'Oh.'

My mother knew what staying with Valentina meant – that's what I'd told her last time I'd broken up with Kryštof. The distance between us made it impossible for her to interrogate me. She'd barely have been able to broach it were we face to face. 'How did your debut go?' she asked instead.

'Oh good, yeah, great.' She was straining to decipher my state of mind from my tone of voice. So I adopted an upbeat tone of voice, which set her on high alert. 'Listen, Mum, have you got a pen handy and I'll give you Valentina's number.'

She murmured that, hang on, she thought there was one in the drawer. A clunk as she put the phone on the table, then the sound of her heels clicking across the wooden floor. The mantel clock chimed the quarter hour. Dusk in New York City, night-time at home, the smell of wet leaves and coal smoke on the air. The rummaging noises in the background grew angry. It was no longer a search, but a shoving of things around in frustration. My mother was punishing the drawer for not containing a pen.

'Mum,' I called, knowing she couldn't hear me. 'Mum, come on, stop.' I couldn't bear her tension, her repressed rage, which was never quite repressed enough for my liking.

Slam, the drawer was shoved shut in disgrace. Her heels again on the wooden floor. 'Eva, I'll call you back. I can't find a pen.' Her voice was tight.

33

'Mum, you can't call me back – you don't have my number.'

'Jesus.'

'I'll ring you again in half an hour or so. You'll find a pen somewhere. Try Dad's study, okay?'

'Okay.'

'I'll talk to you later, Mum, okay?'

'Okay.'

'Bye.'

'Love,' she said, and I hung up.

I didn't call her back. I knew I wouldn't. She knew it too. I was just like my father. Valentina returned to the apartment and held out a white box displaying my name. I lifted the lid. A chocolate torte. 'Welcome!' she said, but her gaiety made things worse. I asked her to cancel my students for that week, then I sat beside her chewing my nails as she made the calls. The painkillers had run out two days ahead of time, and with them the cosy delusion that everything would be all right.

Nobody believed the real story of how I found the Magdalena. Her origins, like Daniel's, are suspicious at best. I got her from a Russian. At least, I thought he was Russian. He was a giant of a man and blond as a child. His name, he told me, was Alexander, and I followed him into a derelict tenement building in search of an alleged Stradivarius because I had nothing left to lose by then. That's how bad it got in the wake of breaking up with Kryštof. I stumbled along drunkenly behind the Muscovite thinking: So what? So what if it all ends here? It's all over anyway. Besides, there was a remote possibility that what he'd told me was true. Alexander, as he unlocked the door, took a look at my face and laughed. 'You will like it, don't worry, yes?' he said.

I encountered him in a bar done up like a KGB office, or a New York bar owner's impression of one. Red lights, black walls, yellow scythes, the Cyrillic alphabet. We all looked like shit. Some rooms enhance you, some rooms don't. This room scraped you out like an airport lounge. It exuded the stale air of the morning after, of curtains drawn against the persecution of dawn. Valentina and I had ended up there because it was simply too cold to go further. We'd been aiming for the Bowery. I'd bamboozled the girl into thinking it was her moral duty to accompany me. 'I can hardly go out drinking alone,' I argued, thereby shaming her into coming along. It was like dragging a child around by the ear.

Valentina had long since given up on trying to lift my spirits. She'd done the whole you've-been-through-a-lot routine, to which I'd responded with grunts. She rotated her bottle of beer around on the counter in silence. Around and around with fierce perseverance, as if trying to bore a hole through the

35

wood. I shredded another beer mat and added it to the pile, then banged my bottle on the bar and swivelled around on my stool to face her. 'This is bullshit,' I shouted (the music was loud). 'It's Saturday night. How can we be having a shitty time on Saturday night?'

Valentina didn't know either. At least, that's what I took her dismissive gesture to mean. I scowled at her in fury. My eyes were watering. I'd been up since seven that morning. The rehearsal earlier had been desperate. Hannah kept patting me on the shoulder, assuring me that I'd get back on form, but Richard had been straight up. 'You should not have cheated on Kryštof,' he said. 'That was a big mistake.' I could've put his head through his cello. I hadn't told him I'd cheated on Kryštof. I hadn't phrased it to anyone like that. But tomorrow was Sunday, so I didn't have to work. My mood brightened at the prospect.

'We'll have another drink,' I informed Valentina, and signalled for two more beers. She'd been sending her bottles back three-quarters full, as if I wouldn't notice this sabotage. I placed a fresh one before her. 'Finish it this time. You're making me feel like a lush.'

'I'm making you what?'

She'd heard me. I took a swig from my bottle. 'Forget it.' She stood up. 'Oh great, so you're walking out on me now?'

'I'm going to the restroom, Eva, if that's okay with you.'

I shrugged; suit yourself. A long hard look at me, then she went.

Never before had Valentina been angry with me, and I might have felt mildly conciliatory if she'd actually expressed it, but her peaceableness was an underhand attack on my drunken aggression, I decided. I spun around balefully on the barstool. That's when I spotted Alexander. Five guys were sitting around a table listening to him. He wore a cream cable-knit turtleneck and was gesticulating wildly. He looked like a sailor. He delivered the punch line and the five guys roared with laughter. They looked like sailors too. I wanted in on the joke.

My arm was nudged. A middle-aged man in leather trousers

36

had hauled himself onto Valentina's barstool. It was a horrific transformation. 'Hi there,' he said, 'is this seat taken?' I slid off my stool and brought my beer over to Alexander.

'This place is a shithole,' I told him when he turned around. Alexander sat back in his chair and frowned. 'It's a dump,' I added, by way of clarification.

His face lit up. Ah, dump. Yes, dump. Now he understood. 'Let me see.' He stroked his chin in deliberation. His accent was consonant-heavy like Kryštof's, but more glottal. He tried to see, but failed to, and so shook his head. 'New York,' he concluded, 'is not that bad.' Nodt thadt badt.

I rolled my eyes. 'I wasn't talking about New York.'

'What? All of America is a dump?' He shrugged the way Estelle shrugged, and I nearly walked away. 'You should try Russia.' He jerked a thumb at the window, as if Russia was that way, then pulled out a stool from under the table. 'Haff a seat,' he instructed me. 'What is your name?'

'Jane.'

He held out his hand. 'I am Alexander. Pleased to meet you, Jane.'

In fairness, he did seem pleased. I shook his hand and he all but broke mine. 'Jesus,' I protested. Alexander didn't notice, or if he did, didn't care. He was not a man, I don't think, who had much time for frailty.

'You are not a happy woman, Jane. You must tell me what is wrong.'

'Hang on.'

Valentina had returned to her barstool and was blinking at the man in the leather trousers. I called her name across the room, and the myopic way in which she cast about for my face filled me with remorse. The gentleness of her, the patience. I had to wave before she located me. Alexander's buddies smartened themselves up at her approach.

'Valentina, meet my new friend. His name is Alexander.'

'He's very handsome,' she whispered into my ear. I looked at him with renewed interest.

37

Alexander pulled out a second stool. 'Haff a seat, Valentina.'

The girl saw her chance. 'No no,' she protested, 'I'll leave you two alone.' She kissed my cheek and was out of there.

Alexander indicated the extra shot glass that had appeared on the table. 'Vodka, Jane'. We clinked glasses and knocked it back. A warm feeling sparked in the centre of my chest.

He was hardly what you'd describe as a shy man, holding forth upon a range of topics to which I didn't exactly listen. It was difficult to hear him over the racket of the bar, and his accent presented a challenge. I just smiled when he smiled, laughed when he laughed, and he kept my glass topped up from a bottle under his seat. He was most attentive in this regard, it has to be said. I quickly felt myself to be in the presence of a friend. The thin wire frames of his glasses lent him the aspect of a man of letters. He was excited about everything and waved his hands about a lot. There appeared to be something wrong with one of them.

I couldn't say at what point he started telling me about violins. About four shots in, give or take. It is possible I prompted him, but I can't think how, seeing as he was the one doing all the talking. He was banging on about Russia in the eighties, about dollars, about how he'd had to attain dollars in Russia in the eighties – 'American dollars, you understand, Jane?' I nodded gravely: Yes, American dollars, I'm with you. 'Exactly,' he continued. He'd had to attain enough American dollars to finally be able to defect.

'Wow,' I said, trying to sound like I meant it. It was the kind of thing he presumed Americans liked to hear. I'd never been taken for an American before.

Alexander looked sadly at the small stub of a glass in his hand. 'I was very depressed in Russia,' he confided, shaking his head at how depressed he'd been. He recalled a day in the winter of '89 when he realized it was a matter of life and death that he get out. Something about looking up and seeing that there were no leaves on the trees. The end of the road. He couldn't take it anymore. Wouldn't have been alive today had he remained there much longer, he reckoned. Would've thrown himself in the Moskva, had it not been frozen solid. 'Like rock,' he said bitterly, rolling the r. 'Water hard as rock, and just as grey. Merciless. Without mercy. Do you understand, Jane?'

I nodded without looking at him. Oh yes, I understood. I knew what he meant, all right. I hated stories about depression. Depression was contagious, as far as I was concerned. Incurable and contagious. It sprang from one person to the next and never stopped going. The warm feeling in my chest had petered out. I felt inordinately tired all of a sudden. So inordinately tired that I wasn't going to have the energy to make it home. I drained my thimbleful of vodka and yawned.

'But,' Alexander interjected. He leaned forward and confided this next bit as if it were a state secret. The bar had emptied out somewhat, so he no longer had to project. 'But,' he repeated with a note of pride, 'I haff very good friends.' He sat back triumphantly and interlaced his fingers. He nodded at me in case I didn't believe him. I believed him.

'Congratulations,' I said.

I stooped down to rummage in my bag, but my inhaler kept slithering through my fingers like a fish. So I upended the bag and shook the contents onto the table, grabbed the inhaler and wheezed on it twice. Is that, I wonder, when Alexander saw something? I glanced at him, curious as to why he'd fallen silent.

He was staring at my stuff. Was there a clue there? In amongst the keys and coins and make-up and dirty tissues, and all the other bits of crap that accumulated in my wake, was there a clue as to who I was, a clue to what would make me greedy? Some reference to the chamber orchestra, or the violin? I still can't think of anything that might have tipped him off. Could it possibly have just been luck? I swept my bits and pieces back into my bag.

'Ups,' said Alexander. He reached into the maw of the bag

and picked out a beer mat. 'You don't want to take that home, do you, Jane?'

'No, Alexander, I don't want to take *thadt* home.'

He smiled and flicked the beer mat back onto the table, then leaned in and began to speak conspiratorially once more. My seat seemed to be lower than his.

'Listen,' he said, and pointed at the ceiling. 'I haff many very good friends, yes? From all over the world. I haff very good friends in Europe. I haff very good friends in Russia, and I haff lots and lots of very good friends in New York City.' He eyed me knowingly. 'They get me things,' he added, 'all kinds of things. Everything is for sale in Russia if you can pay in US dollars. People come out of nowhere with these things salvaged from the old days, things they've been hiding in their families for years. Russians,' he informed me, 'are cash poor but asset rich. My very good friends help the Russians to liquidate their assets.' A profound nod, as if liquidating assets were transubstantiation, or a form of alchemy. 'Paintings,' he continued, 'clocks, jewelleries, whatever you want.' Alexander waved his hand in an arc through the air. 'Furnitures, silvers, antiques, rugs, violence.'

'Violence?' I repeated. 'What, like, punishment beatings?'

'Violence, yes.' He lifted his arms to play a few bars of air-violin. 'Italian, mostly. Sometimes German. Once belonging to the Russian aristocracy.' He examined the expression on my face, then sat back and smiled. He had me. I knew that he had me, and he knew it too. He slapped the table. 'You like the violence, Jane, I can tell.'

The warm feeling was back. A log-fire on the inside. Alexander felt it too. He clasped his hands behind his head and stretched out his legs. Yes, he reflected, his friends were very good friends. They brought him the violence and he sold them to Europeans. And now Americans. They were not difficult to export. 'Small. Not metal. Not *detectable*.' He transported them out of Russia on trains. 'Like mice!' he bellowed, and slapped the table again. 'Real Stradivarius violence sneaking on the trains like mice!' He choked like it was just too funny. I didn't get it. Mice didn't ride trains. And so, he'd attained a large amount of US dollars, until one day he had enough to defect. Boom, he was out of there, and on a plane to New York, depression gone, just like that, magic.

I raised my glass. 'God bless America.'

'To America, yes,' he agreed, and we drank. He refilled our glasses. The vodka bottle was now empty. Alexander returned it to the floor.

'So tell us,' I began after what I judged to be a respectable silence, 'do you still sell the violins?'

Alexander retracted his legs and sat up. Suddenly he seemed angry. Then he smiled, he wagged his finger, as if I had nearly, just nearly, caught him out. 'Ah, but can I trust you, Jane?'

I tried to look trustworthy. 'Of course you can trust me, Alexander.'

He reached over and grasped my left hand, ran his fingertips over the calluses on mine. 'So, Jane, you play a stringed instrument?'

'Yes,' I said hesitantly. How strange to be touched like that. It was surprisingly intrusive.

'You play the violin?'

'Yes.'

'And now you want to buy one, Jane?'

I took back my hand and said no. 'Why? Have you got one for sale?'

He beckoned me forward, and forward I came. 'I haff several, Jane, but I haff one very special one.' One fairy special one. He did that nod again, the meaningful one: Mark my words. 'I haff a Stradivarius.'

I laughed. 'Of course you have.'

'I haff.'

'Hey, I believe you.'

'Good. You are wise. You are wise woman, Jane. I will drink to that.'

'So will I,' though I'd have drunk to anything by then. We

41

emptied our glasses and banged them down on the table. The lights flashed last call. Alexander went up for a final round.

'Listen,' he said when he returned with the drinks, 'why don't you come to my apartment, and I show you the Stradivarius? I haff another bottle of vodka there. My car is outside.' He sat down and put his mouth to my ear. 'I imported this violin only last week, Jane.'

He sat back to gauge my reaction. I laughed. Importing violins was funny. He leaned forward once more.

'To be honest,' he told my ear, touching it with his lips, '*import* is not the correct word. The more accurate word is *smuggle*.' I laughed again. Smuggling was also funny, particularly at that hour of the night. He got up and stood over me then, and I gaped at his height. He must've been six foot six. 'Come, Jane,' he said, 'let's go.'

It was all a bit abrupt, and there was so much to organize: my bag, my scarf, my coat. 'What, you want to leave right this minute?'

'Yes, come, come Jane. I show you the violin, and I drive you home.' He hooked his hands under my arms and whooshed me to my feet. The chair fell over behind me and I looked at it in surprise. I spotted my scarf.

'My scarf,' I said, and pointed at the floor. Alexander picked up the scarf and wrapped it around my neck. I opened my mouth to tell him something important, but instantly forgot what it was.

Alexander tied the scarf in a big bow for a joke, then helped me into my coat. He buttoned it up and knotted the belt around my waist. He brushed down my shoulders and straightened my lapels. 'There,' he said, 'very pretty.' Fairy pretty.

Out we went, his hand on the small of my back. We had forgotten to say goodbye to his friends. It had been snowing again. I knew I was in bad shape because I couldn't feel the cold. I wanted to lie down right there on the sidewalk. 'Ahhh,' said Alexander, taking a deep breath and surveying his surroundings, 'sometimes New York is just like home, Jane.' It was a sentiment I couldn't share.

We crossed the street and he unlocked the passenger door of an old navy car. In I climbed, the big blue bow tied around my neck as if I were something he'd won in a fair. It wasn't my scarf. That's what I'd wanted to tell him back in the bar. 'This isn't my scarf, Alexander,' I'd been trying to say. I attempted a second time to point it out, but he'd already slammed the door.

It was dark under the coating of snow, like sitting in an igloo. His smiling face appeared before me as he cleared off the windscreen with his bare red hands. 'Hello,' he sang out when he saw me, 'my name is Alexander.' He lowered himself into the driver's seat and inserted the key into the ignition. The engine wouldn't start. It growled like a dog warning us to back off. He gestured at the unobliging bonnet. 'Just like home, Jane,' he said again, and laughed his big bear laugh. It was my last chance to jump out. Then the engine started up with a clatter, and my last chance was gone.

That's when the gravity of the situation dawned on me, and questions toppled down on me like bricks. Could I really be in the passenger seat of a battered car, driving at speed over the East River, with some complete stranger behind the wheel who was almost as drunk as I was? It was tempting to try to deny it.

And yet there I was, hurtling across the Brooklyn Bridge, then swaying left and right as we negotiated an intricate series of turns. It hadn't occurred to me before agreeing to get in the car that Alexander didn't live a few blocks away. Everyone I knew lived a few blocks away. And no one owned cars, because everything was a few blocks away. Until now.

I looked over my shoulder. In the backseat window, the Manhattan skyline was sinking. I had never seen it from that angle before. For all my years of living in New York, I knew next to nothing of the vast conurbation surrounding the island itself. I could've found my way to the airports and back, and possibly have located the New Jersey Turnpike. That was it, though. All a blank. I gazed out at the streets and they were about as familiar as Calcutta, and nearly as rundown. Then the car steamed up and I saw nothing at all. Alexander rubbed clear a patch on the windscreen about the size of a dinner plate. I would have given anything for my phone.

It seemed I had no choice but to jump out of the moving car. Alexander must've read my mind because he kept his foot on the gas. 'We're going too fast,' I told him as we broke another red light.

'But it's cold,' he protested, as if speed defeated cold. A car swerved to avoid us and he sounded the horn. I strapped on my seat-belt, as if that would save me. My nail bent backwards as the catch clicked. 'Okay, Jane?' Alexander looked across at me, a dirty big grin on his face. He was in great humour, the bastard.

'This better be some violin.'

'Believe me, it is. You will not be disappointed.'

Disappointment was the least of my worries. 'Why don't you just give me your address and I'll come visit you tomorrow, Alexander?'

'Because I won't be here tomorrow, Jane. Besides, we're almost there. Just another corner.' Another corner, then he pulled in. 'See?' He wiped down my side of the windscreen.

We were up some poorly lit side street and there was not a soul about. No traffic, either, and we were far enough away from Manhattan to have escaped the Manhattan snowfall. My stomach turned over with fear. Alexander switched off the engine and rubbed his palms together. I was no longer so determined to leave the car. My feet seemed glued to the floor.

'Why don't you bring the violin out to me, Alexander?'

He screwed up his face in disbelief. 'What? Bring a Stradivarius out here?' He gestured at the vacant lot across the street. 'Are you crazy? Crazy Jane? These people are animals. These people carry knives and guns. Come, it's better inside. Besides, it's cold. It's fucking freezing, no?'

He produced a large chain from the backseat and I nearly bit the dashboard. He wrapped it around the steering wheel and padlocked it into place. 'Okay then,' he announced, 'we go.'

Things were even worse once out of the car. The sidewalk was a skateboard. I could barely stay upright. Alexander was right – it was fucking freezing. I could feel the cold now, which meant that I was sober, or at least approaching it. That should've been a good thing, but it was not. I wanted to be drunk again. I wanted to be insentient. I wanted to come round when it was all over. The morning was a hell of a long way off.

It crossed my mind to scream for help, but it just wasn't that kind of neighbourhood. What was I thinking, going to look at the fairy special violence of some seriously dodgy Russian, or whatever Alexander was? ('I'm not Russian,' he'd informed me at some stage of the journey. 'I'm from Chechnya.' 'Oh, you're Chechnyan?' I'd enquired in a respectful little voice, as if I'd understood the cultural niceties of the distinction. The only distinction I made was that this, in all likelihood, made him more dangerous. 'Not Chechnyan,' he'd snapped. 'Chechen.' I had an image of a fluffy dog.)

There was a street-sign up ahead on the corner. The letters wriggled and pulsed. Just a few more yards and they'd be legible. My eyes practically tipped out of my head with the effort to read them. B something Street. Or was it an R?

Alexander stopped at a doorway and put his hand out to halt me. 'We are here,' he stated.

The street-sign was still undecipherable. I searched for a number on his door. There was no number. On one side was an old storefront, its windows boarded up. The building on the other side had been demolished. Last week's snow was scraped into heaps on either side of the stoop, and the heaps had frozen into stony grey drools. Two squat trolls guarding the mouth of the cave. The stoop itself was slick with ice. I held onto the railings for safety.

Alexander had to open three locks to get inside. 'Quickly quickly,' he said, ushering me in like we were cops on a raid. The interior was pitch-dark. I needed a gun.

'Is there no light?' I asked.

'Shh,' he hissed. 'No light.'

'What is this place, some sort of crackhouse?'

But Alexander was now a man with a mission, and too busy to answer questions. 'Shh,' he hissed again. 'Straight on.'

He was right behind me, tall enough to breathe on the top of my head. His hand was on the small of my back again, hustling me along. 'Hurry hurry,' he said, and I hurry hurried. I stumbled along the black corridor, my hands outstretched for guidance.

We arrived at a stairwell. A weak yellow glow was coming from the floor above. 'Upstairs,' said Alexander, 'then left.' I turned around and looked at him. I didn't want to go. 'Jane,' was all he had to say. Upstairs I went, then left.

We came to a dead-end door with a brass number on it. Six. I hadn't noticed any doors numbered one to five. I got out of Alexander's way and he unlocked it. 'Ladies first,' he said, and I stepped into his lair.

A dim light was emanating from the room off to the right. A man was sitting in the darkness in the corner to my left. I stared at him in fright, but he didn't speak or move. Alexander locked the door and dropped the keys into his pocket. He pulled across chains and bolts. He peered through the peep-hole and satisfied himself that there was no one on the other side. Only then did he switch on the lights.

We were in a kitchen, a shabby one. A table, two chairs, a portable television set on the draining board, empty spirit bottles and take-out cartons on the floor. No man in the corner. It was just a coat. A heavy, black wool coat. On the table was an ashtray full of cigarette butts, and a corkscrew.

'Take off your coat, Jane. I will get the vodka.'

'I don't want any more vodka.'

Alexander shrugged. 'So? I do.' He disappeared into the room on the right. I swiped the corkscrew from the table and slipped it up my sleeve.

'Okay then,' he said when he came out. He unscrewed the cap and swallowed down two shots in a row. 'Are you sure you don't want any, Jane?' He offered his glass.

'I'm positive.'

'Right: to business. The violin.'

Yes, the violin. There was no sign of the violin. There was no sign of any violin, let alone a whole illegal trade in them. 'In here, Jane,' he instructed me, and I followed him through to the bedroom. 'Oh where did I leave it?' he muttered in a singsong voice, and I froze. He was acting, I knew it, he was trying to appear casual. There was no violin.

I slid the corkscrew down into my hand. I held the spiral between my ring and middle fingers. He would get it in the eye, yes he would. There was a concertinaed grate padlocked onto the window, like the gate of an old elevator. The iron bars of the fire escape were visible on the other side.

Alexander started digging through the clothes and blankets heaped on the bed and floor. I stood behind him, sick with fear, wondering what in the name of Jesus he was about to produce. A knife, another chain, a Kalashnikov? There'd been some article in the paper recently about white slavery. I thought of Kryštof. I thought of my mother. I thought of my father, who was maybe watching somehow.

'Here it is,' he finally said, straightening up and turning. Yes, here it was; I braced myself.

It was an old black leather violin case.

Alexander held it out like a cushion on which a crown is placed. He nodded at me. 'Open it, Jane.' I tucked the corkscrew back up my sleeve and unclicked the two locks. Whatever was in that case would decide, well, everything. I raised the lid.

It was a violin. It was the Magdalena, though it wasn't yet the Magdalena. It was just a violin, but I'd never been so grateful before to see just a violin. I was not going to die. I was not going to be raped or murdered or sold. Alexander laughed at my expression.

'See? I told you, Jane. Stradivarius.' I saw then what had troubled me back in the bar: he was missing his ring finger.

'Smuggled,' I said.

He winked. 'Imported. Take it out, Jane. Go on.' He jerked the case at me. I didn't move. He sighed like my mother (Do I have to do *everything*?) and put the case on the bed. I transferred the corkscrew into my pocket and rolled up my sleeves.

Alexander passed me the bow first, a big clunky factory job, an agricultural tool. I knew it – rubbish. I'd been dragged here for nothing.

'This is a piece of shit, Alexander.'

'Wait.' He unstrapped the violin, picked it up like a baby, then lovingly held it out.

I took it by the neck and turned it over, trying not to look impressed. I didn't have to try hard. It was not devoid of merit like the bow, but it was filthy. 'State of it.'

Alexander threw his eyes to heaven. 'Quality,' he enunciated carefully, like it was the word to beat all words.

I put down the bow to take a closer look at it. I was surprised to discover that it was in fact a quality violin. In relatively good condition, too. No damage that I could detect. Old, definitely. Possibly Italian, as he'd said, but it could've been Bohemian, German, even Russian. I'd never had to appraise the origin of a violin before. They always came with certificates of provenance. Lists of previous owners, too. I was guessing, however, that this one didn't.

The set-up needed looking at – the bridge, fingerboard, new strings – but nothing was actually wrong with it, as far as I could see. I tried to put it under my chin, but the big blue bow of the scarf got in the way. I pulled the scarf off angrily and threw it on Alexander's bed. 'That isn't my scarf,' I told him.

'I know, Jane.' Alexander retrieved the scarf and wrapped it around his own neck. 'It's mine.' He pulled a red scarf out of his pocket and threw it on the bed. 'That's yours.' So it was. The man was inscrutable.

I put the violin under my chin and plucked the strings. Dull as dead elastic. Nobody had played this thing in some time. Which meant that Alexander hadn't shown it around yet. I was the first. A warm glow of excitement. I lowered the violin and rubbed at the grime.

'No really, Jane,' he interjected, as if I'd been arguing with him at length, 'we do terrible things to violence. We buy ones as young as say seventy years old and we age them. We knock them about. We cover them with dirt. Buried one once, but that was a mistake. We stick false labels inside, take genuine labels out, replace them with better labels. Better fake labels, that is. I don't need to tell you this. You know violence, I can

49

tell. But not with this one. This one, we didn't touch. This one, we didn't need to touch. It is the real thing, I promise you, Jane.'

'And what's your promise worth, Alexander?' He didn't even pretend to look insulted.

I tuned the violin up, holding it at arm's length. The strings were so old, I worried they'd snap in my face. Alexander, solicitous now, and delighted to see me showing a bit of interest, handed me the bow, piece of shit that it was. I started with the Tchaikovsky we'd been rehearsing that morning. That was the point at which I began to suspect what I had. Right there in that hole of a room, and still partly in fear for my life. The clarity of the high notes, the remarkable projection. I started to wheeze.

Clink, the neck of the vodka bottle hit the glass again. I glanced at Alexander. Now he was the one who looked nervous.

'You are the first to see it, Jane.' He gulped the contents of the glass down in one. The room was so quiet that I heard the anatomy of his swallow. A strained, wrenched noise, more like a choke. I put bow to string again and played.

Was it because I was so relieved that there *was* a violin that it sounded so sweet? I had never heard such sweetness come out of a violin before – at least, not when I was the one playing it. How drunk was I? Was it like one of those dreams in which you think you can fly? I'd been drinking for seven hours – I was blind drunk – and yet I felt sober. I felt so sober, it hurt. Tomorrow morning's hangover was already setting out its stall. In which case, the violin should've sounded shrill and hard. It did not. I played the pieces I played regularly on my own violin. It made it easier to gauge the difference between the two. The difference was vast. Diamond and glass. My wheezing was getting worse.

In the intervals between the pieces, Alexander issued statements.

'You play very well, Jane,' he said.

'This violin suits you, I think.'

'You should haff this violin.' Clink, swallow.

'This violin is for you.'

'You are made for this violin.'

'The violin and you are one.'

'Yeah, enough, Alexander.' I lowered the violin to take another look at it. 'This isn't Italian,' I pointed out with authority, though I had no idea what it was. 'This violin is French. Late nineteenth-century French. I have one just like it at home.'

'Excellent, Jane. Buy this, then you haff two Stradivarius violence at home.'

'I need to get someone to look at it.'

'Absolutely not, Jane.'

'What do you mean, absolutely not? What are you trying to hide?'

Clink, swallow, smirk. 'Myself.'

Alexander wasn't a messy drunk like me. In fact, the drunker he got, the more neutralized his accent became. He'd eased up on the consonants. He was beginning to sound, well, familiar.

I raised the bow again. I was dying to let rip, but I didn't want to showcase the violin too much, seeing as we hadn't yet set the price. It was highly unlikely that Alexander had heard it played before – it hadn't been tuned. I wanted to get it cheap, so I deliberately played poorly but still it sounded good. I was spellbound.

So was Alexander. The more I played, the more his face lit up. The clinking of the glass against the neck of the vodka bottle accelerated. The man was celebrating. The dollar signs were multiplying in his head. He placed the bottle and the glass on the floor and applauded. 'Bravo, Jane. Encore!' I wanted him to leave the room so I could really get going.

'Did you say you were making a cup of tea, Alexander?'

'No cups, Jane.'

'I'll drink it out of a jam jar.'

'No jam jars.'

'A fucking tin can, Alexander. Anything will do. Go out there and see what you can find.'

But he was having none of it, the obstinate shit. He stooped to retrieve the bottle and glass from the floor. Clink, swallow. 'I have no tea, Jane.'

Have. He'd said have. Not haff. But it wasn't an American accent either.

'Oh come on, Alexander, just get out of the room.'

Never a good move to reveal what you want. Alexander pretended to consider my request for a moment, then shook his head and said no.

'Okay, fine, whatever. Suit yourself. I'm finished playing.'

My wheezing had escalated to a worrying level. I put the violin on the bed and rooted in my bag for an inhaler. Alexander watched me closely. I hid my face from him. I let my hair conceal it. Because I didn't want him to read the thought now burning in my brain. Burning so brightly that it might well have been legible all the way through to my forehead: This violin will change my life.

He cleared his throat. 'You haff finished playing, Jane?'

Haff. We were back to haff.

'That's what I said, Alexander.' No sign of my inhaler. I must have left it in the bar. How long could I manage without it?

'So.' He picked the violin up even more lovingly and returned it to its case. 'What are your thoughts, Jane?'

'I don't feel well.'

'Yes yes, but what are your thoughts about the violin, Jane?'

'Oh that? Very nice. You should be able to hock it, no bother.'

Alexander snapped the locks shut. 'But do you want to buy it, Jane?'

'Not without getting an expert to look at it.'

'Not possible.'

'So you tell me.'

Silence. Surely I was an expert? That's what I was thinking, and so was Alexander. I couldn't carbon date the thing, or make conclusive observations about its provenance, but I could evaluate the sound, and the sound was extraordinary.

'This is a Stradivarius violin,' Alexander stated. 'I am selling it at the price of a good copy. What is the problem, Jane?'

'Well, look, let's talk about this, Alexander. Exactly what price are you asking?'

Suddenly he no longer seemed drunk. Or desperate. Or familiar. 'Six fifty,' he said. Six hundred and fifty thousand dollars. Approximately half of what I estimated the violin would fetch on the open market, if it were in fact a Strad. Which it no doubt wasn't. I didn't care about that right then. It was a very beautiful instrument.

I put my hands on my hips. 'Five.' I was haggling with money I didn't have.

Alexander laughed. 'I shouldn't haff brought you.' He tucked the case under the bed.

The sight of the case disappearing made me panic. 'Five fifty,' I blurted. The case stopped moving.

'Six hundred thousands. In cash.'

There was no conceivable way I could've laid my hands on such a sum. Yet if the violin was what he claimed it to be, it was a knockdown price. Oh, the added allure of it being a bargain. Lungs like a wet sponge. 'Alexander,' I wheezed, 'I don't have that kind of money.'

He shook his head gravely. 'Can you get it, Jane?'

Of course not. Not a chance in hell. I chewed at my thumbnail. I could raise a certain amount, sure. The money my father had left me, which had been stashed away for the best part of eight years, plus whatever I could get for my old violin at short notice. Barely even halfway there. It wasn't going to happen. 'Maybe?' I said. Alexander raised a sceptical eyebrow. 'All right, yes.'

'Maybe or yes? Which?'

'Yes.' Jesus. A whistle in my chest.

'How long will it take you?'

'I don't know – a month?'

'Jane Jane Jane! It won't be here in a month.'

I believed him. I did. Any fool who heard that violin would immediately snap it up. It was merely a matter of showing it to the right person. But how merely was that merely? Was Alexander capable of locating the right person? He didn't look especially capable, standing there in his dump of a bedroom. This was not a man who'd been making lucrative deals of late.

But what of his very good friends? Who were these very good friends? Were they capable? Could they locate the right person? They were unwilling to show the violin to experts, I already knew that much. Which was good. It cut out the lion's share of the target market. Which left . . . well, who did it leave? What sort of person invested in violins of suspicious provenance? Just how big was the black market? And just how much would the black market pay? The vast amount of variables in the equation was overwhelming. I was out of my depth, but there was no question of letting this violin go. Not without at least trying. 'How does a fortnight sound?'

Alexander shook his head. 'A week.'

Forget it. 'Go on, a week.'

'Good, Jane. We meet in Tompkins Square Park. I will see you on a bench by the Seventh Street and Avenue A entrance on,' he consulted his watch. 'Sunday the nineteenth, two p.m., okay?' He'd done this before. It was routine. 'Okay?' he asked more loudly when I didn't respond.

'Okay,' I said quietly. Checkmate.

'Excellent. Here.' He took an inhaler out of his pocket. 'You left this behind in the bar.'

'Fuck, Alexander, why didn't you give it to me earlier? Can you not see me gasping?'

Alexander seemed offended. 'I wouldn't haff let you die.'

We travelled in silence. It took a lot longer going back than it had coming out. By the time we reached Manhattan, I was tired and sour. It was like the end of a one-night stand. The unsavoury intimacy of it, the rush to be in a room on your own. I directed him to an address on the Upper East Side.

54

'Slow down,' I told him, 'I live here.' I pointed at a canopied apartment entrance. The concierge inside was asleep.

'You live here, Jane?'

'Yes,' I lied.

'You are no Uptown girl. But I don't blame you not wanting me to know where to find you. So I drop you here, if that's what you want, Jane. I will see you next Sunday.'

I got out of the car. 'Sunday,' I said, though I had long since decided I wanted nothing more to do with him. He could shove his violin; I didn't care how fairy special it was.

I slammed the door. He leaned across the passenger seat and rolled the window down. 'You are a brave girl, Jane,' he told me, and slapped the dashboard. 'The fighting Irish, ha!' I looked at him blankly. I hadn't told him I was Irish. I opened my mouth to, I don't know, object, argue, complain, reprimand, but he rolled up the window and sped off.

Once he was out of sight, I bent over and vomited between two cars. The vomit melted a hole in the snow. Steam came off it. I could feel the cold now, all the way through. I needed to warm up. I needed a cup of tea. I needed to be safe in my bed.

I wandered towards Fifth Avenue in search of a cab. The night-time sky was beginning to pale. I was incredibly relieved to be back in Manhattan. It even felt, for the first time, a little like home.

I wondered, fleetingly, if all this meant I had a drinking problem. It was my gambling problem that should've worried me more, as it turns out. There was something unfamiliar in my pocket. I ran my fingertip over it. Something cold and sharp.

Alexander's corkscrew.

It was worse than a one-night stand, I realized as I woke on Valentina's couch the next morning. Alexander's corkscrew glinted on the coffee table. I missed Kryštof so much I thought I was going to be sick again. It was worse than a one-night stand because it didn't have the clean getaway, the tacit acknowledgement that you'd never see each other again. A follow-up date had been arranged. A standing-up had to be perpetrated. I wanted nothing more to do with Alexander or his skanky apartment. I would definitely not be in Tompkins Square Park the following Sunday afternoon.

Which is why it came as such a surprise to find myself on the phone to my bank in Dublin the following morning, checking the balance on my father's bequest and ascertaining how long a transfer would take. It would be in my US account on Friday, they told me, if I arranged the transfer now. I arranged the transfer now. The giddiness I experienced issuing the instruction was unnerving.

I was doubly surprised to discover that what had once seemed like a fortune and a lifelong safety net had evaporated, in the space of twelve hours, into less than enough – Dad, I don't think you'd counted on me having such big dreams. When I rang around looking into the price I would get for my own violin, even upon receipt of an offer several thousand higher than the current insurance valuation, especially in light of my insistence on a shotgun sale and payment in cash, it still felt like an unholy rip-off. The sums would not add up to the magic number: six hundred thousand. I was one hundred and forty thousand short.

I needed to think, but my mind was elsewhere. My mind was in a decrepit tenement building an hour or so's drive away.

It was under a bed, locked into an old leather violin case that belied the value of its contents. I had to buy that violin, I knew by Monday night, because the alternative, not buying it, was unthinkable.

I spread a sheet of newspaper out on the kitchen floor and emptied the trash bag onto it. I picked through the contents with a knife and fork. Finally, right at the bottom: Daniel's business card from that night in the Madera. I wiped the coffee granules from it. Raised navy print, corporate bank logo: *Daniel Jackson. Vice President, Investments.* Investments. I knew I hadn't imagined that word.

I dialled the cell number he'd written on the back. He didn't sound in the least bit surprised to hear from me. He confirmed that yes, absolutely, he'd be delighted to attend my trio recital that night, and then he invited me to dinner the night after that.

I put in a strong performance. Had to. Vice-President of Investments Daniel was seated in the eleventh row. The prospective purchaser of my violin, David Rivers, was sitting bolt upright at the front. He was one of my old students and had just been accepted into Juilliard. He was an ambitious and talented boy who needed a decent violin.

I wanted David Rivers to feel about my violin the way I felt about Alexander's. I wanted him to lie awake all night doing the maths in his head. Sometime around dawn, I wanted him to be seized by the conviction that he had to possess it, whatever the cost, and then I would raise the price. Just by a few grand. Every small progression was a progression towards Magdalena. I was in the race.

The day after the trio recital was filthy wet, but my spirits were unassailable. For the first time in years I didn't have my violin, and therefore didn't have to practise, or feel guilty about not practising. David Rivers's father had collected it that morning for his son to try out at home.

I sat in the creaky chair by the phone and Ming leapt onto my lap. There was a message from Valentina on the notepad. She always wrote with a sharp pencil. How the girl always had a sharp pencil to hand, I did not know. She came to her life prepared. The grace with which she formed her characters revealed her alertness to the true wonder of symbols. She could have been a scribe, recording the word of God. There was nothing lovelier than a sheet of music written in her hand.

'Kryštof called last night,' her note said. 'He'd like to meet up and talk.'

The chair screeched as I sat back to consider this. Valentina had pencilled down his number. I'd lived with the man for two years. I knew his number. It had been my number too. The inclusion of the area code was a step too far. Kryštof lived five blocks away. Was he alluding to the distance he now perceived between us? Or was he just being snide? Either way, both he and Valentina knew better than to include the area code. He shouldn't have dictated it and she shouldn't have transcribed it. Valentina was my friend. Kryštof had no right to recruit her against me in this manner. I balled up the note and binned it.

There were other matters to hand, matters of destiny and fate. I phoned David Rivers. 'Hey,' he said warmly when I told him who it was. I asked him what he thought of last night's trio recital. 'Awesome, yeah, really awesome.' He'd brought his whole family along to hear the violin and they all thought it was very beautiful.

'Yes,' I agreed, 'it's quite something.'

'Absolutely,' he concurred.

And how was he getting on with it himself? I enquired. Oh great, he told me, everything was totally great. He'd just been playing it when I called – it was right there on his knee (he plucked the E string to illustrate) – and he was pretty excited, all in. Excited, I thought. Excited is good.

So, he continued, he'd, like, given it some thought and discussed it with his family, and they'd come to the decision that this was the right violin for his future. He was going ahead with the purchase.

'That *is* awesome,' I said, and the chair creaked happily. 'That's great news, but –' I squeezed my eyes shut to make it less intrusive – 'there was something of a development this morning.'

'A development?' David Rivers's exuberance evaporated instantly. Clearly a boy used to things falling flat.

'Yeah,' I said ruefully. 'Sorry to spring this on you, but there was a dealer in the audience last night, I'm afraid, and this dealer . . . Well, he sort of rang me up earlier and, you know, placed a good offer on the violin.' I bit my knuckles. He sort of rang me up and he sort of hadn't rung at all.

'Oh,' said David Rivers. There was the seashell sound of his hand covering the phone, followed by muffled muttering in the background. A female voice and a male. Wait, two females. No, just one angry one. A big angry female. I had pissed his mother off. David Rivers removed his hand.

'So how much did the dealer offer?'

I took a deep breath and told him the new price. 'A hundred and sixty.' I made a face at Ming. Ming blinked calmly. She didn't think it was that big a deal.

David Rivers unfortunately did, though he hadn't the gumption to curse. Well, not properly. 'Jeez,' he said, 'I don't know. Jeez, I don't know, that's a lot.' More muttering in the background, this time not muffled by the hand: 'Mom, she says she wants a hundred and sixty now,' and his mother exclaiming 'She *what*!'

I reminded him of my other stipulation: that I would need payment in full in cash by Friday. I bit my knuckles again.

He didn't have to consult Mom on that one. He said straight out that that definitely wasn't an option, not the extra ten grand. The hundred and fifty, yeah, he could just about go to that. The arrangements were almost in place. But a hundred and sixty? Forget it. He'd already reached his limit.

I took my knuckles out of my mouth. 'That's a shame.'

We were of a mind there. 'A real shame,' he agreed.

I explained that if I didn't raise one sixty, I wouldn't have the means to acquire the violin I was chasing, in which case the whole thing would have to be called off, because if I couldn't get the new violin, I was going to stick with the old one, because the old violin was a great one, whatever way you looked at it.

David Rivers was silent. 'What's she saying now?' his mother wanted to know. 'Nothing, Mom. Drop it.'

I stared out at the sodden street and was confident, all of a sudden, that David Rivers would find the extra cash. David Rivers wasn't confident, but then, he wasn't the confident type. He had yet to discover the extraordinary lengths to which human beings were prepared to go when confronted with their deepest desires. It was all ahead of him. It was all downhill.

He plucked the E string again. It sounded mournful this time. 'See?' I wanted to say. 'See what an expressive instrument it is?' Eventually he said he'd look into it, but that he didn't think it was possible to go the extra whack.

I didn't bother replying to that. Of course it was possible. If I was going to conjure up a hundred and forty grand out of nowhere, he and his family could manage a pissy ten. He could have a whip-around amongst the relations.

'What kind of violin are you buying?' he asked out of interest.

'A Strad.' I was taken aback by the determination in my voice. So was David Rivers.

'Whoa,' he said. 'A Strad. Scary.'

'Yeah, it is scary, but it'd have to be some violin to make me part with my own one, right?'

'Right.' He plucked the A string several times in quick succession. Ding ding ding, an alarm bell going off. 'A Stradivarius, though. Man, that's epic.'

Now was not the time for listening to the voice of reason. I did not need to be reminded of how outrageous it was. So I told David Rivers that I had to go, and that I needed my violin back by six that evening, because the dealer sort of wanted to look it over. 'Later,' said David Rivers and hung up, but not before I heard his mother launching into an invective.

I called Zach and invited him to a late lunch. He didn't want to come out because of the torrential rain. I said it was important. He said he had to be on a plane for Cincinnati at five-thirty, but that he'd meet me for a coffee at Marco's in half an hour if I 'really insisted'. I think he just wanted to hear me 'really insist'.

'It's about a Strad,' I told him. He said he'd see me there.

I put on two coats, a wool scarf, snow boots and my hat, the one with the earflaps that made me look like a cretin. Ming sat by the door monitoring my preparations. A small animal should not have to look so sad. I picked her up and kissed her and assured her I'd be back shortly. She'd heard that one before.

I arrived at the diner ahead of Zach. It was most unlike me to be early. A full quarter of an hour early, according to the clock on the wall. I felt virtuous and together. Everything was under control. I chose a booth by the window and organized the condiments. I ordered a burger and coke from the laminated menu, keeping an eye out for Zach.

The weather was apocalyptic. All but dark outside, though it wasn't yet three. The figures that struggled past were of indistinguishable gender, hunched up inside big coats and bent against the wind. It was too fierce for umbrellas. A broken one skated around the sidewalk like a dying bird. People stepped over it and glanced back in surprise. Pellets of hail lashed against the windowpane, louder than even the traffic.

It was a lovely sensation, being inside. I thought of the violin tucked under Alexander's bed, safely hidden away from the storm, and that too produced a lovely sensation. Zach came in on a blast of wind. He was five minutes early and didn't bother looking around for me, presuming I'd be late. He slotted himself into a booth with a clear view of the door. He looked much better wearing a hat.

'Hi, Zach!' I called brightly, and stood up and waved. Several diners glanced in my direction to see who could be so cheerful on a day like this. They looked me up and down. Goddamned tourist, you could hear them think.

Zach didn't smile. I pointed at the empty seat in front of me. 'I've saved you one,' I called across the room. 'Look, it's by the window!' Zach shook his head as if he couldn't believe the shit he had to endure. An old guy lowered his newspaper. He couldn't believe it either.

Zach dragged himself over and removed his camel coat. He

stood there staring angrily at the embossed silk lining. Water stains were creeping up from the hem. It was a brand-new coat. He'd brought it back a month earlier from Milan. Already it was beginning to ruckle.

He carefully draped the coat over the side of the booth. It smelled like a wet dog. Even the dank smell was a source of joy. It reminded me of being a small child on a wet school morning, back in the days when kids got there on foot, so that when it rained, we showed up soggy. Forty soggy children in a small stuffy room. We'd dry our coats and shoes on the radiators. Our little tiny coats and our little tiny shoes and our little tiny hats and scarves. The condensation trickled down the windowpanes as the tiny items of clothing dried off, but we didn't know what condensation was. Each droplet was a universe and unending source of awe. We'd sit there with our mouths hanging open because the world was astounding. And the world hadn't changed, that was the thing. It was the same astounding place it had been when I was five. I beamed across the table at Zach. The improbability of my happiness only made it more intense. If I could be happy on such a bleak day, I could be happy on any day.

'How the hell are you, Zach?'

He threw me a black look. 'I cannot believe you dragged me out in this storm.' He peeled his wet trousers from his calves. 'I just picked this suit up from the cleaners.' Zach hadn't had the foresight to wear snow boots and two coats, like me. I may have looked like a cretin, but I was invincible. The waitress placed my burger before me. There is nothing to beat the sight of a big American burger. I put the pickle on the patty and squirted ketchup and mayo at it. I sandwiched on the bun. My happiness was complete.

'I'm really sorry,' I said, and bit the burger. Ketchup squelched out the other end.

'You don't look really sorry.' He had a point.

'Well, I am really sorry. I'm really sorry your new coat got soaked. Let me buy you a burger. They're very good.'

'You know I'm a vegan.'

'Sorry, forgot. How about a coffee?' I flagged down the waitress and ordered him a coffee. 'Here, have a fry. Vegans eat fries, don't they?' I pushed my plate towards him. He shook his head and scowled out the window, though I could tell he really wanted one. 'Ah Jesus, have a chip.'

'You brought me out here to discuss a Strad, right?'

I nodded and gulped some Coke. 'I'm buying one.'

He laughed.

'It's true. I've come across this exquisite violin which is being sold at half its open market value: the Magdalena Stradivarius.' She became the Magdalena right then – the name materialized out of the air like whispered encouragement.

'Never heard of it.'

'That's because it's lain undiscovered for years.'

I ran the story past him, or at least, a version of it. A Russian dealer breaking into the US market; the Strad he had for sale which, because he had no decent contacts yet, was going for the price of a good copy; the sound that was so beautiful, it felt like I was dreaming it. 'Come on, Zach, don't look at me like that. It's fate. I just happened to be in this bar –'

'Imagine that,' he said flatly. 'Eva Tyne just happening to be in a bar.'

'What's that supposed to mean? Valentina dragged me out. Anyway, I ran into this Russian guy, and we went back to his place and he showed me this phenomenal violin. No really, it's amazing. Wait until you see it, you'll love it, trust me.'

Trust? Zach liked that. Trust was about the last thing on his mind. 'How much is the guy asking?'

'Six hundred thousand.'

He whistled. 'Can you raise that kind of money?'

'I've a substantial amount already put aside from my father's estate, plus I'm good for a loan, and I've secured an excellent price on my own violin.'

'You're selling your own violin?'

'Yes. On Friday.'

'For this one?'

'Yep.'

'That you saw when you were drunk?'

'What makes you think I was drunk?' Had Valentina been talking again?

'You were in a bar, Eva. That means you were drunk.'

'That's a racial slur.'

'Excuse me?'

'I was sober by the time I saw it.'

'You only think you were sober. What's its chain of ownership? What do the documents say?'

'The dealer didn't show me any documents.'

'Oh my God, this stinks. If you go ahead with it, you'll have lost all your money, your own violin, and you'll have acquired a sizeable debt.'

'And I'll have a new violin. A very old new one.'

'Some obscure Russian one.'

'Strads are Italian.'

Zach sighed wearily. 'It couldn't possibly be a Strad.'

'It is. I know.'

'How do you know?'

'Instinct, gut feeling. I just know. Just like you'll know the second you hear it.'

'I don't want to hear it. There is no such thing as an unknown Strad. It's either a fake, or it's stolen. You have of course considered the likelihood that it's stolen and will be seized from you the minute the rightful owner steps forward.'

'Of course I have.' Of course I hadn't. 'The Magdalena isn't stolen. The dealer told me it's been hidden away in the same family for years. It originally belonged to the Russian aristocracy.'

'Russian mafia, more like. Can't you just wait until our mini-subscription series is over?'

'No.' I couldn't wait. I absolutely couldn't.

'Who is this dealer, anyway?'

'He's just a dealer. A Russian dealer.'

'I know most of the dealers. What's his name?'

'I told you.'

'So tell me again.'

'Alexander.'

'Alexander what?'

'I can't remember. It ended in an *ich*.'

'They all end in an *ich*. An *ich* or a *ski* or an *ov*. Shostakovich, Tchaikovsky, Rachmaninov. And half of them are called Alexander, too. How long did you play this violin for?'

I thought back to Alexander's bedroom and the way he kept butting in. The weird dogmatic statements that disrupted my concentration. 'This violin is for you.' 'The violin and you are one.' 'You must haff this violin.' Was he simply nervous, or was he trying to distract me from a flaw?

And then, as it happened, I didn't want to play too much because the dollar signs were multiplying almost audibly in his head. His big Chechen head, which needed a smack. So I couldn't let rip, not with him standing there on percussion, clink swallow, clink swallow. I couldn't push the violin to its limits lest it rocket out of my price-range altogether, or even further out of my price-range, as the case may be.

And why wouldn't Alexander allow me to consult an expert? What was he trying to hide? Maybe it was a cultural thing. Perhaps he was just stubborn in the way that I was just stubborn. 'The fighting Irish,' he had laughed in delight, then skidded away in a cloud of fumes, leaving me to puke in the snow.

So how long had I actually played for in the end? Fifteen minutes? Ten? 'A good half-hour,' I told Zach.

'A good half-hour?' he spluttered. 'Eva, for six hundred thousand, you'd need to examine it for a month. And run it by an expert, get it appraised.'

'I am an expert.'

'Oh come off it.'

Surely it was in the violin's favour that ten minutes of playing had convinced me so thoroughly of its merit? 'I knew, Zach, okay? I played a few bits and pieces and I just *knew*. It was like love at first sight, or something.'

'You had an emotional response.'

'Yes. I had an extremely emotional response.'

'Because you're in a bad space right now.'

'No. Because it is a supremely expressive instrument and it would be impossible not to be moved by it. When you hear it, you'll have an emotional response too.'

He shook his head. 'Eva, you look like shit. Are you eating properly these days?'

'Of course I am.'

He looked at the burger. It sat there reproachfully with only one bite taken out of it. 'I'll bet you played this violin in a small room, right?'

'It wasn't that small.'

'But small enough that there was an intensity?'

'There was a ferocious intensity, yes.'

'That might not transfer to a two-thousand-seat concert hall?'

'Why wouldn't it transfer? The room was full of soft furnishings that dampened the sound. The violin will come into its own in a concert hall.'

'Tell me, did you examine it for structural damage?'

'I gave it the once over, yeah.'

'The once over?'

'That's what I said.'

'Was it a dark room?'

'I wouldn't call it bright.'

'So they could've covered anything up?'

'Zach, they didn't have the bloody thing tuned. If they'd gone to the kind of trouble you're suggesting, they'd have had the bloody thing tuned. They'd have put new strings on it, given it a bit of a shine, teamed it up with a quality bow, for God's sake. You want to have seen the state of the case it's kept

67

in. There is no cover-up. No doubt it has some damage – it's nearly three hundred years old – but I didn't spot anything majorly wrong.'

'The more I hear, the worse it gets. It's either fake, or worse – it's the real thing, and the Russian guy doesn't have a rightful claim on it, in which case someone is looking for it as we speak, and it'll be seized within days of your first performance. Have you considered what that will do to your career? Being linked with a stolen violin and the Russian mafia? You'll be finished, Eva. You might even be arrested. You'll be deported from the States at the very least.'

Zach spoke with the authority of one who had been around and knew that this world held no surprises. *There is no such thing as an unknown Strad.* The absoluteness of his voice, the surety of his manner. I was sick of the whole thing, all of a sudden, sick of the relentless temporariness of my life. How long could I go on dragging such a makeshift existence out? I didn't even own a bed.

'Your own violin is a concert-standard instrument, Eva. You were excellent on our debut night, and there's been great feedback on your trio recital. Stick with it and there'll be a recording contract and bigger venues and an East Coast tour. A real Strad will eventually be loaned to you by one of the big foundations, and you won't even have to pay for it. It'll come with a nineteenth-century photograph of an old guy in a bow-tie perching it on his knee, and you'll be able to frame it and hang a photo of yourself holding the same violin next to it. Think of what your grandchildren will say. It'll just take time, Eva, and you're so young. You're still only a baby. Hang on to your money and put this craziness out of your head.'

Everything he said was right. Logical, reasonable, fair and right. I couldn't refute him. And yet I couldn't allow myself to agree with him. I shook my head. 'My mind's made up.'

Zach pushed his coffee cup away. 'Jesus Christ, if your mind was already made up, why did you drag me out here in a rainstorm?'

'To let you try and talk me out of it and then see if I was still sure. If anyone could talk me out of it, you could.'

'So are you still sure?'

If I bought the violin, would somebody come knocking on my door, claiming rightful ownership? Not if it had been stolen from somebody who'd stolen it themselves. And not if it had been lost; not if it had been seized from the Russian aristocracy a century ago and found its way into the hands of someone who didn't fully grasp what it was. Just another fiddle in a country full of fiddles. It was feasible. Highly unlikely, but feasible.

There'd been any number of wars during the violin's lifetime, huge savage wars spilling right across Europe, in which everything had been uprooted and lost. Napoleonic wars, world wars, cold wars, a plethora of revolutions. Things had come loose from their moorings; paintings, jewels, even people. And the difference with paintings, jewels and people was that they were identifiable by sight. A violin wasn't. Not unless it had distinctive ornamentation. Magdalena had no distinctive ornamentation. At least, not that I could recall. I racked my brains, but remembered no markings at all. Only dirt, grime, the formidably alluring patina of neglect. It was just about possible that I might get away with this.

'Yes,' I told Zach. 'I'm sure.'

Zach considered this information carefully. 'Do you have any idea of what this will do to the group? A brand-new orchestra being associated with a stolen violin?'

'I'm not a member of your orchestra.'

'You're the soloist we opened with on our inaugural performance, and there are two more concerts featuring you to come. Do you know how hard I've worked to set this orchestra up? Do you understand how entirely dependent we are on keeping our sponsors happy? Do you care about how many begging letters I have to write? Fifteen alone today. I spend my whole life grovelling, and you're about to jeopardize it.'

'The violin isn't stolen,' I said quietly.

Zach scrutinized my face for traces of doubt. This could be it between us, I suddenly realized. This could be the end of our working relationship. I had wasted his time, dismissed his advice, he had every right to wash his hands of me.

He stood up and put his ruckled coat and scowl back on. 'We're probably going to fold anyway, so do what you like. We didn't have this conversation. I have a plane to catch. Just do one thing, Eva.'

'Name it.'

'Just ensure for your own sake that this violin isn't stolen. I'd hate to see you stripped of every last thing you possess.'

It is calculated in the standard text on Stradivari by the Hill Brothers that his workshop produced one thousand one hundred and sixteen instruments after 1666, of which over six hundred and fifty are still in existence. Other texts say fewer. The topic is surrounded by vagueness and surmise, and this vagueness fuels the myth of the lost Stradivarius. Everyone suspects that the violin in their great-aunt's wardrobe is priceless. More than four hundred and fifty instruments remain unaccounted for. The majority of these instruments, perhaps as many as four hundred, are violins. Four hundred missing violins. They can't all have perished. They are made of wood, not paper or silk. A few must still be out there.

Many were kept, often unused, in palaces and wealthy homes. According to my research, a surprising number found their way to Russia. Some ended up lying half-forgotten in churches and attics, whilst others were fêted internationally. It was often a matter of luck, which ones made it and which ones didn't. And the Magdalena, when Alexander dragged her from under his bed and lifted her out of that dirty scuffed case, didn't look lucky to me. The Magdalena didn't look like anything to me. But I heard something when I put bow to string. Drunk or otherwise, I heard something that unveiled an Aladdin's cave of possibilities.

Which is why, at dinner that evening with Daniel, I could barely sit still. The situation, to my mind, had escalated into an emergency. By agreeing to pay Alexander six hundred thousand dollars, I had confirmed that his violin was indeed no ordinary instrument. With this endorsement, he might take it elsewhere, seek a higher price. The minute he ascertained I didn't have the money, it would be over.

I took out my inhaler, but didn't raise it above table level. The restaurant was too quiet, too formal. Two limp hands and an inhaler on my lap. My feeble lungs in my weak chest and all my brittle bones, piled one on top of another like kindling. I was wearing a cocktail dress with silver shoestring straps, and I knew by the way the other faces had taken me in as I'd crossed the floor that I was overdressed. Or underdressed. Too much skin, an excess of bare neck and arms. I'd overdone it again. It was just a Tuesday in January after all, and a storm was raging outside. I smiled a small smile at Daniel.

He regarded me thoughtfully across the linen and silverware. Daniel had a gift for stillness, as if the world were a painting hung for him to appraise. He swirled the wine in his glass, then pushed my glass closer. 'Try the wine, Eva.'

I'd been trying very hard not to try the wine. There'd been an excruciating palaver with the wine steward and his list. When the nominated bottle arrived, it took both the steward and the host to stand over Daniel as he tasted it. Two grown men holding their breaths in case the damn thing was sent back. I couldn't bear to watch.

Daniel was at ease in the midst of it. The world was there, after all, for him to assess. He savoured the wine for longer than was necessary. Either the bottle was corked, or it was not. He swallowed, and the glimmering irises were replaced by the sheen of his eyelids. There was more of the performer in him than in me.

He pushed his glass towards the steward and nodded. No smiles, no appreciative words. The steward proceeded to pour. Daniel looked at me as my glass was filled: Look at what I have brought you, behold these wondrous gifts.

'Try it,' he coaxed when the waiters retreated. I hadn't taken a drink since that night with Alexander. Three whole days. Don't know why it felt like an achievement.

I sipped and agreed that it was indeed an excellent choice, as if the wine reflected Daniel's good taste, not his spending power. 'Thank you,' he said solemnly, as though he'd fermented it himself. A waiter set down our starters.

'So, Eva, you never mentioned the night we met in the Madera that you played the violin.'

I smiled. I had. Told him three times. 'Did you enjoy last night's recital?'

'I thought it was divine. I tried to call you last week.'

'Did you?'

'Yes I did, but I kept getting your voice mail. Then I remembered that your purse had been stolen, and that your cell was in your purse.'

'Ah, of course.' I thought back to our dismal leave-taking, the taxi driver sneering, the snow seeping up my socks, the fear that Kryštof was watching it all from upstairs. That morning seemed terribly remote.

'I would've left a message,' he continued, 'but there wasn't any point. But I rang a bunch of times to hear your voice on the voice mail.'

'Really? That's sweet.'

I didn't tell Daniel that I knew he was lying, that he couldn't have heard my voice mail since the phone number I'd scrawled out in the Madera had been concocted on the spot. I had no notion of seeing him again. 'I'll call you,' he'd said in the back of the cab, and we'd both smiled politely because we knew there'd be no call. Our case was hopeless. Two solitary drinkers on a perishing Saturday night. It was a delicate matter, and Daniel had been delicate. He had put his arms around me and helped me through the night. Perhaps I had in some way helped him, too, but come morning, neither wanted to see the other again. And yet here we both were, as if the world had been calibrated.

'What's the big smile for, Eva? What are you thinking about?'

I laughed. What was I ever thinking about? Magdalena, hopefully still under that bed. 'I am thinking of a violin.'

'A violin!' Daniel marvelled at the word. 'Such a complex instrument.'

'Are you a fan of classical music?'

'Of course.'

'And what kind of stuff do you like?'

'I liked what you were playing last night. The uh . . .' Daniel drew a circle in the air. 'The uh . . .'

'The Bruch? You liked the Bruch concerto?'

'Ah, the Brook concerto, that's it.' It wasn't, he'd lied again. It wasn't Bruch and it wasn't a concerto. 'I liked it very much.'

'I like it myself. The way it builds up and undulates in incremental cycles – sometimes when I'm playing that section, the momentum is such that it feels if I put the violin down and walked away, the sound would sustain itself and keep on spooling out into infinity, and they'd hear it years later in outer space.'

'I could tell you liked it. You played divinely. My client thought so too.'

'Your client?' I hadn't made note of the person seated next to him.

'Yes. He said you played wonderfully.'

'What kind of client is he?'

'A rich one. I invest his money. I'm an investment banker.'

'An investment banker? Really?' Like I didn't know.

'Yes,' Daniel said proudly. 'I'm the youngest vice-president in the firm.'

'Vice-president? I'm impressed. Congratulations.'

'Thank you.' We drank to Daniel's success. The waiter removed our plates.

'So, what sorts of thing do you invest in?'

'Oh, the usual. Stocks, shares, bonds, foreign currencies. Occasionally we buy out companies.'

'Do you ever invest in the art market?'

'Not for my clients, no. I'm thinking of investing in it for myself, though.'

'In paintings?'

'Yes. I like art.'

'Would you consider investing in violins?'

74

'Violins?' He sounded puzzled. Why would anyone invest in violins?

'Yes, violins. Eighteenth-century Italian old master violins. Stradivari, Amati, Guarneri.' I'd seen a window, after the chicanery with the wine. And that deplorable statement: I like art. Here's a guy, I decided, who's open to bullshit.

The entrées arrived. Daniel shook his head. 'I don't think so.'

'Hey, that's a shame. They represent an excellent investment. It's a question of supply and demand. Value is proportionate to scarcity. The supply is finite since the masters who made them are dead, so you can be assured that the market won't be flooded by new Strads. The price, therefore, will not decrease. It can only increase. It's watertight. I'm completely stunned that you haven't heard of this.'

Daniel wasn't completely stunned that he hadn't heard of this. 'It's not really my area,' he said, dismantling his main course.

'As it happens, I'm looking for an investor at the moment.'

Daniel didn't look up from his plate. 'That so?'

'Yeah. I'm buying a new violin.'

'That's wonderful news, Eva.'

'Well,' I corrected myself, 'I'm hoping to buy it. It's expensive. It's a genuine Stradivárius, but it's been offered to me at a fraction of its market value.'

'How come?'

'Because the guy who's selling it doesn't realize it's a Strad.' I laughed at the stupidity of Alexander, who was probably in some bar laughing at the stupidity of me. 'He has no idea what he's got on his hands, because the violin has no documents, no certification of attribution.'

'How do you know it's real, then?'

'By playing it. An experienced violinist knows by playing it, by assessing how it behaves. It doesn't respond like an ordinary violin; therefore it isn't an ordinary violin. It doesn't sound like an ordinary violin, either. As a musician, you instinctively sense when something is special.'

I shrugged, as if it were a simple matter. As if genuineness were a tangible quality that could be discerned by eye or ear. As if authenticity resonated at a specific pitch, or showed up under certain wavelengths of light. As if there were no grey areas at all.

Here's what I didn't tell Daniel that night: that Italian eighteenth-century violins immediately acquired an almost legendary reputation, so much so that the violins of the Bohemian, German, French, and English schools, also full of musical merit, were proportionally disenfranchised. So unscrupulous violin dealers regularly ripped out the real maker's labels and substituted them with Italian labels, whilst some violinmakers made exact copies of Strads and stuck in Strad labels, so much so that a label reading *Antonius Stradivarius Cremonensis Faciebat* – Antonio Stradivari of Cremona made this – came to mean, in the violin trade, 'Made in the style of Antonio Stradivari of Cremona.' There was no definitive way of telling who made what, neither then nor now. It was entirely a matter of educated guesses, and of old-fashioned connoisseurship.

'The guy who's selling it thinks it's nineteenth-century French. It's truly remarkable – this precious violin has somehow or other slipped through the net. I have to get my hands on it before anyone else so much as catches wind of it. Then, when it's legally mine, I'll have it certified by a recognized authority. Its value will double overnight. Maybe even treble.'

'Why can't the guy get it authenticated himself?'

'He's an illegal immigrant. He can't afford to draw attention to himself.'

This was met with silence. Daniel continued to work through his main course. I picked up my cutlery and prodded at mine. His silence was huge in my ears. His non-reaction said it all. I glanced up at his impassive face and saw, refracted through it, the sad reality of my delusion. Of course the violin was a fake. Of *course* it was a fake. There was no way a masterpiece could have ended up with the likes of Alexander. It was that simple. That's how simple it was. It was so blindingly simple that I couldn't see it. I had to go through the humiliation of reading it on a stranger's face. Whilst on a date with him. A date for which I was overdressed, because I'd hoped for too much. My expectations from life were immoderate and would have to be downwardly revised. I wheezed the air out of my lungs, a drab and dreary sound, and inhaled some Ventolin.

Daniel raised his eyes from his plate. The Ventolin had marked a turning point for him too. He started to nod, cautiously at first, but he built up momentum. 'That's very interesting, Eva,' he said. 'That really is very interesting.'

Was he being sympathetic? I examined his face. No, this wasn't sympathy. This was greed, lovely human greed. We two, I realized at that second, were alike. Daniel didn't think me deluded after all, so maybe I wasn't.

'It is interesting, isn't it?' I said to him. 'It's the most interesting thing I've ever heard in my life. It actually causes me pain, the white-hot fear that I might lose this violin, the horrendous suspicion that someone else will get there first, the very real risk that Magdalena might slip through my fingers, and that I will have missed my one and only chance.'

'Magdalena?' he asked. Yes, the whole restaurant wanted to know at this stage who Magdalena was.

'It's the name of the violin. The Magdalena Stradivarius. All the old violins have names, and Magdalena is this one's name.' I sat back in my chair. 'I just need to have the money in place by Sunday.' Like: just. Minor clause. I made a throwaway gesture with my hand to illustrate how trifling it was.

The waiter cleared away our plates and a second waiter took our dessert order.

'How much does this guy want?'

'Three hundred thousand.'

I don't know why I lied. It just popped out. I tried not to look surprised. I was hoping to make it seem less outrageous, I think. Less outrageous to myself as well as to Daniel. It was so terrifyingly fragile that if I told him the real price, I was scared he might take flight. Worse – I was scared I might take flight. I could only get through this with my eyes tightly shut.

'I have most of the money already secured,' I added. Another lie, yes, but only just. I would have most of the money secured once David Rivers came through for me, even if he only produced one fifty.

'So how much do you think this violin will be worth once it's authenticated?'

'Who knows? Anywhere between one million and two.' I didn't tell him that this estimation was academic, that the violin would never again be for sale.

Daniel nodded appreciatively. One to two million dollars out of three hundred grand? Not a bad day's work. But then, for no reason that I could discern, he appeared to lose interest. His gaze became vague again. He ran his thumb over the curve of the wine bottle. 'Dust,' he said, rubbing it between his fingertips.

The desserts arrived. I spooned pannacotta down my throat without tasting it. Daniel worked methodically through his pear and quince crumble, and patted his mouth with his napkin when he was done. The waiter cleared away our dishes. We were offered coffee. We said we wanted tea. Tea, as if we were civilized. As if we were two civilized human beings sitting down together for a meal.

I took another fifty-dollar sip of wine and pretended that I too had lost interest in the violin. I pretended that the pain in my chest was no longer raging. I pretended that a cup of tea was the only thing on my mind. The discipline, the years of restraint of a musical training: it had its uses.

The tea arrived in a porcelain pot, which Daniel commandeered. 'American tea is generally awful,' he said, pouring. He handed me my cup and stirred sugar into his.

'Nice restaurant,' I offered, to break the silence.

'Do you like it?'

'Yes, it's lovely.'

'It is, isn't it?'

'Yes, it's just . . . lovely.' What did he want me to say?

'Thank you. I can go through the figures with you, if you like.'

At last. 'The figures?'

'For the violin.'

'Oh, okay. You mean now?'

'Why not?' Daniel asked the waiter to bring him a pen and paper. 'Right,' he said, uncapping the pen, 'let's start with the amount you presently have.'

Oh man, why had I lied? Now I had to divide everything by two in my head.

'Well, there's . . .' (my father's three hundred and thirteen thousand divided by two?) 'one hundred and fifty-six thousand, five hundred and forty-two dollars from my father's estate.' One five five, wrote Daniel and I felt this insurrection. My father gave me twice that, I wanted to protest, as if Daniel had in some way belittled the man.

'That it?'

'No,' I said morosely. 'I'm hoping to get around –' (half of one sixty?) – 'eighty thousand for my present violin, worst case scenario seventy-five.'

Seven five, wrote Daniel.

'Which equals . . .' Daniel drew a line under the seventy-five. 'Two hundred and –'

'Call it two thirty.' He wrote down two thirty.

'Two thirty,' I said. 'That's what I have.'

'Pretty good. And how much did you say you agreed to pay for the violin?'

Last chance to tell him the truth. Say six, do it. 'Three hundred thousand.'

Three zero zero, he wrote, and I could've punched my nose. 'So you basically need seventy more, Eva.' He drew a dollar sign before the seven zero, and a K after it. 'You basically need me to find you seventy thousand dollars.'

'Yes.' No. I basically need you to find me one hundred and forty thousand dollars.

He tapped the pen against the paper. He drew a circle around the $70K and added an asterisk to either side. 'That's manageable,' he concluded, nodding at the figure. Of course it was manageable. The man had just spent several hundred dollars on a dusty bottle of wine. A few more bottles, and we were away.

'Do you think you can get it?'

Daniel replaced the cap on the pen. 'Sure.'

'By Sunday?'

'I'll write you a cheque right now. How does that sound?'

An amount that substantial mightn't clear in time. 'I need it in cash.'

Daniel shook his head. 'I never handle cash.'

'I'll pay it back to you within the year.'

He narrowed his eyes. 'Pay it back?'

'Of course.'

'Eva, is it a lender or an investor you want?'

'This is very romantic.'

'I'm an investor. You understand that, don't you? I'm an investor, not a moneylender. Which do you need?'

I needed anyone who would stump up the cash. 'I need an investor.'

'So you understand that I'll retain part ownership?'

'Yeah, you can have the bow.'

'I'm being serious. You understand that I will retain quarter ownership of the violin?'

A quarter of the ownership for less than an eighth of the price. Another wave of resistance engulfed me. This would be the violin that my father bought me. His gift, his enduring legacy. And yet I was in no position to refuse. 'That's understood,' I nodded. 'You will retain quarter ownership.'

Daniel reached across the table and took my hand and kissed it. 'I will bring the money to you before close of business on Friday. In cash, since you insist.'

'I do.'

'I'll draw up papers for you to sign.'

'Okay. Thanks.'

The evening was wrapped up fairly swiftly after that. Daniel signalled for the bill. He inserted his credit card into the book-let without first checking the amount, then surveyed the room in a territorial fashion. I finished off my wine. My glass had not been topped up all night. This should've afforded me more gratification than it did.

We waited in silence behind the glass doors of the foyer, watching the busboy getting soaked as he hailed us a cab. His black trousers were soon as glossy as garbage sacks. The cabs sailed on past, every last one of them occupied due to the rain.

Finally one drew up and the busboy dashed back. Daniel tipped him, then turned to me.

'There's your cab, sweetheart.'

So, he wasn't going to share it with me. He wasn't going to attempt to come back to my place, nor coax me to join him in his. He must've had somewhere better to be at that hour.

'Well, it was great to meet you once more,' I told him.

'Thank you. Let's talk on Friday.' We shook on it.

Daniel was gracious with the air of one who has overseen matters to his complete satisfaction. From the backseat of my cab, I studied his expression as he spoke on his cell phone. I failed to decipher the tenor of this conversation, despite tremendous effort.

That night I dreamt of Sandpiper. I was standing at the bay window, gazing at the long lawn, when the first bomb whistled down and exploded. A deluge of them then, pounding down on us without respite. I rushed along the corridor and threw open the door, but my mother was no longer seated at the kitchen table. There was no kitchen table – the back of the house was gone. It was literally gone, not so much as a wall stood, no trace of what had been there only seconds before.

East Ninth Street glittered in the Wednesday morning sunlight when I awoke, gasping for my inhaler. Yesterday's storm had washed the dirty old snow away. A new message had appeared by the phone.

'Kryštof called again last night.'

I crumpled up the note and threw it away.

I had an hour before my student showed up. I set myself up with the Stravinsky music. This was what was called for – hard work, concentration. Ming took up her post by my feet as sentinel and kept our audience in check. The audience doesn't put a foot wrong when Ming is on the job. Normal cats can't tolerate violins. It has crossed my mind that Ming is partially deaf. Either that, or she loves Stravinsky.

I was still nearly sixty thousand dollars short. Seventy, if David Rivers didn't cough up the extra ten. A quarter of the new violin was already beholden to some banker. What did I want with three-quarters of a violin? Why would I trade that for four quarters of my own? Plus all of my father's money. No violin could have sounded that good.

I decided to stick with Stravinsky. It blocked everything else out. I didn't notice the phone ringing. I didn't hear David Rivers leaving a message. That he'd like to arrange a meeting.

That he would have the money as specified. The full one sixty, in cash by Friday. That perhaps we could arrange the transfer of ownership then. He'd appreciate it if I called him back as soon as I got this message.

I didn't call David Rivers back. My student came and went, then I had to be at the City Opera for a run-through at two, as I was deputizing for a second violinist for four nights on *Billy Budd*. I was looking forward to sharing the perfumed darkness of the pit with sixty other string musicians, maybe five of whom knew my name. I would take my seat at the back where no one could see me, or discern my sound from the sound of the others, and where, for a change, nothing would be required of me other than to keep up with the conductor.

I rang Daniel's cell phone on Thursday morning. There was another message from Valentina by the phone. David Rivers had called twice the night before. I'd have to face him sooner or later, now that I'd made a decision. Not to buy, not to sell.

I turned the page over. Nothing new from Kryštof. A lurch of emptiness that I deserved.

Daniel seemed surprised to hear from me. Not pleasantly surprised, just surprised. 'Eva,' he said curtly. 'How can I help you?'

'Well that's just it,' I told him, 'you can't.' I explained that I wouldn't be needing that seventy grand after all, seeing as I was no longer going ahead with the purchase. I'd made a huge mistake in the calculations, I said. It turned out I was in fact many tens of thousands short.

Daniel didn't respond for a few seconds, then said that listen, he couldn't talk right now, I'd caught him at a bad time, that he was in the middle of closing a deal, and that it wasn't going well. He took down Valentina's number and said he'd call me back.

He didn't call me back. David Rivers did. David Rivers called me back several times, but I let the voice mail take it. I taught my students, I practised my Stravinsky. Igor Stravinsky in the morning, Benjamin Britten at night. Benjamin Britten, or Aunt Britten as Stravinsky called him, composed *Billy Budd*.

The intercom rang as darkness was falling on Thursday evening. My first thought was that it was Kryštof and I jumped up to answer. It was David Rivers and his father.

We sat around Valentina's table in the gloom. I didn't invite them to take off their coats. I didn't offer them tea or coffee. I just showed them where to sit and, sitting across from them, explained that the deal was off. I hadn't secured the rest of the finances necessary to acquire the Strad, and I therefore couldn't sell my own violin to them. I thought for a strange moment that I was going to cry.

David and his father listened to this information obediently. They didn't demonstrate frustration or disappointment. They didn't demonstrate anything at all. They just nodded solemnly, and I was acutely aware of their powerlessness. I felt like a doctor delivering bad news.

When my speech was over, they didn't immediately move. I waited for them to get up, but they did not. They simply sat there, bundled up in their coats and scarves like children. Someone was coming up the stairwell. The footsteps paused outside our door and I thought that Valentina was about to appear, but whoever it was started walking again and went up another flight.

Mr Rivers scratched his eyebrow and said that he could go an extra ten. I looked at him blankly. 'We'll pay one hundred and seventy in cash,' he clarified, though I knew what he meant. There was no strain in his voice. No flicker of surprise in the son, either. This was an eventuality for which they'd evidently prepared. They must've surmised that my alleged dealer had put in a higher bid. They'd been going through the same torment as me these past few days.

I explained that the shortfall on my part was a significantly larger sum than that, but I thanked them for their kind offer all the same. I promised that once I was in a position to sell my violin, they would get first refusal. David needed a new violin immediately, though, we all knew that. I apologized for wasting their time.

They neither accepted nor declined my apology. They left soon after. David hadn't opened his mouth. He was already beginning to lose his hair, though he couldn't have been more than nineteen. Soon he would look just like his old man.

Daniel finally rang back on Friday afternoon. 'So how much is the shortfall?' he asked in a harassed tone of voice, as if I'd been badgering him about it for days.

'Sixty grand.'

'I can raise it.' This was not welcome news. 'How does that sound?'

'But then you'll own almost half of the violin. I don't want you to own almost half of the violin.'

Daniel considered this for a minute. There was a lot of noise in the background. Bells, announcements. Sounded like he was in an airport. 'All right, I'll set up a loan for the extra sixty. The first seventy will still stand as an investment, that is, quarter-ownership of the violin. The extra sixty will be arranged as a loan. You'll pay it back at a competitive interest rate. My percentage of ownership of the violin will not go above the quarter mark. I think it would be a real shame to let this opportunity pass us by.'

I shook my head as if he could see me. 'It's too much debt, Daniel. I can't get into so much debt. I just can't do it. I'm sorry.'

Daniel said he understood, though he didn't sound like he understood at all. He sighed and said he'd call me back, that he had to go, that there was another call coming in. I put down the phone and felt lighter. I filled the kettle and placed it on the stove. I set out my Stravinsky music.

The phone rang again as soon as I raised my bow. Zach, calling from Cincinnati. 'So? Did you buy the violin?'

'Zach, I haven't the balls.'

He assured me he felt certain whatever decision I reached would work out for the best. It was a meaningless sentiment. He told me he was putting our Stravinsky rehearsals forward to four o'clock instead of three because of a rescheduled meeting with the Cincinnati board that Monday morning. I said I'd tell Valentina when next I saw her. She'd taken to avoiding me in case I dragged her out drinking again.

The apartment seemed awfully quiet when I put the phone down. A quarter to three. The bank would close at four-thirty and not reopen until Monday. If I wanted to withdraw my father's cash, I would have to do so soon.

I turned back to the Stravinsky concerto. The progress I'd made the day before was lost. The shape I'd discerned had sagged. The minutes ticked past. The sky darkened. At dusk, I put my head in my hands. I had to get the money out of the bank. I couldn't bear to leave it there.

I put away my violin and pulled on my coat. Just because I was withdrawing the cash didn't mean I had to spend it, I counselled myself. I could return it to my account first thing on Monday. I think this is what alcoholics tell themselves as they merrily pile vodka into their shopping baskets. I don't have to drink it, I'd just like to know it's there. Besides, they were expecting me in the bank. I'd requested that the money be ready for collection.

I brought along a Key Foods bag in which to transport the cash. The money wouldn't look so conspicuous if carried in a supermarket bag, I reasoned. I went back for a second bag in case one bag was snatched. I'd never been mugged before, which now struck me as a glaring oversight. Adrenalin was pumping through my blood as if a race had begun.

I only just made it to the bank on time. The security guard turned the key in the door to prevent other latecomers slipping in. I was much relieved to see it locked. The process of counting out the money was hampered by the bank-teller's nails. They must have been an inch long and were embossed with blue gems. What a stupid thing, I thought, to spend your money on.

The cash was accompanied by a statement indicating that my account was now empty. I instructed the teller not to close it, since I'd be returning the full amount on Monday. The account address was that of the apartment I'd shared with Kryštof. I didn't update it, so as to prevent the bank staff from knowing where the money was being brought.

I signed the forms and packed the money into the supermarket bags. The bills were visible through the thin white plastic. The teller gave me envelopes to help conceal them, but they still didn't look like groceries.

The security guard unlocked the door, and it struck me that he could well have a criminal past. He wished me a great weekend. I tried to detect irony in his voice, but he just sounded bored. I rushed back to Valentina's and pulled the safety chain across her door. I closed the blinds and set about stashing the cash. I hid some of it under the sofa and some of it in the casserole pot. The rest went into the salad drawer of the fridge.

I didn't exactly feel alone in the apartment, though I knew it to be empty. Sometimes I believe in ghosts. The phone rang and I jumped. I let the voice mail take it, but the caller left no message. My muscles trembled as if I'd set down a heavy load. I wondered if I was coming down with the flu.

Ming leapt into my arms but I put her straight back down. She climbed into the Key Foods bag and caught her head in the handle. Valentina had swung by and gone out again during the half-hour I'd been at the bank – the cupboards had been restocked. I debated whether to tell her about the cash, then decided against it. But what if she found it? What if she lifted the lid of the casserole pot or shifted the sofa?

I dialled her number and her coat started ringing. She'd left her cell behind. There was no way of contacting her. If I left a note, an intruder would find it, and therefore the money. I picked up the pencil anyway.

'Stravinsky rehearsals put forward to four on Monday,' I scribbled. 'And please keep your cell on you in case . . .' In case what? I didn't know. 'In case I have to talk to you.'

I put the pencil back on the writing pad. I didn't mean the note to sound so imperious, I just wanted the girl to know how much I needed her these days. I hadn't called my mother in ages. Too late now. There was barely time to get changed for the opera.

I locked the door and looked down at the key in the palm of my hand. How could something so tiny be all that separated the outside world from everything my father had left me? I dropped the key into my bag and hurried down the stairs. I was not cut out for this.

Saturday morning. I was standing in a shaft of sunlight, practising the Stravinsky concerto's Toccata when the intercom buzzed. I raised the bow from the string, then decided I must've imagined it.

I was about to return to the buoyant rhythms when the intercom buzzed a second time, and I didn't have the wit to ignore it. I didn't have the sense to recognize that the room was complete as it was, and that any intrusion would only injure that completion. It was Daniel, of all people. I buzzed him in, and he showed up at the top of the stairs, panting.

'How did you get this address?'

'Your roommate told me. I spoke to her last night. She sounded really nice. She sounded like a really nice girl. She said she'd leave a message for you.'

I'd seen the message by the phone, all right. 'A "Daniel" called,' Valentina had written. 'He says he has a present for you.'

'I have a present for you.' He handed me a gift bag. 'It's a new cell phone. So, are you going to invite me in, or what?' *Watt*. Daniel never pronounced the *h* in what. He was too busy.

'Come in,' I said, and he walked past me into the living room. He placed a fat envelope on the coffee table and threw himself on the couch, arms outstretched along the backrest Jacuzzi-style.

'What's that?'

'That's Ming.'

'Wow. That's one funny-looking mammal.'

'She's Siamese.'

Ming jumped onto our guest's lap to welcome him, and

raised her nose to his face.

'Look at that. She wants to kiss me. I'm great with animals.' He put Ming back on the floor and brushed imagined fur off his knee. 'I thought you lived on East Fourth.'

'I moved.'

'Right. I have a really great apartment on Fifth Avenue.'

'Well done.'

'Thank you.' He nodded at the music stand. 'You practising?'

'I was trying to.'

'Good. It's important to practise.'

'Is it?'

'Yes. You must focus.'

'I didn't know that. Thanks for the advice.'

'No problem.' Then his expression changed. 'Is that a hickey on your neck?'

'This mark? It's from the violin.'

'Oh.' Daniel settled back into the couch. 'Anyway, sweetheart, that's what I'm here about, the violin. The Stradivarius one. I've looked into the matter, and I think you should go for it.'

'Oh do you?'

'Absolutely. I believe this opportunity is just what your career needs. So I have the cash. I have it right here.' He lifted the flap on the brown envelope. He wasn't joking. There was a whole lot of money in there. 'Where are you meeting the guy?'

'Tompkins Square Park.'

'What time?'

'You're not coming.'

'I didn't say I was coming. I just asked what time you're meeting the guy.'

'Two o'clock. But I'm not meeting him. I'm not going anymore – I told you that yesterday.'

'Great. Listen, there's one hundred and thirty thousand dollars in this envelope. Seventy as investment, sixty as loan, as discussed. You're going to be in that park at two o'clock tomorrow, and you're going to come out with the Stradivarius violin. I need for you to sign this affidavit to acknowledge that the cash is here. If you don't go ahead with the sale, you return the cash in full on Monday, and we tear up the affidavit, okay?'

'Tear it up now. I already told you I'm not going ahead with the sale.'

'Why not? You have the capital now. You should be thanking me. I'm helping you achieve your dream.'

Achieve your dream. Did he never listen to himself? 'It's too big, Daniel. I'm not prepared to take the risk.'

'So I was right.' He jumped off the couch and stood by the window with his hands on his hips, shaking his head. 'I knew it. I knew you'd turn chickenshit on me. I'm so intuitive. I cannot believe how intuitive I am. That's why I came down here. To stop you making the biggest mistake of your life.'

'Daniel, come on.'

'Biggest mistake of your life, sweetheart, biggest mistake of your life.' He threw himself back on the couch. 'You want to make it to Carnegie Hall or not?'

'How would you know how to make it to Carnegie Hall?'

'I know how not to make it. I just want what's best for you, Eva. You are positive it's a Stradivarius, right?'

'Yeah, but –'

'Great, then I definitely think you should go ahead and buy it. So call me when you have it, say tomorrow around three, and I'll take a look at it. My number's programmed into your new phone.'

'Jesus, Daniel, I don't want your money. I don't want it in the apartment. What if someone breaks in and steals it?'

'So find somewhere clever to hide it. Use your imagination – you're the creative one. Here.' He pulled a sheet of paper out of the envelope and handed it to me. 'You need to sign this before I go.' It was the affidavit. I handed it back.

'I already told you, I'm not buying that violin.'

'Fine, then I will.'

'What?' A jolt of alarm.

'I'll buy it if you won't. What's the guy's name?'

'You're joking.'

'Where's the joke? What's funny? If you don't want the violin, I'll take it.'

'I didn't say I didn't want it, Daniel. I said that I didn't want to take the risk.'

'Well sometimes you have to take the risk, honey. What's he look like?'

'Who?'

'The Russian guy.'

'He looks Russian. Look, he's not the type who'll accept a cheque, and you won't have enough cash on you by tomorrow. The banks are shut.'

'Who's to say I didn't take the precaution of withdrawing the entire three hundred thousand in cash in case you turned chicken, like I figured you would? If you're not buying this violin, Eva, I sure as hell am.'

Thank God I'd had the foresight to lie about the real price. Still, there was an outside chance that Alexander might settle for three hundred thousand in the absence of a better offer, what with his soft spot for US dollars.

'What use is a violin with no provenance certificates going to be to the likes of you, Daniel? Nobody's going to purchase an unknown violin from a banker. At least, not for the market value of a Strad.'

'I'll get it certified myself, sweetheart. I'm not some illegal peon who has to hide from the law. I'll bring it to a luther.'

'A luthier. This is bullshit. I was buying the violin to play it, not sell it. That's the whole point. Show me that document again.' Daniel handed back the affidavit and I glanced through it. If I held onto his money until Monday under the pretext of purchasing the violin, it would at least prevent him from acquiring it. 'Are you sure this isn't some sort of rip-off scam?' Like he'd tell me if it was.

'If anyone gets ripped off here, it'll be me, Eva. I'm the asshole putting my money on the line.'

That was true. He was the asshole.

'What if I run off with your money?'

'Don't worry, I'll find you.' He displayed a row of implausibly perfect teeth. I reckoned he'd find me, all right. I took his pen and signed my name. Daniel folded the affidavit in four and slotted it into the inner pocket of his coat. 'Wonderful. Call me on Sunday at three to let me know how things worked out.' We did the handshake thing again. 'You're prettier in daylight. Anyone ever tell you that, Eva? You're even prettier in daylight than you are at night.'

'So are you.'

'Don't be smart.' He tipped me under the chin with his finger. 'And don't disappoint me.' Off he went. I shut the door. Don't disappoint me? Not even my mother had the right to say that.

The gift bag started ringing. I unwrapped the new phone. *God calling* . . . read the screen display.

'Don't let this opportunity pass you by,' Daniel warned. 'If you're not going to buy the violin, let me. That's all I'm asking you to do, sweetheart. I need for you to do that for me, okay?'

'Jesus,' I sighed, 'okay.'

'Great. Another call coming in. Gotta go.'

'Hey Daniel.'

'What?' *Watt.*

'This cell phone. Who's footing the bill?'

'I am.'

He hung up and I dialled my mother. There was an international block on the line.

The problem with being a musician is that as soon as you establish a routine, the routine is broken, because no performance can go on for ever, nor even for very long, no matter how successful. You have to move on, and on and then on, whether you want to or not. It's like life, only faster. You play with different musicians each evening, and you play different programmes, and you play them in different venues, and nothing stays the same. Not even the music. The arrangements are fluid, and even if you believe you've perfected the definitive version, it'll be thrown out of the window the next time around.

I was dejected out of all proportion on Saturday when the last night of the opera came. I'd been content, for once, sitting at the back of the second violins, watching the audience instead of having the audience watch me. The order and cohesion of the operation appealed to me, as did the feeling of security induced by the paycheque. The lack of challenge was precisely what I needed. I was an exhausted woman, and it had been an exhausting month. But now the nightly routine was over. It was back to the state of flux.

A wrap party was organized, but I didn't much feel like attending, so I kept my head down and packed up. The stagehands were already hammering apart the set as I left. Another crowd would be in the pit tomorrow. I wanted to be there tomorrow. Out I went into the freezing night and caught a cab on Columbus Avenue. The first flakes of snow had started to fall.

I sat in the backseat with my arms wrapped around my violin case and gazed at the people on the street, just as I had gazed at them on the trip home for four nights running. But whereas it had given me comfort before, knowing they were all out there going about their business, now they seemed sinister. The exact same people doing the exact same things, as if trapped in a routine they couldn't break. There are two recurring notions that trouble me: the first, that life is so big as to be unmanageable; the second, that it is so small as to be inescapable. It'll either tie me down or cast me adrift, and I don't know which frightens me more.

I took a deep pull on my inhaler. I needed to talk to someone. Valentina wouldn't fully understand the unease I felt, not being prey to such fears herself, but Kryštof might, because it lay at the core of his being too. Twelve days had passed since we'd parted. It was time to face him, I finally accepted, and redirected the driver to East Fourth.

The lights in our old apartment were on. It crossed my mind that it was too late to disturb him. Terrible, to have to worry about protocol with Kryštof, to feel like an intruder at your own door. I buzzed the intercom. He'd already removed my name.

'Hello?'

I blinked. It was a woman's voice. I wasn't expecting that. Deserved it, but wasn't expecting it. I turned and hurried away.

The snow, which was falling heavily now, made it difficult to find my way, and I felt myself to be lost, though I was not. The sidewalks had cleared. The few cars caught out in it glided along First Avenue as stately as ocean liners, and I ducked into a doorway to hide.

After a time, I took out my new phone. *God* was the only listing in the address book, and I almost called him, but the fear that Daniel would also have company prevented me. It was Saturday night, after all.

I phoned Valentina, but my old friend didn't answer. She must've already been asleep. So I rang David Rivers instead. It was the only other number I could call to mind. A snowflake alighted on my lash and I tried not to cry. It didn't look like anyone was home in the Rivers household either. It was going on for midnight. Was I the only soul alive?

'Hello?' At last. David Rivers, groggy.

'Listen,' I told him, 'your father said he could go the extra ten. If he can get it to me in cash, then the deal is back on. I need it by tomorrow morning.'

'Who is this?'

'It's Eva.'

No response.

'Eva Tyne. Look, David, it turns out that I can sell my violin to you after all, so long as you get the cash to me by tomorrow morning.'

'We're not here tomorrow morning. We've got something going on.'

Well fucking well cancel it, I wanted to scream. I needed to get indoors before I froze. 'How about tonight, then?'

'You mean, like, now?'

'Yes, I mean, like, now.' It was unkind to mock him. He knew it too. 'David, do you want the violin, yes or no? You must decide this minute.'

He sighed. 'It's snowing.' I didn't say anything. He sighed again. 'Uh, hold on. I have to talk to my father. He's asleep. I'll call you back.'

'Call me at the apartment. I'll be there in ten minutes.'

They came all the way from Mohegan Lake. I'd forgotten that they lived so far away. They'd missed the last train, so had to travel by car. It took an hour and twenty minutes because of the snow, but, David's father told me, they'd managed to find a parking space right outside my building. He regarded this as some sort of achievement. David's father didn't like driving in the city, but I did. At least, I liked the idea of him driving in the city. I liked the idea of father and son journeying through the snowy night in pursuit of a violin. Contemplating this image of them together had made the waiting easier.

They had the money, including the extra ten, on top of the other extra ten, which I wouldn't have insisted on, but which I accepted all the same. One hundred and seventy thousand dollars in cash. My parents had bought me the violin a decade earlier for forty-two thousand Irish pounds, a currency since deceased.

I counted out the cash on the coffee table and handed over my old violin. A deeply unsettling moment. I presented the Rivers with the certificates, and then we shook hands. I wished them all the best with it. They wished me all the best with the Strad. 'Oh that,' I said. 'Yes, thanks.'

I showed them to the door, and experienced an extreme pang of regret to see my violin go. You've really done it now, I realized. You've really gone and done it now. I watched father and son descend the stairs, then rushed over to the window and waited for them to emerge at street level. Ming was in my arms, purring as hard as she was able.

The blizzard outside was quite something. David and his father shuffled towards their car. Mr Rivers unlocked the passenger door and David got in, his arms wrapped around the violin case just as mine had been a few hours earlier. They fussed over the seat-belt, then Mr Rivers carefully shut the door on his son. This display of paternal heed did not make matters any easier for me. For the first time since the age of five, I did not own a violin. It was like losing an arm. Ming cried out because I was holding onto her too tightly.

When they'd driven away, I didn't know what to do at first. No point in turning to the rigors of the Stravinsky concerto. Nothing to play it on now, and two bows with which not to play it. The shock of that woman's voice on Kryštof's intercom, as stinging and as personal as a slap across the face. 'Hello?' I kept hearing it, the voice of my replacement.

It was two in the morning but there was no question of sleep. I paced around the apartment, Ming's head resting in the crook of my neck. I wanted to go back to Kryštof's to see what she was like, this woman who had taken my place. Was she prettier than me? More gifted? Easier to be around? I still had the key to his door. I could sneak in on them as they slept and stand over them for a while.

97

But it was nothing to do with me anymore. I had to remind myself of that. 'It's nothing to do with me,' I said out loud. 'This really has nothing to do with me anymore.' My voice had no conviction.

I sorely needed a distraction. No violin. The cash. I'd count it out.

I retrieved the money from its various hiding places and assembled it on the kitchen table. The one hundred and thirty from Daniel, the three thirteen from my father's estate, and the one seventy from Mr Rivers and his son. Six hundred and thirteen thousand; I'd outdone myself. A Frankenstein's monster it made when joined up, a slovenly torn heap, as commanding a presence as any creature with eyes or a mind. More than I was worth, and potentially my ruin; nearly a quarter of it, after all, was debt.

I set about dividing it into three stashes, though it was only money and possessed no inherent identity in itself. And yet it possessed distinct identity once separated. There was the Daniel stash, the David stash, and the Dad stash, and each stash embodied a specific emotional resonance. The Daniel stash swaggered, and the David stash was to a minor extent self-made, but the Dad stash towered over them both, and I was pleased about that.

I sat there for a good half-hour chewing my nails. Rearranging the cash stash and chewing my nails. It was a good thing that Valentina was already in bed. How would I have accounted for this?

I went to the bathroom and nearly died when I came out. There was a cup on the counter that hadn't been put there by me.

'Valentina?' I whispered.

No answer.

Her bedroom door was still shut. Ming was perched on the arm of the sofa. Were someone in there with us, Ming would have been after them like a shot. I turned on every light in the apartment.

I placed the cup in the sink and put my head in my hands. Post-fright tears were welling up. I could still hear that woman saying 'Hello.' Not a woman's voice, but a girl's. And now this huge transaction tomorrow, this obscenely huge transaction. Everything my father had left me and more for a violin I'd played while drunk.

The cash formed an unwieldy bulk. How was I to transport it safely to Tompkins Square Park? What was to stop Alexander from grabbing it and making off? My God, Alexander mightn't show at all. That eventuality only dawned on me then. In which case, could I retrieve my old violin from David Rivers? I knew that I could not. I had no idea what I'd do for a violin for the Stravinsky concerto on Monday. I had no idea what I'd tell Zach, never mind my mother when she discovered the ransacked account.

I made a cup of tea and sat at the kitchen table with my palms pressed against the scald of the cup. Owl-eyed Ming helped me keep vigil, purring all the while. I left every light burning. We sat there, the pair of us, as the small hours got bigger, and at daybreak I swept the money into one large pile. I made a big pyramid of it, a drift of autumn leaves. Now it had no separate identity. It was just counters in a game.

Sunday dawned still and bright. It was not, I imagined, unlike facing major surgery, something from which you might not return. I showered and organized the money. Saturday night's blizzard had deposited an icing of snow. New York has a way of seeming brand-new sometimes. Tompkins Square Park was a two-minute walk. I put on my runners in case I had to run. Ming was distraught at being left behind, having kept watch with me all through the night.

At twelve forty-five I left the apartment, having scribbled a brief note to Valentina, who was still in bed. 'Meeting Alexander, the guy from the Russian bar. Shouldn't be long.' It crossed my mind, as I signed my name, that this note might end up in a police station, being passed from hand to hand in ominous silence. I should've made it say more than it did, but I was not thinking clearly that day.

I stepped out onto the street and was confronted by the suspicion that my appearance had triggered a response. Was someone watching my door? I immediately dismissed the notion. It was natural to feel jittery around money. Last night in the apartment, for God's sake, I'd thought I wasn't alone. I put on my shades and headed for Tompkins Square Park. In my hand was a tightly packed Key Foods bag.

The faces around me looked fresh in the bracing whiteness. I tried not to look in their eyes lest they detect the alarm in mine. The pressure of walking around with such a large sum was breathtaking. I had the very distinct feeling that someone was trailing me. This very distinct feeling followed me around the corner and jogged through the traffic in my wake onto Eighth. I couldn't shake it. I told myself that I was being paranoid. In retrospect, it has to be said, I'm no longer so sure.

I had to queue for longer than usual in Odessa's due to my insistence on a seat by the window. That way, I could keep an eye on the entrance to the park. The Sunday brunch trade was as brisk as ever. I got a table at last and ordered pancakes. The lid fell off the maple syrup bottle and syrup glooped all over the plate. My pancakes were ruined. This cheered me up, if anything. I was too nervous to eat. I'd only ordered them so as to be allowed to sit there.

I drank the coffee and accepted refills from the waitress, all the time worrying the handle of the plastic bag on my lap. Half a million dollars. If I returned Daniel's cash on Monday, I'd be left with nearly half a million dollars to my name. Half a million dollars with which to buy a legitimate violin.

A man in a black overcoat walked right past, not a foot away, so tall that he momentarily eclipsed the window. In his hand was a violin case, an old leather violin case that belied the value of its contents. He crossed the street to the park. Thump thump thump, went my heart.

I took out my inhaler and wheezed piteously. I didn't have to give him the money if it wasn't the same violin. Or even if it was the same violin, but just didn't seem as good anymore. That's what I told myself. I don't have to do anything that I don't want to do, but it still felt like my fate was sealed. I picked up the plastic bag and left ten dollars on the table, put on my sunglasses and hurried out.

Alexander scanned the benches and, having established that I had yet to arrive, embarked on an anti-clockwise circuit of the park. I went directly to the Seventh and A entrance so that he'd catch me on his second lap. There was a faint warmth in the January sun that shone on my face. I wiped snow off a bench and sat on it.

Alexander still hadn't spotted me. I watched him making his round. I couldn't have run away if I'd wanted to. My hands in my lap were like two dead puppies. Between them was the plastic bag. I was happy, that's the odd thing. It was like sitting in a darkened cinema waiting for a slasher movie to begin.

Alexander trudged doggedly through the snow. Sharp black suit under the overcoat. Shafts of sunlight spilled through the trees onto his ash-blond hair, causing it to flicker like fire. How well he suited this landscape.

His pace picked up when he clocked me. He cut through the centre of the park, the collar of his overcoat turned up around his face. The mad skinny height of him, the length of the shadow he cast across the snow – with the bare trees behind him, he could've been back in Moscow. It wasn't a scene that belonged in my life.

One of his eyes had been punched black and blue. I tightened my grip on the Key Foods bag. Within it were three fat brown packages. What was to prevent Alexander from snatching the bag? Nothing at all, not a thing. I knew that. He knew it too. If Alexander wanted the bag, he just had to grab it. He could've kept the violin as well. I couldn't have stopped him. I wouldn't even have tried.

I sat there limply waiting for him, a big stupid smile on my face. There was a big stupid smile on Alexander's face too. Silly, really, two grown adults beaming at each other like children. I suppose neither of us thought the other would show. That both of us had turned up seemed like uncanny good fortune. I was delighted to see him again, I realized, and not just because of the violin. Here was a comrade, a brother in arms, someone who really knew the score. 'You wouldn't believe the shit I've had to put up with this past week,' I wanted to tell him, because Alexander would have understood. He'd instinctively have known exactly what I meant, and we'd have sat in comfortable silence over a drink or ten. Maybe it was because we were both outsiders in New York, maybe it was because he patently had troubles too. His eye looked pretty bad.

'Hello, Alexander,' I said.

'Hello, Jane.'

Jane. I'd forgotten about that.

He sat down beside me and let out a companionable sigh, then placed the violin case by my feet. It wasn't a good idea to leave it on the snow. I didn't feel in the least bit scared of him anymore. I knew that Alexander wouldn't hurt me. He might steal from me, cheat me, but he would never hurt me. At least, that's what I thought.

We studied the branches of the tree on the other side of the path. Squirrels were scampering up and down. A set of railings around the base of the tree kept the enclosed snow pristine. The sky was as blue as a summer's day.

Alexander pointed at his black eye. 'Fucking squirrels, Jane.'

He laughed, so I laughed too, though I didn't get the joke. His wire-framed glasses were still intact. They'd removed them before punching him. I wondered at the mentality of that.

'Nervous, Jane?'

I shrugged. He shrugged back.

'Only natural. Inhaler?' He took one out of his pocket and held it out. 'I brought one for you just in case, Jane.'

I shook my head. 'That's very considerate of you, Alexander, but I remembered to bring my own this time.'

He raised his eyebrows at the wisdom of this. 'You are smart.' He nodded at how smart I was, then put the inhaler back in his pocket. It was remiss of me to have forgotten his corkscrew.

'Alexander?'

'Yes, Jane?'

'I have to ask you something before we do this.'

He tilted his head to indicate that he was listening. 'Proceed.'

There was no other way but to come straight out with it. I pointed at the case on the ground. 'Alexander, is that a stolen violin?'

Alexander shook his head. 'No, Jane. Bought fair and square from the owner.'

'Did the owner have rightful claim to it, Alexander?'

'Excuse me?'

'Did the owner own it?'

'Of course, Jane. He was the owner.' He pulled a face to indicate that the question was dumb.

'So why, if it's a genuine Strad, did the owner sell it to you cheaply?'

Alexander drew himself up to his full height, clearly taking exception to the question. 'He did not sell it cheaply. I paid a large amount of money, Jane. Do not think I bought this violin for a cheap amount.'

'Yeah, but the guy didn't sell it to you for the market value of a Strad. How come?'

'Many reasons, Jane. Because I paid in US dollars. Because he was a fool. Because he wanted a house and a car. Who knows? The price I paid for the violin was the value of the violin in Russia.' He'd probably taken it off some serf's hands for a couple of grand.

'Did you buy it from a little old lady, or something?'

'No,' he reassured me, 'her son.' He picked up the violin case and placed it across my knees to indicate that there would be no more questions. It was the same old leather violin case from his apartment. It looked even more scuffed and torn in daylight. 'Your violin, Jane.' Alexander patted the case. I put a hand out to stop it sliding off.

Jesus, I thought as I sat there contemplating it. A gooey noise came out of my chest. My heart started to race again, but I breathed deeply and it slowed down and down, until soon it seemed to be hardly beating at all. There is a point at which you must accept the inevitability of things. I'd learned that lesson years ago, first from my father, and then, on a lesser but incremental scale from the stage. Certain events have their own momentum; they are bigger than you. The orchestra and audience waiting, your mother saying you'll never see your father again. You must submit, whether you feel prepared or not, and there is strength in that submission, because it is the opposite of running away.

I listened to the laughter of the children in the playground, the cooing of the woodpigeons, the barking in the dog run. If I was about to make the biggest mistake of my life, then so be it. I was meant to make it here on this snowy day which possessed a quality of perfection. I was young. I'd bounce back. I always did. I looked at Alexander. He nodded at the case. 'Open it,' he grinned, as if it were a carefully chosen gift.

I put the Key Foods bag on the ground and wedged it securely between my ankles, then lifted the lid of the case. It looked like the same violin, all right. Dirtier in daylight. It was certainly the same crappy bow. My hands came alive. They unstrapped the violin and took it out. They groped it and mauled it and ran their fingers over the curves. They were tempted to put it in my mouth.

Alexander took the case off my knee and returned it to the ground. He unclipped the bow and passed it over. I fine-tuned the strings and hesitantly sounded the high notes. How ethereal they were on the icy air.

'Would you mind?' I handed Alexander the bow and violin, then stood up to remove my coat so that I could fit the violin under my chin. I kept the plastic bag tightly trapped between my ankles at all times.

'Nice coat, Jane,' he said, though he had seen it before.

'Thank you, Alexander. I like your suit.'

It was the first time since childhood that I'd played outdoors, and in the frozen world of Tompkins Square Park, the sound was startlingly pure. I began with the Stravinsky concerto's Aria II. Woodpigeons exploded into flight on the opening chord, whipping snow from branches. I took my time with the slow melodic passages. I didn't rush. You have to be so careful with valuable musical instruments in public places, and it's a real burden, a real strain, the constant worry that they'll be snatched out of your hands.

But for once, I wasn't inhibited. I didn't give a fuck. If anyone tried to steal that violin, Alexander would maim them. His presence granted me temporary immunity. I sent notes spiralling into the chilly sky, intertwined with imagined flutes, absent cellos. I was almost laughing, almost crying in wonder at the loveliness of the sound. It was without question the same violin. It was without question extraordinary.

A few people had stopped to listen. Alexander was vigilant as a hawk. When I was finished, and just for the hell of it, and in honour of Alexander being Russian, or whatever, I played Prokofiev's *Dance of the Knights*.

'This one's for you,' I told him, and sawed out the swinging notes of the violin section. He took up the bass line, singing dourly, but doing a pretty good job for a man keeping the world at bay. 'Wah hey,' shouted some homeless guy who'd been drinking with his buddies. He goose-stepped around the chess tables and the buddies joined in.

Alexander scowled, but never dropped the bass line. A dog in the dog run had started to howl. I couldn't wait to get at the violin with a decent bow. On the finishing flourish, there was applause in the park, from Alexander too. I handed the violin back to him, and he returned it to the case.

'You bring a tear to my eye, Jane,' he said, dry-eyed, clicking the lid shut. 'Now, the money.' He indicated the Key Foods bag. 'This is it, yes?'

'No, Alexander, the money's in here.' I took my coat off the bench and removed an envelope from the pocket I'd stitched into the lining the night before. The crafts my mother taught me as a girl were not entirely wasted. 'And here.' I removed another envelope from another such pocket on the other side. 'And here.' I lifted my jumper and pulled the last envelope out of my waistband. 'There's two hundred thousand in cash in each one.'

'You Paddies, you are wily,' he sniffed. 'A wily nation full of cheats and pretty girls.' Alexander opened each envelope in turn and leafed through the cash. 'Do not,' he warned me, 'marry an Irishman, Jane.'

'Take your time and count the money out properly,' I told him, but he didn't, which was just as well, because we were starting to look suspicious. Alexander nodded over my shoulder, and I turned and saw another man dressed in a black suit and coat standing outside the park. We were separated by the railings. The man nodded back.

'Who's that,' I joked, 'Igor?'

'No, Igor's in the car. That is Nikolai.'

'One of your very good friends?'

'Nikolai?' Alexander snorted mirthlessly. 'Nikolai is nobody's friend.'

He stuffed the envelopes into his pockets and stood up. The almighty size of him. Nikolai made for the gate. I hurriedly pulled my coat back on, and Alexander thrust out his hand. He was wearing black leather gloves, one of the fingers of which sagged emptily. And so the spell of his protection was over. Now I was the sole custodian of the violin. Don't leave me in this place on my own, Alexander, I wanted to implore. Just see me safely to my door.

'Best wishes, Jane,' he said in his clunky English.

'Yeah,' I told him. 'Good luck.'

He gripped my hand too firmly again, but this time I didn't complain. He nodded in a faintly military fashion, grinned like a boy, and seemed about to say something significant. I leaned in to hear it, but he released my hand and off he went, just like that. It was done.

The violin was mine. I stooped to pick it up from the snow. Suddenly there were a lot of tall men in black suits and coats. They approached Alexander from various directions, converging at the Seventh and A exit like a bunch of undertakers. Five of them in all. One short of a pallbearer team.

They discussed something with Alexander, picked at the contents of the envelopes, then narrowed their eyes at me. That's when I noticed the sixth guy, muffled up in a hat and scarf. He kept his head down and left the park via the St Mark's Place gate. I didn't catch sight of his face. It's possible that he wasn't with them at all, but he looked just like them. Same black coat. Though a black coat is just a black coat. And it was Sunday, after all. Church day. Perhaps it was only a coincidence.

I tightened my grip on the case and hurried away. I wanted to get the hell out of there before Igor, wherever he was parked, decided to intercede. But then I remembered the Key Foods bag, which I'd left behind in the snow. It was full of paperbacks belonging to Valentina, old French paperbacks patterned with coffee rings. I'd packaged them up in brown envelopes the night before.

When I reached the bench, the Russians had already gone. Off to the next funeral. How bare the park exit looked without them. As if they had never been.

It was a privilege to at last be alone with her. There was something miraculous about that violin, almost occult, as with all great works of art. She demanded deeper resources from me. She required that I become a finer violinist. I recognized that I was blessed. It could've been anyone Alexander met in that bar that night, or the next bar the next night. But it wasn't anyone. He'd met me.

I sat backstage the following Monday evening, staring at Magdalena in a sort of horror. The privilege had come with a price. Zach and the group were onstage playing the overture. I had owned this violin for thirty hours and was afraid, suddenly, of its power, afraid that I would fail to match it. It occurred to me that I might not be worthy of Magdalena. I needed to lock myself up with her for a hundred years. Only then would I master her range.

This burden was immense, as if the violin were made of rock, and me of paper. Soon they would come for me. Zach would call my name. I didn't think I'd find the strength to raise Magdalena from my knee. She was not the fake; I was.

My thoughts turned, as was their wont, to my father. His money had bought this violin. Magdalena was a gift, not a burden after all. This knowledge spurred me on to reach the violin's depths. I vehemently desired to bring out of that superior instrument all it had to give, as if some lost quality of self drew breath within it. I'd glimpsed something that drunken night in Alexander's apartment. I had seen beyond the confines of my life.

Applause for the overture, then the stage manager came to summon me. Zach smiled and held out his hand. I crossed the stage and placed the violin's great weight on my collarbone, locked into an uncharacteristically solemn state of mind.

'RECENTLY REDISCOVERED STRADIVARIUS' ran the headline of the *New York Times* review two days later. Zach had called the critic personally, and by some miracle, she'd actually come. The piece featured a large reproduction of my publicity photograph, the one of me lying down with the neck of my old violin laid across my hair. 'Eva Tyne with the recently rediscovered Magdalena Stradivarius,' read the caption.

The photograph had been taken on a day when New York was limp with heat. I'd just come out of the shower and was towelling my hair. Kryštof was seated at the table with his camera equipment laid out. 'Lie down,' he'd said softly, then knelt beside me and spread my hair across the floorboards. He placed my violin on the fanned-out coils, then stood over me with the camera. The picture that resulted was striking. Very intense, very intimate. We were in love back then.

'New Discovery,' read the subtitle of the review, referring to both the violin and me. Ming was asleep on my lap. Magdalena was on the table in the ragged old case, the lid open so I could glance at her from time to time. The sky had thickened into matt grey. It was about to snow.

'The New Amsterdam Chamber Orchestra tackled the Stravinsky Violin Concerto in D with the power of a full orchestra, and the precision of a smaller group. There were occasional lapses in the soloist's technique, but Eva Tyne's great lyrical powers carried her through. The two Arias were chillingly affecting, almost bleached out . . .' (I was thinking of Tompkins Square Park, of waiting for Alexander in the snow) '. . . But the highlight was the finale. Tyne's tendency to over-dramatize was here replaced by a seeking out of the internal colors of the music, the rhythmic nuances of a phrase, the inner life of a melody. The music breathed and glowed.'

I took my time cutting out the review. The edges, when I was finished, were perfectly straight. This was a document of consequence. It would have resonance for years to come. Other people would look at it. My children, for instance, if I ever had any; at that moment I felt certain I would.

I slotted the review into a cardboard-backed envelope. The volume on the phone was turned down. I battled my way through the swirling snow to the Cooper Union Post Office and mailed the envelope home to my mother.

I took off Daniel's clothes for the first time that night. His body was like his face; smooth, silky, dark. He had a silky Latin build, my satin Latin boy. I put my face against the dip of his chest and pressed myself into it. I clasped him, stroked him, committed him to memory. There were no sharp angles to his body at all, not like us thin and bony Irish, all strung together like violins. Daniel was nothing like a violin. He did not feel hollow. He was the opposite of me. How was it that we could be members of the same species? 'What makes you think we're from the same species?' he asked, then laughed loudly. He only came up with punch lines when they were fed to him.

I returned his sixty grand that same evening, telling him I didn't need the loan after all. His quarter share in the violin still stood. I placed Magdalena on top of his tallboy where we could both see her. It was our second night together, but it felt like our first.

There was some sort of a problem that I didn't want to hear about regarding the violin's status. Zach rang on Thursday morning. He told me two things: one, that there was some sort of a problem regarding the violin's status, that the Entente des Luthiers wished to discuss the sale; and two, that we'd secured our first Carnegie Hall gig.

The second piece of information outshone the first. The news beat down on me like the sun. The concert wasn't until the fall, but that didn't diminish the exultation. I barely gave the Entente a second thought.

~

I tried to insure Magdalena the next morning, quoting the woman on the phone a valuation of one and a half million dollars. I'd plucked this figure out of the air, and gathered from the woman's reaction that I'd pitched it too high. She wanted details from me – receipts, certificates of provenance, a recognized expert's analysis, that sort of thing. The sort of thing I didn't have. 'We can't just call it a Stradivarius because you tell us to, ma'am,' she informed me.

'Why the hell not?'

I was talking to the hand after that. 'You don't have a receipt, ma'am?' She repeated the question several times in incrementally incredulous tones.

'No receipt,' I confirmed, 'no documents, nothing.' I don't know why I sounded so pleased with myself. The insurance woman didn't know either. She sighed and said I'd need official authentication if I wanted my violin insured for that amount.

My old policy was terminated right there. A new one would not be issued until I submitted the pertinent documents. Which meant that if Magdalena were damaged or stolen in the meantime, I'd bear the loss in its entirety. A pain in my stomach then like I'd eaten a bag of ice.

I got back on to Zach. He said he'd been about to phone me, as he'd been getting more calls from the Entente. These words rumbled like distant gunfire. 'They're not going to go away, Eva.'

'What do they want?'

'They want to know which dealer sold you the Strad, how much he charged, and they want to examine the certificates.'

'Fuck, Zach, is it any of their business? Do I have to comply?'

'I don't know. I don't know what legal jurisdiction they have, if any. The Entente's a cartel. They set the prices on stringed instruments. If someone sells a prestige violin cheaply, it undermines their monopoly. They want all the big sales to go through them. Hence their determination to investigate this. It's their livelihood.'

'So, because the sale didn't come through them, it would be in their interest to declare my violin a fake, so as to scare off anyone else thinking of purchasing from a dealer outside their circle?'

'Oh,' said Zach, 'I guess it would. I hadn't really looked at it that way.'

Ming whimpered and her fur bristled. She was having a nightmare. I stroked her back and she began to purr. I couldn't tell whether she was still asleep or not. There was an argument going on downstairs. A woman was shouting, a door was slammed, an ambulance hurtled past. These events seemed connected.

'Don't give them my number. I want nothing to do with them. I'm sorry about this, Zach.'

'We'll talk tomorrow,' he said.

I put the phone back in its cradle and paced around the apartment. I'd known, even as I'd stooped to pick that violin up from the snow, that I would have to fight to hold onto it. I'd understood, carrying it out of Tompkins Square Park, that I would never be left in peace. It had been too easy. I had come by it too easily. The world didn't work like that.

I booted up Valentina's computer and ran an Internet search. There were thousands of hits on stolen Stradivarius violins. Listings from Interpol, Europol, the FBI, various museums and dispossessed owners. One site showed an empty glass display case, the side pane of which was shattered. A ghost violin was superimposed inside it. The accompanying text was in the Cyrillic alphabet. '1996' was the only part I could recognize. Alexander had defected some time around '89.

I went down to the hardware store and returned with a padlock and chain, but I couldn't find anything to chain the case to. There was only the radiator pipe, and the heat would damage the violin. I felt like handcuffing it to my wrist. I'd decided by then to keep the old Russian case, which belied the value of its contents. It was something of a talisman to me, an emblem of the extent to which this violin had been overlooked in the past, an auguring that it might continue to be overlooked, that I might just get to keep it. I knew from the off that the chances were I would lose it.

Perhaps that's why our relationship was so intense. Because our days together were numbered, right from the start. That violin was as miraculous to me as the magnetic streamings of the aurora borealis, only she was smaller and more constant, and I could take her wherever I went. I had risked my life for her. I had mined the depths of the underworld. I had entered that crackhouse and stepped into Alexander's lair. I had handed over my father's bequest and more. That violin was my birthright. I would not relinquish her easily. I would hold onto her with my teeth, yes.

So I bit her. Very gently, just enough to leave the most shallow depression, one that only I would find. The violin was too wide to fit in my mouth, so I left an indentation of my front teeth next to the chinrest clamp. The taste of varnish was pleasantly familiar. I'd chewed a church pew once as a child. Got a slap on the head for my efforts.

I examined my tooth marks so that I would recognize them anywhere, then ran my fingertips over the twin indentations like Braille. I turned Magdalena over and buffed her with my polishing rag. That's when I spotted the hairline crack.

Âme, Seele, anima. Three translations for what is termed in English the soundpost, but in the languages of the great composers is called the soul. The soundpost is a small stick inside the violin connecting the belly to the back. It carries the tiny vibration of the strings via the bridge to the body, where it is amplified, creating the big sound that we hear. I explained the situation to Zach over the phone. That there was a crack over the soul of my violin.

'The back or the belly?' he wanted to know. 'Thank God,' he sighed when I told him it was the belly. 'That's serious, obviously, but it won't devalue the violin. Get a soundpost crack in the back, however, and you're done for. Or wait, hold on, is it the other way around? Shit, I can't remember; I'm really sorry.'

I needed to consult a luthier as soon as possible, but I couldn't go to my regular guy since my regular guy, the one used by the majority of string musicians in New York, was no less than the president of the Entente des Luthiers, an organization that, despite its moniker, was motivated as much by dealer interests as by violinmaking and repair. The Entente kept a track on prices and on each other. They'd sent me a letter via Zach. There was my guy's name in the list of directors at the bottom of the page: Honorary President, Eduardo Vedres.

I scanned the list and recognized two more names. Johann Vogl and Bob Johnston. If you didn't use Eduardo, you went to Johann or Bob. 'We write with regard to the recent appearance of the Magdalena Stradivarius. We have no records of a Stradivarius so-named, and wish to discuss this discovery in full.'

It hadn't taken them long to get on the case. It wouldn't take them long to get to the bottom of it. They wanted to know when would be convenient to inspect the violin. Any known Stradivarius, they said, would be added to their database, which would greatly enhance its value. They didn't point out that the value of my violin would be very much undermined were it to be excluded, that it would make me notorious as the peddler of a fake. Or worse, that were Magdalena to match up with the measurements of a stolen Strad, legal proceedings would ensue. The *New York Times* would cover the story again, but from an entirely different angle.

What made me think I could evade my fate, I'll never know. It would clearly be foolhardy to bring the violin to President Eduardo, yet every other luthier advertised was affiliated with the Entente. 'Members meet regularly and are committed to a code of practice,' read their website. If one of them decided that my violin was a copy, or identical to a missing Strad, the news would be everywhere.

Yet it seemed I'd no choice but to subject Magdalena to their scrutiny, the soundpost crack being a matter of urgency. Then Konrad suggested Claude Martel. I had never heard of him; nor had Zach. 'He's cheap,' Konrad told us, 'obnoxious, but cheap.' I checked the Entente website. Martel wasn't registered. What should have been a warning acted in his favour.

Martel was based in Dumbo, Brooklyn. Zach was already waiting on the corner of Jay and York Street when I drew up in the cab. We set off downhill in a businesslike fashion, making a conspicuous pair amongst those rusty, derelict factory buildings. It was a curiously barren and depopulated place, considering its proximity to Manhattan.

'Just for the record,' Zach informed me, 'I didn't accompany you on this trip, you got that? The Board of Directors cannot –' The roar of a train crossing the overpass drowned him out.

'I'm nervous,' I told him once the train was gone. Nervous was not the right word. It was more than that.

'You're always nervous,' he responded without slowing his stride. He didn't mean it unkindly. Neither of us liked being out on the street with the violin, particularly in a neighbourhood like this. Zach knew about the insurance difficulties. A car drove past, sounding on the cobbles like it had four flats. Tramlines were set into the stones.

'No, I mean, I'm like doctor's-surgery nervous. It's not adrenalin; it's a sort of powerlessness. I don't know what this guy is going to say to me. I don't know what the diagnosis will be. What if he looks at the crack and tells me the violin is finished? What'll I do then?'

Zach put his hand on my shoulder. 'The information will not leave his workshop, okay? That's the deal I made with the man. If it's a fake, we don't use the word fake. We call it a copy, an excellent copy made in good faith, and we don't let anyone discover it's a copy until after the Carnegie Hall performance. You can't possibly show the violin to the Entente until after your Carnegie Hall debut, right? You need it around the clock to practise. They can't subpoena the damn thing. It wasn't used in a bank robbery.'

Three things became clear to me from Zach's response: firstly, that he hadn't listened to my question; secondly, that he was more concerned about the authenticity of the violin than about the crack; and thirdly, that he didn't actually believe the violin was the real thing anyway. Neither of us addressed the real fear: that Martel might recognize the violin, might say, why, this is the Strad that went missing from the glass case in Moscow in 1996. Or from backstage in the Musikverein in Vienna in '98. Or from Mrs Edel Winter's Park Avenue apartment only last Christmas.

We arrived at a stoop that led up to a heavily riveted metal door, numbered 215 in gold hardware store stickers. Zach looked at Konrad's scribbled instructions, then back at the door. NO PARKING NO PARKING NO PARKING was slathered in white paint across the steps, as if anyone would be so stupid as to leave an unsupervised vehicle around there. Aluminium shutters rattled in the wind, and a Coke can trundled past at a fair clip. I stood back to get a better look at the place and stepped on something crumbly. I lifted my boot:

117

frozen dog shit. A couple of windowpanes were broken and patched with plywood.

Zach glanced up and down the empty street. 'This seems to be it,' he said with great reluctance. It was too cold to stand there debating. We climbed the unrailed stoop, and Zach heaved open the riveted door into darkness. I was really glad he'd agreed to come along.

'Hello?' he called up the stairwell. Martel shouted down in a French accent crossed with Bronx – '*Fronx*,' Zach whispered in my ear – to get in the elevator and take it to the sixth floor. The workshop was at the top of the building.

The elevator landed with an inexact clang and the doors slid apart. It was an unprepossessing sight. Someone had wallpapered it back in the seventies. We stepped inside and I swallowed two headache pills. I'd been swallowing a lot of headache pills of late.

'You should always take water with those things,' said Zach, and pressed 6. 'And I didn't accompany you to this place either, okay?'

'Okay.'

'I know nothing about any of this.'

'All right.'

Claude greeted us gruffly when the elevator opened onto the top floor. He led us into his workshop, or his 'atelier,' as he termed it. It was an unexpectedly bright room, long, narrow, and high-ceilinged, windowed all the way down one side. This was a significantly smaller operation than Eduardo's. Eduardo had four or five assistants, Claude just one. He was down at the far end with his back to us, whittling, and didn't look around to check us out. Eduardo's walls were lined with autographed concert posters of virtuosi dating back to the fifties; Claude had a calendar with nothing filled in on the days.

A workbench ran the full length of the room, various tools and clamps suspended from the rack above it. The air was sweet with woody smells. A pale violin-shaped coffin was propped up on the desk, a belly without *f*-holes next to it. The wooden floor had a quality of paper, upon which the sun formed glowing shapes. It was a room I would very much have liked to practise in. The light, the elevation, the warmth and pliancy of the wood. I would have felt buoyant, free, like a dancer.

A train rattled past in the distance and the windowpanes quivered in response. An unseasonable wasp was hurling itself at the glass, and I was seized by an overwhelming conviction that I'd been there before. I'd stood exactly on that spot. With my father, as a child. He had held my hand and we'd walked along the line of windows, pointing at things on the other side.

The surge of happiness stimulated by this memory was unusual. Thoughts of my father generally made me sad. I only remembered him as an adjunct to the catastrophe of his end. In my many recollections of him, he was already a ghost, an incarnation of what had been stolen from me. But not this time, not here in this room, with its blazing parallelograms of sunlight serried across the papery floor.

I knew I'd never been in Claude's workshop before, though. I'd never been to the States with my father. It was just the wasp banging against the row of sunlit windows, and that smell, like pencil parings. They called something to mind. A train journey, maybe, at the end of the summer holidays, on one of those old carriages with crimson velour seats. My father must have taken me on a trip sometime. I didn't recall my mother being there.

Claude led us to the workbench on the shadowed side of the room. He was a small man, defensively small. He stood with his legs apart in a bid to elongate, which made him wider, yes, but shorter. Zach and I were like wading birds beside him. Claude scratched at his face with stubby fingers. 'Please,' he said in his clipped Fronx, and nodded at the bench.

I put the violin case down and unlocked it. It was noticeably colder on that side of the room. Claude kept his distance from the case as if it were diseased. He cleared his throat and folded his arms.

'Where did you get this violin?' The Fronx was compelling. I wanted to be able to speak it too.

Zach had outlined on the phone that we didn't know much about the violin's provenance. That was the official line. 'We don't know much about its provenance,' I said.

'Yes, yes, but who sold it to you? What is his name?'

'Alexander.'

Claude stiffened. I saw that I'd made a mistake. 'Alexander what?'

'I don't remember his surname.'

'Did he tell you he was Russian?'

'Possibly. I don't recall.'

'Was he a tall bastard?'

I threw a glance at Zach. This wasn't supposed to happen. 'I have no idea. He was sitting down.'

Claude blinked incredulously. 'All the time?'

'Pretty much. I wasn't really paying attention. I was excited about the violin.'

'Was he scrawny and yellow-haired and missing part of a finger?' Claude held up three and a half of the four fingers of his hand. A toxic taste flooded my mouth. The aspirin. None of this had anything to do with music.

'Mr Martel, would you just take a look at my violin?'

'Answer my question. Was this Alexander blond?'

'No, he was bald. He was as bald as Zach.'

Claude regarded Zach's scalp with suspicion.

'Listen, Mr Martel, this is my new violin, for which I have paid an awful lot of money, and three days ago I discovered a hairline crack over the soundpost. Now, are you going to take a look at it, or do I have to bring it elsewhere?' It was chilly on that side of the room. I wanted to go and stand in the sun again.

Claude grunted. 'Okay, let us see this famous violin.' He rolled up his sleeves and lifted the lid. His forearms were as thick as mutton shanks.

We stood in silence as Martel breathed heavily upon Magdalena. He took her to the row of windows, frowned, picked at the crack, looked miserable, shook his head, tutted.

My head thudded with pain. I could have cancer, I thought, and not even know it. Claude glared at us over his bifocals.

'Slip slap drip drop,' he said accusatorily. He brought the violin back and indicated the blackened glue-lines. 'Inexpertly applied. Whoever last owned this violin paid no care. Half the work I do is repairing what's been badly done by others.' He put the violin back on the table, cracked his knuckles, selected a knife from the rack. 'Now, I pop it open, take a look inside, okay?'

He went at Magdalena with the knife. I snatched her off the table. 'Are you joking me? Jesus Christ.'

Claude threw back his head and laughed. 'Women!' he roared at Zach. 'No sense of humour.'

Zach smiled bashfully. The assistant down the back kept sanding. He didn't miss a beat. It occurred to me that he might be deaf. But were he deaf, would he not sit facing the room?

Claude relinquished the knife and planted himself before me. 'Replace the violin on the bench, mademoiselle.' He issued it like a challenge. He was standing too closely, defying me to disobey. He put his hands on his hips and grinned. It was a lopsided grin, as if his jaw was off its hinge on one side. 'You do not trust me? But I am the best. The things that I can do with my hands . . .'

He leered suggestively. I replaced the violin on the bench.

'It is true,' he admitted ruefully, 'I have had some difficulties.' This was an entirely unsolicited statement.

'What kind of difficulties?' queried Zach, but Claude ignored him. He picked up the violin and started tapping it with his knuckle.

He tapped it all over, head tilted to one side as he listened. Occasionally he stroked it with his palm. He kept returning to the soundpost crack. 'It will take a month,' he concluded.

'What will?' I asked.

'A full restoration.'

'But I don't want a full restoration, I just want the crack fixed.'

'And we want to know if it's a Strad,' added Zach.

Claude held firm. 'No, I am sorry, you must have a full restoration. This violin has been neglected.' He ran his fingertip along the thin black line. 'The crack will cause difficulty if not immediately addressed. The violin will lose tension, the sound will become dull. When it looks very bad, it's often not so serious, but when it's very serious, it often doesn't look so bad. This crack is an emergency. It will very soon grow.'

I took a blast of my inhaler. 'There isn't time, Mr Màrtel. I need it every day, I need it every minute. I have to rehearse.'

Panic flared on the word rehearse. Yes, I had to rehearse alone in a room with Magdalena for a hundred years. There would never be enough hours in the day for the amount of rehearsing I had to do.

'Borrow a violin,' said Claude.

'I need this violin.'

Claude raised a hand in resignation. 'Okay, I have warned you, I have tried. Off you go. Rehearse. You press upon the fingerboard over and over, you play fortissimo with the bow, you bump it around, the crack wakes up and sets off like a snail.' He wiggled the pad of his index finger across the violin's belly by way of demonstration. 'Slowly, slowly, until it gets to here.' He tapped the tailpiece. 'And then, kaput, floppy violin. The crack wins. You lose. But you have already decided. I understand. Go. Thank you. Goodbye.' Claude put Magdalena back in the case.

How had I not noticed the crack when I'd bought the violin? Now it was all I could see. Magdalena was two bits of wood arranged around a fissure. Was she going to cave in onstage? Or was I being taken in? Was Claude playing on my fears? I needed to sit down and think things through, but the man had commandeered the only other stool. He dragged it out from under the bench and picked up the white belly of the instrument he'd been working on. How implausible it looked without soundholes.

'Is it a Strad, Mr Martel?' Zach persisted.

'It is a fine instrument,' he replied without looking up from his work.

'Yes, but –'

Claude cursed and swung around on the stool. 'How can I tell without looking inside? The violin must be opened for examination. This requires patience and skill. I will insert the knife carefully underneath the glued edge – only an expert like me can do it – and then, as I said, pop.'

'That's just not an option right now, Mr Martel, I told you that.'

'The crack will not survive many performances. I told *you* that.'

'Jesus,' I whispered, and covered my eyes. My brain was rhythmically shouldering against my skull, trying to hatch out.

Claude put down his work and stood up. 'You are worried,' he said. 'A beautiful girl should not worry. I can do an emergency repair. Just glue, no knife. It will hold for a number of weeks.'

'Perfect, we'll do it. How long will you need?'

Claude peered into the case and ran his fingernail over the crack again. 'For one thousand dollars, I can start on it this minute. It will be ready in a week.'

I shook my head. 'Too long.'

'Not long! Next week is short. I need to rub hot glue into the crack, clamp it, clean off the excess glue and let it dry. Then I need to restore the surface with several layers of transparent varnish and colours, scraping and polishing until the repair is invisible.'

'Can you not just stick it back together like you did Konrad's bass?' asked Zach.

'A double bass is carpentry. Hammer hammer, knick knock. My boy down there could do it with his eyes shut. This is a surgeon's job.'

I looked at Zach. 'I don't know.' I was thinking it was time to call Eduardo, do things legitimately, get it out in the open, stick with those you trust. A fake Strad was better than a botched one. But maybe a botched one was better than a stolen one. 'I don't know,' I said again. 'I need time to think.'

'This crack won't hold while you think. For two thousand dollars cash, I can work through the night. I will have it back to you this time tomorrow. No varnish, no polishing, just glue. Your violin will not go floppy. Leave it with me now.'

'The glue won't affect the sound, will it?'

'How would the glue affect the sound?'

'I don't know. Resonance and . . .' I couldn't think of anything else.

Claude rolled his eyes. 'How can a violinist know so little about a violin? You people don't deserve the violins – we deserve them. We, who appreciate their true sublimity. The glue won't affect the resonance because I will not use a chemical glue. I will use an animal glue, glue that is made by boiling tendons and hides. What makes tendons and hides so strong?'

'I don't know.'

'Of course you don't know. Collagen. Collagen is strong and flexible due to its long molecules. Structures produced by animals and plants possess mechanical properties which are superior to substances created by man. Wood is one outstanding example. It consists of cellulose. Can you think of another example?'

'Wire?'

He grabbed my plait. 'Hair, the protein keratin. Your bow is strung with the tail of a white mare. A mare's tail is more suitable because it is coarser than a stallion's. The surface is jagged and sticks to violin strings. But why would you want to know this? You only play the thing for a living.'

I didn't react. It is the fate of young women to be lectured by old men.

'The violin is not just a phenomenon of physics,' he finished. 'It is a triumph of the natural world. Did you know all this?'

'No.'

'See how stupid you were?'

'Yes. Thanks.'

'No problem. Now you are not stupid anymore. I will not

charge you for this valuable service.' He was standing too close to me again. Grey chest hairs bristled at the neck of his shirt. 'The repair won't dampen the sound, because the collagen in the glue will vibrate with the cellulose of the wood. So I fix the crack, agreed? Twenty-four hours, mademoiselle. That's all I need.'

'And two grand,' said Zach.

'Precisely. In cash. And then later, we pop it open, fit a soundpost piece, okay? You come back tomorrow, same time.' He started to walk us to the door.

'Wait, do I not get a receipt or something?'

'A receipt?'

'Yeah, a receipt.' That insurance woman's incredulous whine: You don't have a receipt, ma'am?

Claude searched the pockets of his smock, as if he might find one there. 'One moment.' He took a booklet down from the shelf and scribbled on it, then tore out a blue docket and handed it to me. 'There's your receipt. Goodbye, goodbye, goodbye.' He held open the glass door and hustled us out. The last thing I saw was the boy in the corner, still not looking up.

The elevator descended with ponderous jerkiness, as if we were being lowered manually into a hole.

'Didn't you think it odd, Zach, that Martel had no old violins lying around? There were only bits of half-made new ones. Doesn't this guy do repairs?'

Zach shrugged. 'Maybe he keeps the old ones locked away.'

The elevator shaft groaned like the hold of a sinking ship. The cry of distressed metal set a despondent tone. 'Since when do you need to open up a violin to tell who made it? They don't dismember them in Sotheby's.'

'Yeah,' said Zach.

'And what about that boy who was rocking away in the corner the whole time? Wasn't that freaky?'

'What boy?'

'Ah come on, Zach, the boy in the corner. You couldn't miss him.'

But apparently you could miss him. The boy hadn't so much as glanced our way when we left – I'd been watching. I was dying to see his face. How could you not turn around when something was going on behind you? That wasn't normal behaviour. Could he have been a bit simple?

'Why isn't Martel registered, Zach? Why is he the only luthier in the tri-state area who isn't listed on the Entente directory?'

'Maybe he had a run-in and they disbarred him, or something. You heard him say he's had difficulties.'

'Yeah, what did that mean?'

Zach didn't know either. The elevator halted abruptly and we lurched out of the building. The sun, which had been beating down in the atelier, had long since abandoned street level, leaving it stark and cold. It was like disembarking from a plane after a holiday in the tropics. I wanted to stay on the plane, ride the elevator back up. Not having Magdalena to fret over was immensely disconcerting. Leaving her overnight had never been part of the plan.

I caught the subway home, seeing as I was no longer worth mugging. I sat in a slump on the F train and stared at my thighs, unable to imagine a time in my life when I would be thinner.

I took Martel's receipt out of my pocket. It was a square stub of blotting paper, smaller than the subway ticket. I'd gone in with a Strad and come out with a scrap. That had to be a bad move. The receipt pictured an old guy in an apron smiling at a stiletto. 'Shoe repair ticket,' it said. *Vn,* Martel had scribbled on the back.

Images of that poor boy in the corner plagued me all the way home. My back ached, just thinking of the way he'd stooped and rocked over his work. Had he been warned not to look at anyone who entered the room? Or maybe there was something wrong with his face. Was that why he was hunched over? Shame?

It was of course possible that the assistant was rocking back and forth with laughter. That's what occurred to me on the stairs to Valentina's apartment, and the thought stopped me dead halfway up – the thought that the boy wasn't the halfwit in the room – I was the halfwit, leaving behind a violin I couldn't prove I owned. I'd no documentary evidence of it, no electronic tagging, nothing but a set of tooth-marks. What if Martel switched Magdalena? It would be his word against mine.

Ming's small rotund body swelled and contracted with love. She was delighted to have me to herself. No practice, no company, nothing to obstruct her affection. Ming had a lot of obstructed affection. She didn't mind that I played the stereo too loud. Someone banged on the wall and I turned it down. Valentina, as ever, was out.

I turned my cell back on. Daniel had called three times, leaving an identical message three times. 'Hey. It's Daniel. Call me.' I was feeling too morose to call him. The last time I'd sat in that apartment with no violin, I had a big old cash stash for company. The Daniel stash, the David stash, and the Dad stash. I'd spent the night playing shop. Less than a week later and all that remained was a shoe-repair ticket. Even my bows were gone.

I picked up the phone to ring my mother. I wanted to know if Dad had ever taken me on a train, but then remembered that it was the middle of the night back home.

I had wild dreams about the boy in the corner that night. I'd forgotten all about them until Zach and I were walking along Martel's street the following afternoon. The sudden recollection jolted me into thinking for a split second that I'd paid a visit to the atelier during the night. The dreams were weirdly vivid because I wasn't sleeping properly. The boy wasn't sleeping properly either. He had woken in the night and crept up to my violin. He'd seized it and danced the dance of the goblins in the dark.

He could hear me screaming frantically from my cage in the elevator shaft, but my entreaties only made him dance harder. Then I was in the room with him, right up close. His face was the devil's face and he played Magdalena without a bow. The sound came out of his fingers.

Two car seats were humped against Martel's stoop like creatures trying to procreate. They hadn't been there the day before. Zach and I were feeling grim. We were ten minutes early and in no hurry to arrive, so we took the stairs. About three floors up, we heard the strains of music emanating from above. We kept climbing, but climbed quietly, until we stopped altogether on the final flight to listen.

'Is that it?' whispered Zach. 'Your violin?'

'Yes.' That was it, all right. The glue hadn't affected the resonance. It sounded better, if anything.

Zach tilted his head. 'He's good. I hadn't realized he was something of a musician as well.'

Nor had I. I'd have slept a little better had I known Claude played like that. I'd have rested a little easier understanding he was so sensitive to the instrument. He was playing the violin melody from Rimsky-Korsakov's *Sheherazade*. The plangent tones made the hair on the back of my neck rise. How could anyone harm Sheherazade? Who could resist the loveliness of the sultan's young wife?

'Sit with me,' I whispered to Zach, and we sat on the steps. I didn't want Claude to stop. The little blue shoe ticket was clasped in my hand. 'Is that how I sound when I play?'

Zach nodded. 'Yes.'

'I've never heard anyone else play that violin before. When I hear it, it's sharper, you know, because it's right under my ear.'

Zach nodded again, his eyes shut.

Claude didn't sound every note. He must've been playing from memory. There is an unguarded quality in musicians unaware of listening ears. Intimate, hearing the piece like that, played for no one, played from far away, the sound escaping onto a stairwell presumed empty. Sheherazade spun out her tales over a thousand and one Arabian nights. Her tales were her demand for life: I deserve to live so long as I can unravel such intrigue into the world. Do not kill me now. Do not strangle me at dawn.

I wondered if that trapped animal of a boy had left off rocking to listen. That pitiful youth, did he understand rapture? There was a terrible pain across my chest. It was the old pain, the old loss. This paper room at the top of the stairs in which, yesterday, my father had been, and now this unassuming beauty welling out of it, unbidden. Sunlight was spilling through the glass door onto the landing; the dust motes might have been there since time began. It was all immensely delicate and just beyond my reach. There were pockets of wonder all over the earth, I knew, like wild animals in glades, and I happened upon them now and then. Less so in America, because it was not my home, but there were pockets in America, too, and I prized them all the more for their rarity. Once I blundered into them, the wonder took flight; it evaporated like dew. It was a matter of not blundering into them, of letting them be, of trying to live on the brink of them without intruding. I couldn't ask much of them because they wouldn't withstand it.

Once I entered the atelier, as I very soon would, the grace would evanesce. The music would break off, the memories of my father would be proved false. I could only preserve the otherworldliness by remaining just shy of it. Being with my father again was unachievable, but being just shy of him was occasionally possible. We still shared this time, this perpetuity, whatever it was. I was just shy of him there on the stairwell, and the strain was bad.

Zach put his arm around me. 'Hey hey hey,' he whispered, 'don't get upset.' I rested my head against his chest, and he rocked me back and forth.

The elevator shunted into action and Zach and I broke apart. It was three o'clock, the appointed hour. We got to our feet. The elevator doors parted and Claude stepped out, a baguette held at half-cock under his arm. He looked us up and down.

'Oh,' I said. 'I thought you were playing.'

'No. My boy.'

'Your boy? But is he not –' I nearly said retarded – 'a luthier?'

'All luthiers can play. Violinists cannot make violins, but luthiers can play. He is good, yes?' We joined him on the landing.

'He's incredible,' said Zach. 'I'll give him a job.'

'You will not steal my boy from me.' Claude pushed open the glass door and the music ceased.

The boy turned around. I don't know why I'd presumed he'd be disfigured, because the boy was beautiful. It was almost upsetting to find such beauty in that corner. He brought to mind Valentina.

The boy lowered the violin. 'Hi,' he said. Not deaf, then, no, nor simple, nor demonic, but quite perfect, and although the boy had always been perfect, it seemed the violin had trans-formed him.

'My boy,' Claude stated proudly, 'will be a virtuoso luthier.'

Zach ran his palm over the shaved nap of his scalp. 'Your boy could be a virtuoso violinist if he wanted.'

The boy beamed shyly. Yes, he was strikingly like Valentina.

130

He could've been her younger brother. It was his demeanour that recalled her, his artlessness. Music attracted these types, these gentle refugees. His mother must have been a beautiful woman. The boy deserved a violin like mine.

Claude went down to the boy and took the violin. The boy stopped smiling. Claude seemed to hear what I was thinking.

'If he wants a violin as fine as this, he must learn to make it himself. That is what I tell him.'

I glanced at the boy. Yes, the boy understood rapture. He pulled out his chair and bent to his work once more. I believed at that moment that he'd manage to make a violin as fine as mine. He didn't have a choice if he wanted fulfilment in his life. I had gone through my trial to acquire Magdalena. Now it was his turn. That was the way of things.

Claude was bringing my violin to me, triumphant, ceremonial. He bore it aloft like a chalice. The row of windows split the sunlight into shards, and the shards flickered upon the varnish. The violin shimmered towards me, a handful of polished amber. Oh God, it wasn't Magdalena, it was a different violin. I stared at it in panic. It came fluttering across the room, and I reached up.

'Voilà, mademoiselle.' Claude presented it with a flourish. 'Tiger stripes. That is what we found beneath all that dirt. Turn it over.' I turned it over and tilted it in the sunlight. Tiger stripes leapt like flames across the violin's back. 'The repair is good, no?'

The repair? I stared at the bridge. There it was: the repaired soundpost crack. The rest of Magdalena became familiar around the crack. The plain purfling, her shallow belly, and there by the chinrest clamp, the indentation of my two front teeth. Claude would never have known to replicate that. 'Beautiful,' I whispered, and Zach murmured assent. It was some repair, all right. Tiger stripes. Now everyone would want to steal her from me.

'I cleaned away the dirt and polished it,' said Claude, 'because you were so nice.' I looked askance at him.

Apparently, this wasn't sarcasm. 'We will do a full restoration soon.'

'We will, absolutely. Where's the case?' Magdalena had to be concealed.

'You need a new case.' Claude stooped to slide it out from under the workbench. 'This will not protect the violin.'

'No, really?'

'Don't be smart.' He placed the case on the bench and opened it. 'I think you have been too smart with me already, perhaps. This is a Russian case.'

I looked at him as if I didn't know what he was trying to say.

He put his hands on his hips. 'I know where you got this violin.'

Claude stared at me and I stared back. The boy in the corner kept rasping away.

'You have done a wonderful job, Mr Martel,' I said carefully. 'I am extremely pleased.'

I put Magdalena into the case and clipped it shut. I took the two thousand dollars out of my bag and invited Claude to count it. He didn't make the mistake that Alexander had made. He took the money and dealt it out on the workbench like a set of playing cards. He separated it into twenty hundred-dollar piles, then counted it again.

'Thank you.' He restacked the notes and swept them into a drawer.

Zach cleared his throat. 'So?'

The two of us turned to look at him. 'So what?' Claude asked.

'So is the violin a Strad, Mr Martel?'

'I am excited about it, yes.'

'But is it a Strad?'

Claude unclipped the lid of the case again and frowned at the violin. He shook his head in time to his son's sanding. 'How much did you pay Alexander for this violin?'

'A lot,' I told him.

'A seven-figure sum?'

'Not that much.'

'Good.'

'What do you mean, good? Is it not a Strad?'

'Of course this violin is not a Strad.' Claude said this as if it were the most obvious fact in the world. 'Alexander lied to you, as he always lies. Look here at the shape of the tool-marks, the slant of the *f*-holes, the swell of the curves. How could you possibly think that this is a Strad?'

'Because it sounds like one.'

Claude rolled his eyes as if he couldn't credit my stupidity. 'You people know nothing. Only *we* can know anything, we who have handled thousands of instruments in our lifetimes. Yes, I came across a violin very much like it once before. Many years ago, when I was an apprentice in Mirecourt. It had the same curved belly, the same fire in the varnish. A tone of comparable beauty. Hearing my boy play brought me back to that day. This violin belonged to an old man who had acquired it during the Great War when Kaiser Wilhelm of Germany went into exile. The old man produced the certificate, and we young apprentices crowded around. *Joseph Guarnerius fecit Cremonae*, it read, with the insignia of the cross and the IHS. I believe this is a sister instrument. It is worth a seven-figure sum.'

A Guarneri del Gesù. Zach made an involuntary high-pitched sound; a small child being squeezed too hard.

'It is good that you paid less than it is worth,' Claude concluded, clicking the case shut. 'Alexander has been stupid. You have not been stupid. I am happy for you. I am happy because Alexander will be sad.' Claude held out the case and I took it.

'Are you positive it's a del Gesù?' Zach wanted to know.

'I am almost positive. I am as positive as I can be without taking it apart. Do you know why I am so positive? Because my boy thinks it's a del Gesù too. A skilled player knows an instrument by how it reacts to his bowing. You,' he prodded my shoulder, 'knew that this was a special violin by following your instinct. No one can identify instruments with absolute authority, and there is much nonsense spoken, so much non-

133

sense. They even have a violin they say bears Stradivari's thumbprint. It is not Stradivari's thumbprint. It is the thumbprint of the boy in his studio who varnished his violin. A boy like my boy. This is a del Gesù. I would stake my reputation on it.'

Zach and I glanced at each other. What reputation?

'Goodbye, goodbye, goodbye.' Claude ushered us out. I tried to thank the boy, but his back remained turned.

Never did we question Claude's authority, dubious though it was. Not once did we dismiss his diagnosis as the posturings of a chancer. At least, not out loud, and not to each other. He was telling us what we wanted to hear. That was enough for one day. I phoned Daniel. 'I love you,' I told him. I had to say it to someone.

'I love you too,' he responded without a second thought. I noted the quickness in his voice, the lack of fear. I immediately wanted to test it, to push my luck.

'I love you,' I said again, to see if it would spring back to me. It did, without dilution.

'And I love you, my Irlandesa.'

That's when I did start loving Daniel. Not when I said I did, but some moments later when he replied in kind. It was the last day of January. Winter was through.

Giunt'è la Primavera e festosetti
La Salutan gl'Augei

Spring has come and joyously
the birds greet it

from
La Primavera, Spring
Le Quattro Stagioni, The Four Seasons
—Vivaldi

February was a short month of concentration and graft. I cleared my workload, I stayed out of bars. The Hudson froze over. Oh, how it snowed. When it didn't snow, hail fell. Other times, it rained. But for all the precipitation, I never got drenched. The sun didn't shine often, but it shone on me. How quickly I had fallen for Daniel.

The bookings for the fall season rolled in like lemons on a fruit machine – Washington, Boston, Dresden, Amsterdam – the city names were coins tumbling into my paper cup. Six months beforehand it had been a serious struggle. I hadn't yet come into my father's money, nor had I enough decent work. Now it seemed I owned a del Gesù. It had tiger stripes. I was in love with Daniel. He had tiger stripes too. His were in his green eyes, reeds amongst still waters. I slept by his side most nights and he taught me how to cook. I had never known it could be so easy to be with someone. The ease of it was a revelation. It was like getting religion.

It was Daniel's difference to me that was fascinating. I lost whole minutes gazing at him. His simplicity of form suggested that even his internal organs would be less convoluted than mine, less prone to disease, less fickle. I wanted to tear him open and look. The channels through which his blood coursed would be less twisted, the synapses and electrical routes of his brain more upfront. His kidneys, a plump moist handful each – no alcohol damage there; his stomach, stoic and methodical, unperturbed by all he threw at it. His steadfast heart, a heart on which one could rely. He never complained of illness. In the time I knew him, Daniel did not admit to so much as a headache. He was immune to every sniffle I brought home. I could have run my fingers over him from morning to night and still not have had enough. I don't know what would have been enough. To eat him?

He stood at about five foot ten, yet insisted he was six foot tall. He wanted to get that much clear from the outset, and rolled away in a sulk when I laughed. 'Oh come on,' I wheedled when he refused to talk, 'what's the big deal?' I had to cajole him for an age, and eventually concede that I must have been mistaken. About my own height as well as his. We were both taller than I thought. 'All right? Daniel? Are you listening? Friends?' Silence. I chewed at his shoulder (a sheen on it like polished wood) until he finally turned his smile back on. He rolled onto his back and I got to maul him again.

He seemed accustomed to being handled and stroked, as if he were a well-loved family pet. He enjoyed the feel of it, found the admiration soothing. His breathing became deep and slow. 'You're so lovely,' I would whisper, and his eyelashes, his glossy curved eyelashes, would momentarily lower in acknowledgement. His fingernails, as wide as they were long, were as pink as the insides of shells. His feet were broad, but small for a man. I discovered a flaw on his heels. He pulled his feet up sharply when I reached for them one night, and swung his legs off the bed. That was the end of the game. I'd touched them though, the bumps. They were as large as golf balls, one on each heel, and they felt like they were made of bone. His heels were the only part of his body of which he was self-conscious. He never let me look at them after that. At least, he thought he never did. Daniel was a heavy sleeper.

He raised no objections to my projects of measuring him, categorizing him, sizing him up. I clambered all over him aligning our limbs, angled back his head to get a good look at his teeth. Which were perfect. As perfect as every American's, though he maintained he hadn't worn braces. I showed him my fangs and he advised me to get them done. 'If you want to,' he added hastily when he saw my expression. I didn't, I informed him. They were part of my ethnicity.

His skin, like his teeth, was without flaw. It didn't flush or blanch like mine. When he was scared, you couldn't tell, nor when he was upset or angry. I never could detect when he was lying. I held onto him tightly, as if holding onto him tightly might communicate the intensity of my love. I didn't know how else to express it other than by converting it into force. I squeezed him, I crushed him, sometimes I wrestled him to the floor and sat on him, striving to push my soul closer to his. He said that I was hurting him, but I decided he had to be joking.

Often I brought Magdalena over to play for him. He purchased a music stand, saying he liked the way it looked in his living room. I bought duplicate sheet music and left it there. Soon his place was full of music. He said this made him feel close to me when I wasn't around. I wanted him to feel closer, so I brought along more music, whatever I could find, pieces I wasn't playing, pieces that weren't even for the violin. I wanted to wallpaper his life.

He told me he'd studied my pencil marks one night in an endeavour to decipher their meaning. He loved that I had this secret language, and said he took pride in telling people that his girlfriend was a musician. All his friends worked in the financial sector. I mentioned that I'd like to meet them sometime.

Occasionally we got dressed up and went out to dinner, but mostly we stayed in to light the fire and cook. Daniel would sit and listen to the section of *The Four Seasons* I'd been working on that day – we were playing an all-Vivaldi programme to round off Zach's subscription series – and he'd tell me that it was divine. 'That is divine,' he always said, 'divine, divine, divine. I cannot wait to see you up there in Carnegie Hall.' He planned on buying out a full row of seats as soon as they went on sale. Everyone he knew would be invited. The fire illuminated the water-lights in his eyes. I had to step back sometimes to marvel at how blessed I was. This beautiful young man sitting by the hearth, waiting for me to join him. When I looked at him looking at me, it felt like we were bouncing light off each other.

I was scared that I wasn't up to it, that I'd spill the light on the floor. Daniel's love made me anxious, so I'd talk too much and hover like a fool on the other side of the room. I'd babble on about how much better my solo would sound once the group was behind it. 'When I do this bit, they'll be going like this.' I'd play their bars after mine, exhorting him to imagine them being played simultaneously. Counterpoint didn't work so well on your own.

We talked about visiting Ireland together. I told him about Newgrange and Dún Aengus, hoping such names would sound as exotic to his Latin ears as Machu Picchu and the Andes sounded to me. I said that there was this famous basalt rock formation in the North that I'd only seen in photographs. 'Then we should see it for the first time together,' Daniel said decisively. He enjoyed making pronouncements. It fitted in with his ideas about manhood.

One night he arrived home with three Irish guidebooks and asked me to point out on the map where I lived. He longed to see my beautiful Éire, he said. 'Eyrie,' he pronounced it, no matter how often I corrected him. I loved it when he spoke Spanish to his family on the phone. Like me, he'd lost his father when he was younger. His mother had subsequently moved back to Lima, where his uncle owned a horse ranch. We would visit his family's horse ranch after we'd been to see my beautiful Eyrie. He showed me the alpaca fabric he'd brought back from home that Christmas, warning me that alpacas looked cute but they spat in your face. It was his intention to get a coat made from the fabric next time he was in London.

Daniel derived immense pleasure from saying the names of European banking capitals. Geneva, Frankfurt, London, London, London. London, to his mind, was where it was at. He got the British, he told me. He really *got* the whole British thing, and had some very close friends there. So that's where he keeps them, I thought.

He took business trips to London every couple of months or

so. Perhaps we would live in Knightsbridge one day, he speculated, in one of those big white terraced houses with iron railings and bay windows. He would bring the alpaca fabric to Savile Row on his next trip, and pick up the finished coat on the trip after that. He would look like James Bond then, he reckoned, pretty much.

When the call came in the first week of March inviting me to play the Philharmonie in Cologne, Daniel said that he'd love to come along. They needed a soloist to perform Shostakovich's Violin Concerto No.1 the next month, but were vague on the details concerning the previous soloist's withdrawal.

I had never played as soloist against a professional symphony orchestra before. It was a long and profound piece, one that I hadn't attempted since college, and then not with any notable degree of success. I would also have to keep it a secret from Zach because the Vivaldi concert was the following week. Zach would insist that it couldn't be done. At least, not by me. Then I'd get pissy with him and say things I'd regret.

So I didn't tell Zach about Cologne in the end. He would find out afterwards, no doubt, but by then I'd have surprised him, pleasantly for a change. I said yes to the offer without thinking twice, because I couldn't imagine not being able to do it. That's how sure of myself I was at the time. 'Can you do it?' they'd asked. 'Of course,' was my brusque response, as if it were a stupid question. I couldn't conceive of a challenge too large. The world had no fears for me, not with Magdalena and Daniel by my side. An epic Russian concerto was just the job. Something told me my violin would already know it well.

The plan was that Daniel would join me on the day of the performance in Cologne, then we'd fly together to Dublin the next morning to meet my mother. 'Cologne and Dublin,' he said a few times, relishing the names. 'Cologne, New York, and Dublin.' He loved that I'd trained in the Netherlands and France. We talked about nothing but dates and places. South America in summer, Paris in fall. Contemplating the distances we'd travel around the globe made me sleepy. I couldn't understand what I'd been fretting about all my life. I could no longer make sense of the girl I used to be.

I almost wandered into a church one day because I needed so much to give thanks. That's how intense the surfeit of joy became: I nearly entered a church. I needed to make an offering, light a candle, say a prayer. Happiness had caught me off-guard. It burned a hole in my pocket.

It was that church on Tenth Street, St Mark's in the Bowery. I'd walked past it a thousand times, barely registering its existence. I had never been inside an American church before. The gratitude was welling up so high in me that I thought I might burst. I was one step away from hysteria, and so postponed the visit.

Daniel's heart used to stop sometimes. He told me that once while we were chatting away on our cell phones. He was at work, I was out on the street. He said it apropos of nothing and with a casualness more appropriate to an observation about the weather. 'My heart stops sometimes, you know?'

I was horrified. 'No, I don't know. Baby, what do you mean?' I looked around frantically – sometimes I could see his office building.

'Oh, nothing. Just, I get these calls from clients checking up on whether their sale has gone through, and I blank. Until I can confirm that I've made the purchase, my heart stops dead and I can't breathe. I make so many transactions that I can't remember them individually, and I guess I'm kind of concerned that one day I'll forget. The sums of money involved are just so big, you know?'

His father, I thought. Is that why his father died so young? Had his heart stopped too? Was it hereditary? I wanted to say something that would keep Daniel's heart beating, an instruction which would communicate directly with the organ itself, but nothing came to mind. I just opened and shut my mouth.

'But it's okay,' he concluded in an upbeat voice. Someone must've marched over to his desk, detecting weakness.

'I don't want you to die,' I whispered into the phone.

Daniel laughed and said I was sweet. 'You're so sweet, my Irlandesa. Call you later.'

I'd been pressing the phone so hard against my ear that it hurt. Daniel's heart stopped sometimes and there was a crack in my violin. The repair was only temporary. These facts had to be borne in mind. My happiness was tempered by fear for its fragility. I made straight for Barneys and came out with a green silk dress. I'd never spent so much on a garment before. I will wear it around the world, I affirmed. If I wear it enough times, it will constitute a bargain.

The Entente backed off once we withdrew our claim that Magdalena was a Stradivarius. We didn't inform them that we were calling it a Guarneri del Gesù instead. The days lengthened by a few minutes every evening. The Cologne performance was on a Friday, with the rehearsal scheduled for Thursday afternoon. I would fly out of New York on Wednesday evening, with Daniel to follow the next night. There'd be a sweet reunion in the hotel when he arrived on Friday morning, then I'd attend the dress rehearsal while he slept. He'd booked the best seat in the house for the performance, to which he would wear his new suit. I told Zach I wouldn't be contactable after the Wednesday that week. Zach said that was fine, didn't ask where I'd be, so long as I was back by Monday.

The best times were on the stairs in Daniel's building. It was easiest when I wasn't actually in his apartment, but contemplating it from close by. Our love was most manageable when there was no immediate risk that I would wreck it. Often I was overwhelmed by what was happening between us. It made me almost nauseous, as if I'd eaten too much sugar, or was gambling with sums of money I didn't have. I recognized the same symptom in Ming. She couldn't control her excitement at my return if I'd been out all day, so she'd have to hide in a bag until it was safe to come out. Then she'd panic and ricochet all over the place, skidding into walls, banging her head against furniture. It was just too much for her, the onslaught of joy coupled with the threat of its imminent demise. I knew exactly how she felt.

So I liked Daniel's stairs. Liked sitting on them, knowing that he was above. The stairs were hardly pleasant. Too narrow, no natural light, a permanent smell of gas. They hummed like a factory, but I could just about cope with the happiness I experienced there. I would sit on the return with the old leather violin case at my feet, and try to compose myself. At such times, my expression was unstable. Smiles and collapsed smiles crossed my face like Irish weather. I missed it so much once whilst sitting there, the unpredictability of an Irish sky. This incredible longing descended on me out of nowhere, a longing for home, a longing to stand in trembling air. The compulsion made no sense – I hated Irish weather. The rain, the sun, the rain again, the sun again, filling up the picture windows of my every childhood moment. The constant sequence of disappointments and elations had worn me out.

A girl from the salon on the first floor passed by and asked if I was okay. Yeah, I was okay, I assured her. Just about.

Patrice, the salon owner, halted gleefully at the foot of the stairs, like something that had stepped out of my head. A fully formed embodiment of the goblin in my brain. He always asked the same question, and always asked it knowingly.

'How's Daniel?'

'He's great, Patrice.' Asserted with vehemence.

'I'll bet he is.' Patrice was bursting with information it evidently caused him pain to contain. Information about Daniel, his private life. 'Oh, I'll bet he is, girlfriend. I'll bet he's just dandy.' Then the full-bladder squirm.

I smiled my most arid smile. It expired before it reached my eyes. 'Fuck you, Patrice.' I didn't have to say the words. He could read them in the set of my jaw. I tapped them down on him like cigarette ash. 'Fuck you, Patrice, and your invidious little mind.' I'd dealt with the likes of him before, in the schoolyard and the workplace. Full of poison and the desire to spread it. *Eva Tyne, Ovaltine, I know what happened your dad.*

Daniel's door opened. 'Christ, Eva, what are you doing down there?' He ushered me inside. 'Hey, Patrice.'

'Hey, Daniel.'

Patrice sloped off. Someday he'd do more than slope off, of that I was certain. Someday he'd tell me exactly what was on his mind. I hated his insinuation that he knew more about Daniel than I knew. And I hated that his insinuation was true.

Daniel closed the door and kissed me. 'You're so cute,' he said. 'Are all the girls this cute in beautiful Eyrie? Stay away from that guy, by the way.'

Not trusting the happiness was the first step in its destruction. I caught them together once. The very next day, in fact. Daniel and Valentina. I caught them standing too close to each other and that was it, that's all it took. It was my heart that stopped, not his. *I'll bet he's just dandy*, whispered the little Patrice in my brain, and Daniel sure did look dandy that day. He had dropped in to pick me up after a film soundtrack recording session. It was supposed to be a surprise.

I was in the restroom when he arrived. He'd followed the sound of violins, and encountered Valentina perfecting her pretty trill. They recognized each other immediately from my descriptions and greeted one another as friends. 'So, you must be Valentina. I've heard so much about you.' 'And you must be Daniel – hello!'

The conversation had notched up to witticisms by the time I intruded. Valentina was laughing. That's what I heard first when I came around the corner: Valentina's glorious laugh, rebounding down the corridor like something you could reach into and grasp. I arrived at the door and saw not my best friend, but Daniel. He'd never dropped by at work before, and I experienced a swell of pride. I wanted everyone to admire him. I wanted to parade him around.

I was about to go in and greet him, but Valentina laughed once more and I checked myself. Her laugh shouldn't have set alarm bells ringing, but alarm bells rang. Something was shocking about them. Something about the way he leaned into her, the inclination of her face towards his. Something about her blondeness, his darkness; his breadth, her narrow frame. I don't know what it was that I found so alarming, exactly. They looked so right together, they looked so attractive. I had never experienced jealousy before.

Daniel's leg was propped up on the seat next to her. His forearm rested on his knee; a man with his slain quarry underfoot. He was doing his deep-voiced corporate executive thing, sounding authoritative, being expansive. You arse, I thought. You total fucking arse. I'd never had a black thought about Daniel before.

Valentina sat obedient as a schoolchild with her violin on her lap. Her hands worked over it, seeking reassurance in its contours. She looked small, gazing up at him like that. Oh you're so funny and strong, mister. I wanted to kick that chair out from under him. I wanted to hop it off his head.

Daniel passed her a copy of his business card as if I'd willed him to do so. I'd been seeking a sign of treachery, and here it was. This was how he'd started our affair, with the presentation of his card. That's how it had all kicked off.

Valentina took the card and he handed her a pen. She wrote on the flip side, then handed both the card and the pen back. He slotted the card into his wallet and produced a second one. This card, she tucked into the back pocket of her jeans. Jesus, had they just exchanged cell numbers?

My heart beat out war signals. Do something, it screamed, but I was stricken. They were about to get too close, to touch before my very eyes, and it seemed that Daniel was moving in to brush that stray strand of hair back from her face, but Valentina, ever-watchful Valentina, who no doubt had been on the lookout since this illicit conversation had begun, was far too alert. I'd been rumbled.

'Eva,' she said brightly, relieved to have me in sight. 'We were just talking about you.'

I stepped into the room. 'Really? What were you saying?'

'Oh,' said Daniel, turning around and removing his foot from the chair. He kissed my cheek. 'Just stuff. Valentina's going to travel around the world, you know.'

I linked his arm and stood over Valentina. 'No, I didn't know. You never mentioned it, V.'

'Yeah,' Daniel said, 'she's off to India first.'

'India? Wow. You never told me that. Fancy us living in the same apartment and you not telling me that. So tell us, are you going on your own?'

Dear, sweet, guilty-looking Valentina, with that look in her eye and that hesitant manner which confirmed that she was holding back on me – her laughs had thoroughly dried up. 'Nothing's planned yet, Eva.'

I waited for her to say more, but she did not. I punched Daniel's shoulder. 'We should do that, baby. Travel the world. Why don't we do that? We can go to India too.'

'Yeah. Maybe Valentina can recommend somewhere.'

'Yeah, Valentina, maybe you can recommend somewhere?'

She packed up her violin and hitched it onto her back. 'I have to go,' she said, getting to her feet. 'I'm late.' Neither of us responded. 'Sorry,' she added. Only Valentina would be so guileless as to apologize. I almost felt bad. Speak, I told myself. Say it's okay. Tell her you'll see her back at the apartment. I didn't open my mouth.

Tremulous Valentina, off she went, walking that walk of hers on her long thin legs, as if picking her way through a gorge of sharp stones. A tentativeness in her step that had not been there a month ago. Why was she so delicate? Was it just to antagonize me?

Daniel turned to me when she was gone. 'She's from Monaco, did you know that?'

'I live with her, Daniel. Of course I know that.'

'Wow, I never met anyone from Monaco before. Cute accent.'

That pissed me off no end. I thought I was the one with the cute accent.

It was the laugh, I realized, as I lay awake two nights later. I got up and wandered around Valentina's apartment in the dark, picking things up and putting them down again. She had not come home and Daniel was out of town. I pushed her bedroom door open and stared at her empty bed. A weaving at my ankles. Ming, the line of her backbone fluid as a fish in a stream.

I picked up my little cat and pressed my face into her fur. 'It's the laugh, that's what's wrong,' I explained to Ming. Valentina's laugh, sweeping down the corridor like a river that had burst its banks. Nobody laughed at Daniel's jokes that way, not even me, who was in his thrall. He just wasn't funny. He was beautiful, but not funny. Valentina wasn't laughing at his sense of humour, she was laughing at the elation she felt in his presence. It had taken her by surprise, made her feel airborne and girlish. And not a little bit unsure, no doubt. I knew the feeling well.

I waited for him to fall asleep the next time I stayed over at his place. The minute his breathing slowed, I was out of the bed. His coat was in the hall closet and I rifled through the pockets for his wallet. I'd have that card with her number.

No sign of his wallet. It wasn't in his jacket either. Oh, he was clever. He knew better than to trust me. He'd left his phone exposed, however. There it was in the fruit bowl. It took me a while to figure out how to unlock the keypad. *Calls received*: Princess, Princess, Princess. *Calls dialled*: Princess, Princess, Princess. I knew of just one princess and she was the fairest in the realm. Daniel had had Valentina's number barely three days, but had already dialled it three times.

Sunlight on Valentina's wooden floor, the lime trees forming buds outside her window, me in agony, waiting. I tried not to wait by studying the sheet music, but I was still waiting. For the girl with the flaxen hair, in whomever's bed she was waking. Daniel was out of town again. I'd repeatedly tried calling him the night before, but his cell remained switched off.

She breezed in at a quarter past ten. Our rehearsal was scheduled for half past. We were playing four concertos for two violins as part of Zach's all-Vivaldi programme. Ming collapsed at the girl's feet by way of greeting. I thought she only did that for me. Valentina stooped to rub the little creamy belly, and the little creamy body twisted with pleasure. I tapped the bow off the music stand in agitation: Get your hands off my cat. I could smell the quick spring air on her clothes.

'You're back,' I observed. It was a redundant statement.

Valentina glanced up from Ming and smiled. 'Yes,' she said without enmity, without detecting my enmity. Her clothes, I noted, were more casual than usual. Old jeans and après-ski boots, a silk fuchsia scarf knotted around her throat. Ponytail, no make-up. She took off her coat. No bra either. It was hard to miss that fact. Why would Valentina be outside without a bra? Either she'd just come off a *Vogue* shoot, or she'd just been bedded. She locked the door of the bathroom and ran the shower. I listened to the tumbling water with growing resentment.

Twenty minutes later and she was set up before the music stand, hastily tuning her A string to mine. I sighed wearily at her adjustments.

'Aren't you ready yet?' No reply. I sighed again. 'What's the delay?'

'My music.' She was blinking at her music stand. 'I was sure it was here.' She thumbed through the sheet music on the stand and glanced about the floor in case it had fallen to the ground. I checked my watch. It was twenty to eleven.

'It's getting late,' I said quietly.

'I know,' she said even more quietly.

She pulled out a Vivaldi from the stack on the coffee table, but it wasn't the right one. 'Sorry about this.' She went through the sheets one by one in case the right one was trapped. It wasn't. 'I'll check my bedroom. It can't be far. I was practising it yesterday before I went out.'

'You can't have been practising it that hard, otherwise you'd be able to work without the music.' I indicated my stand. No music on it because I knew the concerto inside out, but then, I hadn't had anything better to do the night before. I hadn't been romanced all night. I'd been battering away at my violin like it was the only thing I had in the world. Valentina went into her bedroom and threw things around.

She returned empty-handed. 'I don't understand this.'

'Fantastic.' This was something that should've been sorted out earlier.

She got down on her knees and rummaged through the magazine rack. Something caught her eye. 'Look.' She held up one of my inhalers and I pocketed it.

She pulled out all her old sheet music. There must've been three hundred pages there. It was going to take for-ever to process. 'Jesus,' I muttered. I was too busy for this. I'd the Shostakovich to be getting on with.

Valentina was also muttering, sibilant things. Curses, probably. She cursed in Danish, dreamt in French. She placed each sheet on the windowsill once she'd established it wasn't the Vivaldi.

'Where did you last have it, Valentina?' It was the most annoying question I could come up with.

'On the stand,' she answered, naively mistaking my question for an attempt to help.

I felt quite detached from what was happening all of a sudden. It could've been an episode from someone else's life. Two girls in a room on a fine spring morning. Violins and music stands, metronomes and a Siamese cat. It should have been perfect, that's what was so jarring. It should've been an occasion of serenity and creativity. That ill will was concealed within that sunlit room was what made it so insidious. That, and the fact that only one of the girls was aware of it. Valentina simply didn't see it.

I stared at her back. There was a gap between her jeans and shirt. Valentina's fragile kidneys, which suffered infections at least twice a year. The ones that had her doubled over in pain the week before Christmas, putting a question mark over whether she'd be well enough to travel home. Thierry had just left her. The infection had floored her. Those delicate handfuls deserved better protection from the bitterness of my stare.

A haze of downy hair on the small of her back stood out in the morning sun. I was pleased to note this minor imperfection. All that paternal Viking blood; it had made her sturdy. She would likely coarsen with time.

This prospect produced a lightening of my mood. I almost, for a moment, relented. Ming jumped onto the windowsill and knocked over the relegated sheets. They skated every which way across the floor. Another Danish curse. Daniel was right. It was a cute accent.

Valentina gathered the sheets and slotted them back into the magazine rack. 'But it was here just yesterday,' she kept protesting, 'I really don't understand.' The situation was so deplorable that I nearly said it to her. 'I am not your friend anymore,' I nearly said. The room's mouth would have fallen open. The search would have come to a halt. Valentina would've turned around to face me.

Now she was peering under the couch. Down on her hands and knees with her face practically on the floorboards, her honey-gold hair mingling with the dust. I too should have been searching, but I didn't need to. I knew precisely where the sheet of music was to be found. I had placed it on top of the book-case while she'd taken her shower, deliberately leaving the corner in sight. A small white triangle, that was the clue. The clues were always in front of you. It was just a question of whether you read them correctly, or whether you read them at all.

I read some of them. Valentina's hesitancy, for instance, was a clue. She had never been hesitant before, not with me. Her secretiveness, her nocturnal absences, her inability to look me in the eye. These were all indications that something was afoot. Eventually she would spot the clue too. All she had to do was look up, locate the white paper triangle, and ask herself how it had gotten there. Not by her own hand. Then whose? She'd have turned to me, realizing that I was on to her.

Valentina got up from the floor and pulled down her shirt so that her kidneys were no longer exposed. She held on to the bridge of her nose, her face flushed. She was trying to control her temper. Either that, or she was fighting tears.

'But it was there just yesterday,' she said for the tenth time. 'I left it on the stand. Right there on top, just before I went out last night so that we could start on it first thing. I don't understand this, Eva, I really don't.'

'What's that up there?' I indicated the top of the bookshelf. She looked up and spotted the white triangle. She took it down and stared at it. 'Is that it, Valentina?'

'Yes.' A baffled note in her voice.

'Good.'

The girl wasn't an idiot. She knew she hadn't put it there. Which left me, big old me, squaring myself before her. Valentina raised her eyes from the sheet.

'How'd it get up there?' I asked.

'I don't know.'

'You don't know?'

'I don't know, Eva. It must've . . .'

'It must've what?'

She chewed her lip as she tried to say that it must've been put there by *you*. I dared her to say it. I willed her. I nodded encouragingly to help her along. Don't be shy. Come on, accuse me. Let's have a good fight. Let me give you a thump.

She seemed about to say it, but then broke from my stare and turned away. She placed the music on the stand and picked up her violin. 'I must've done it,' she said without rancour. 'I'm really sorry for wasting your time.'

The acrimony that had been building up over four or five days, disarmed with a show of surrender. Valentina had cheated me of my fury, and how cheated I felt. How cheated, how outwitted, how outclassed.

I sat on Daniel's stairs that evening with my head in my hands. It had been a harrowing day. I'd practised so hard that I was physically confused, as when you step off a boat and dry land feels too steady. My arms without the violin and bow felt too steady. My fingers were bulbous with blood. I couldn't escape the sensation of these bruised, purple fingertips, worse than tinfoil on teeth. I shoved them under my arms and pressed them into my ribs. Nothing felt right, not even Daniel's stairs. I needed to see him before flying to Cologne the next day, but he hadn't come home.

'Hey, sunshine.' Patrice. 'How's Daniel?'

'Fine.'

He didn't arrive home until well after nine. I recognized his footfall on the stairs. At first I was delighted, and then I was terrified. What if he didn't want to see me? What if he thought I was stalking him? What if I was stalking him? He rounded the corner and I got to my feet.

'Eva? What are you doing here?'

'It's a surprise. It's just, you know, I'm going to Cologne tomorrow and I thought it'd be nice to see you before I left.'

'Oh.'

'Aren't you pleased that I'm here?'

'Of course I'm pleased, baby. I'm just tired, that's all.' It was true and it wasn't true. Daniel looked tired, but he didn't look pleased. At least he was alone.

'I'll go if you like.'

'No, sweetheart, come up.'

We went into his apartment. He turned on the television and switched to the Iraq coverage. I followed him into his bedroom. There was a hair on his lapel. I couldn't take my eyes off it.

'You all right, Eva?'

'Yeah, baby. Let me take your coat. Here.'

I helped him out of it and practically ran with it back out to the hall. Held it up to the closet light bulb and picked off the hair. It wasn't one of mine. Too fair to be one of mine. But it wasn't one of Valentina's, either. Too short, too kinked. Was there a third woman, a fourth? I tried to tuck the hair into my pocket. My fingertips still felt horrible, like kneecaps.

Daniel had come out of his bedroom. 'You want a beer?' he called from the kitchen.

'Sure.'

I knew the hair meant nothing. I knew he could've picked it up anywhere. From a taxi, a restaurant seat, the plane he flew in on. From Marcella at work, from any of them at work. My evidence was not evidence, yet it proved something bad.

'Baby, what are you doing out there?'

I hung the coat up and joined him in the kitchen. Shit, I'd forgotten to frisk the pockets. Daniel was leaning on the open door of the fridge, squinting in at the contents.

'Bad news,' he told me. 'Only one beer left.'

'Oh. You have it.'

'No, baby, you have it.'

'No, you.'

'We could always go out and get some more.'

'Yeah. Do you need me to go with you?'

'Uh, no, not really. I can go on my own, I guess . . .' He sounded reluctant.

'Are you sure?'

'Uh, yeah, baby. You order in burritos.'

The door closed behind him. I checked my watch. Nine-fifteen. It'd take him maybe ten minutes to go to the liquor store and back.

He'd taken his phone, so I couldn't examine that. Coat gone too, briefcase locked. I checked under the bed. Nothing, not even dust. I opened everything that had a door. His absolute lack of books, the blankness of his walls. Where did he keep his photographs, keepsakes, birthday cards? There were more clues to my identity in the place than his. Hundreds of ambient compilation CDs that weren't real music – weird amorphous beats for his weird amorphous home. His stuff was meaningless, a theatre set.

Nine twenty-one. I emptied the bedside drawer onto the bed. That's when my hands started to shake. What if he returned early? What if I was caught? I ran to the door and pulled the safety-chain across.

The drawer was full of paired-off socks. They did that for him at the laundry. Film rolls, but no photographs. Business cards; executive this and vice-president that, all male, several Bobs. Condoms, an unmarked floppy disk, keys, small change. A credit card receipt. *Thank you for dining at Japonica, NY, APR 7.* April 7th? Yesterday. But he'd flown out of town yesterday. Valentina hadn't been in her bed last night. I felt a flare of the most intense – I was going to call it rage, but it was more than rage. It was pain, really. Pain that roared off me, an oilfield on fire.

A loud bang at the other end of the apartment, the chain on the door going from limp to taut. 'Eva? Sweetheart? Open up.'

I heaped everything back into the drawer and tried to shove it shut. It jammed.

'Eva? What's going on? Let me in. Christ.'

Oh fuck oh fuck, I chanted, pulling out the drawer and taking aim. It slid in on the third attempt. I ran and unhooked the chain.

'Why is the chain on the door?'

'Security.'

'So why isn't the door locked, if you're so security conscious?'

'Oh. Was it unlocked?'

'Yeah. If you'd just locked it, I could've opened it with my key. Jesus Christ.' I followed him into the kitchen. He put the six-pack on the counter. 'Could you not hear me calling you?'

'I was in the bathroom.'

'What happened to your finger?'

I looked at my finger. It was bleeding. Must've skinned it on the drawer. I licked the blood off and looked at him reproachfully. 'That's your fault for rushing me. You shouldn't shout at me. You know it freaks me out.'

'Oh, baby, come here and let me kiss it better.' He kissed it better, steering well clear of the blood. He handed me a beer. 'Did the burritos arrive?'

I hadn't called for them. 'I thought you were picking them up.'

'You were supposed to call and get them delivered.'

'Oh. Sorry. I misunderstood.'

'Never mind. I'll call.' He went into the living room and I retrieved the restaurant receipt from the drawer. He came back into the kitchen, flicking his phone shut. 'So you're off to Cologne tomorrow? My little world traveller.'

'Yeah.'

'I'll miss you.'

'Will you?'

'Uh huh.'

He leaned in to kiss me but I put my hand to his chest to stop him. 'Daniel, I found this in your bedroom.'

'What is it, baby? I don't have my contacts in.'

'It's a credit card receipt. It was in your bedside drawer.'

He took a step back. 'You went through my bedside drawer?'

'You were in a restaurant called Japonica yesterday.'

'So?'

'So you said you were flying out of town yesterday.'

Daniel took the receipt out of my hand and folded it into his pocket. 'Did you check the time on the receipt, Eva?'

'No.'

'Well, if you'd checked the time, you'd have seen that it's a lunch bill. I had lunch with a client in New York, then caught a five o'clock flight.'

'Oh.'

'In future, get your facts right before going on the attack.'

'I'm sorry.' Daniel just stared at me. I didn't like the expression on his face. Too dispassionate, too composed, no trace of anger or betrayal. It was the first time his geniality had failed. 'I'm sorry,' I said again.

He took the beer bottle out of my hand and put it by the sink. He picked me up and carried me into the bedroom and placed me on the bed. He climbed on top of me and put his lips on my throat. The metallic smell of hunger on his breath. A cobweb clung to the ceiling.

'It's cold in here,' I whispered. It wasn't.

'So leave your clothes on.' One hand rose up my thigh as the other undid his belt.

The intercom rang. Daniel closed his eyes and cursed. The burritos. He climbed off me, and I smoothed down my skirt.

He left at six-fifteen the next morning. I said goodbye at the door and waited for him not to look back as he descended the stairs. Daniel never looked back. I got into his bed again and lay there for a few hours, but sleep wasn't going to return. I dressed quickly and left his apartment without so much as brushing my hair.

I pretended not to see Patrice smirking at me from the salon door.

'In a hurry, Tina?'

I stopped dead, then turned around and walked right up to him. 'What did you call me?'

He looked puzzled. No, he looked like one dissembling puzzlement. He opened his eyes wide and cocked his head to one side. 'Did I not call you "Eva"?'

'No, Patrice. You called me "Tina".'

'Oh, silly me. I do that all the time. Call everybody by everybody else's name. So how's Daniel?'

'Fuck off, Patrice.'

I turned and clattered down the stairs, slamming the street door as hard as I was able. I wanted the glass to shatter; it did not. Outside it was lashing, it was bucketing down. The garbage hadn't yet been collected. Black plastic sacks were piled around the street pole, the oily rain slithering off them. A whole heap of shit. It stank.

In a hurry, *Tina?*

Valen. Tina.

So Patrice had met her. Daniel had introduced them. Some joke going on between the two men, some ugly game. Check it out: Here's another one, friend of the first one. She plays the violin too. They do this "duet". And Patrice loving it. His smirking, his lurking, his greasy grimy glee. 'How's Daniel? I'll bet he's just dandy.'

I took three blasts of the inhaler, but it wasn't enough. I bit down on the mouthpiece and it split. I spat a grey-blue shard of plastic onto the sidewalk. The blare of the city buckled around me, as if there were a cramp in the air. I turned back to Daniel's door, but was gripped by a conviction that I should leave. Something bad would happen if I did not immediately leave. *Something awful,* my guardian angel warned.

With some trouble, I turned around and walked away, my nails gouged into my palms. I stopped at a phone booth a couple of blocks down. Only five quarters in my wallet. I put them into the slot and dialled. An age of clicking sounds and knife-tense silences. It was like ringing outer space. Our little signals to each other so tenuous, so pitiful.

'Hello?' My mother, the miracle of her voice. I nearly cried with relief.

'Mum, hi, it's me.'

'Hello?' she asked again. 'Hello? Anyone there?'

I searched my pockets. There were a couple of dimes in my jacket. I slotted them in. 'Mum?' Nothing. A nickel that I picked up from the ground, which was hardly going to do it, but I fed it in anyway. 'Mum? Can you hear me now?'

'Hello? Is that you, Eva? I can't hear anything. Where are you?'

'Oh Mum.'

That was it, I was out of coins. I cast my eyes about the place in desperation and defeat. People on their way to work. Grim faces staring back at me from beneath an armoury of umbrellas, unmoved by my predicament. The usual relentless aggression in the traffic. Getting down a New York street was personal, not getting down the street was more personal. The stigma of failure was everywhere. I would not like my mother to see this place. I would not like her to see me floundering in this place. 'Hello, hello, hello?' she asked before she was cut off.

I replaced the receiver, and nickels and dimes tumbled into

the phone's guts. My breathing was loud and spongy in my ears. The street was changing. The pavement had begun to tip, the sky whiten, then the pavement whitened and the sky tipped. I sat down on the wet kerb and heaved on the Ventolin. I put my head between my knees and tried not to think about the contraction in my bronchi, my airways seizing up, cutting off. I concentrated instead on the clammy rain, trickling down the back of my neck.

I must have been that way for at least half an hour. The rain had stopped by the time the attack passed. I lifted my head to a world that was brighter, and experienced a moment of euphoria.

I checked my watch – a quarter to ten. The Cologne flight was in five hours. I had to be at the airport in three. I had to be in a taxi in two. Hadn't yet packed.

I took out my cell phone. *Dialling God* . . . God didn't pick up. So I rang his office line. Never ring the office line, he'd warned. His voice mail took the call. 'Ring me when you get this,' I hissed in a voice that scared even me.

I phoned Zach next. He sounded surprised. 'Eva? I thought you weren't around.'

'I'm not. Zach, is Valentina seeing someone?'

'Funny you should say that. I'm thinking exactly the same thing.'

'Who is he?'

'I don't know. She's being totally secretive about him, who-ever he is. I reckon he's married, or something.'

'Zach?'

'What?'

'Fire her.'

He laughed.

'Zach, I mean it: Fire her.'

'All righty.' He hung up.

Fine, I decided. If you won't deal with her, I will.

My skirt had stiffened into cardboard by the time I reached Ninth Street. My hair dangled in rat's tails about my face. I threw open the apartment door so hard that Valentina dropped her breakfast bowl. It was so easy to frighten Valentina. She was always on guard, lately.

'Eva, my God. You're soaked.'

Her muesli was everywhere. The floor, the walls, her shoes, mine. The bowl, oddly enough, was in one piece. I don't know why I'd slammed the door open like that. I was feeling clear-headed and calm. I shut it behind me and pulled out a chair at the kitchen table.

'Sit down, Tina. We need to talk.'

She did as she was told. I placed myself in the seat across from her and spread my hands out flat on the table. 'I can't take this anymore,' I began.

Valentina started chewing her lip. First she was chewing at the inside of her mouth, then she was gnawing at her bottom lip. She had funny little teeth, small and white as a child's. Ming furtively lapped up the spilt breakfast milk. An oat flake was stuck to her back.

'You're my best friend,' I continued. The chewing accelerated. 'We've been through so much together and I love you like family. I deeply appreciate your kindness these past months in taking me in after my break-up with Kryštof, and I hope you can forgive me for having been so obnoxious to you in recent weeks. I know, however, that the last thing you'd ever want is to hurt me.'

I waited for her to say something. *I'd never hurt you,* some shit like that. I hadn't prepared my speech beyond this point, presuming such emotive words would provoke a defence. Valentina kept on chewing. She needed another prompt.

'But I don't think you've been entirely straight with me of late.'

Silence.

'In fact, I believe you're hiding something.'

Nothing. Not a word. Wasn't she going to demand to know of what she stood accused? Her teeth had drawn blood. She explored the punctured skin with the tip of her tongue, then

163

started chewing again, fast as a rabbit. I couldn't bear to watch, no matter how much I wanted her to destroy her pretty lips right then.

'Stop that,' I snapped, and she stopped. Unsure of what exactly she was supposed to be stopping, Valentina stopped everything and froze. She stared at me with big apprehensive eyes. There was a quality of green to their brown, like the velvety moss found on riverside stones. The blood was spreading.

'Your lip. You've cut it.'

'Oh sorry,' she muttered, as if it was my lip she'd bitten. She rummaged in her bag and produced a tissue, which she pressed to her lip. This was not going according to plan.

'Are you fucking him?'

The words sounded outrageous, even to me. Not the words, but the use of them on Valentina. Valentina didn't fuck boys. She enraptured them.

'Are you fucking my boyfriend, Valentina? Are we fucking the same man?'

She peeled the tissue away, emitting a tiny noise of pain.

'Just answer me.' Shouting now. 'Are you fucking Daniel?'

Her mouth dropped open. 'Of course not. How can you even think that?'

'Why did Patrice call me by your name?'

'Who?'

'Patrice. Why did he call me *Valentina* as I was leaving Daniel's apartment this morning?'

She shook her head in bewilderment. 'Who is Patrice?'

It was a convincing performance. I wasn't convinced. 'So where the hell are you every night of the week? Why won't you tell me? I know what he's like. I know how he makes you feel. Like a princess, I understand, but it would hurt me more if you betrayed me than if he did.'

She started in on her lip again.

'Would you lay off your lip already? It's making me sick.' I jumped up from the table and stood by the window, stared at the crowns of the trees. Neither of us spoke for a while.

164

'I'd never do anything to hurt you, Eva.'

'Good.'

'I am not sleeping with Daniel.'

'I'm glad to hear it.'

She ran her palm over the wood-grain of the table and raised a shoulder. 'I just.'

Here it was. I came back over and sat beside her and stared right in her face. 'You just what?'

Her eyes darted between mine, trying to gauge me. They were darting too fast, though, a runaway train rocking on its tracks. It was almost epileptic. Something big was coming. I felt uncommonly anxious at that point in time. What was about to step into the room?

'Say it, Valentina.'

She looked anxious too. Her eyes kept shuttling back and forth, and I wanted to lay a hand on her arm to steady her. Her poor ruined lip, as if I'd punched it. She broke eye contact and made this little defeated gesture with her hands.

'I just want you to be happy, Eva. I want everyone to be happy.'

We sat there for another thirty seconds or so, then Valentina excused herself from the table. She got out the bucket from under the sink and filled it with water from the hot tap. She measured out a capful of one of those untrustworthy American cleaning products, something that fluoresced green and smelled of pine.

I watched her mop the muesli up, and she knew that I was watching her. Her movements lacked intent. They weren't about the mess on the floor. Valentina was aware that she was navigating landmines. We were both navigating landmines. And if Valentina, who believed in forgiveness, couldn't bring herself to confess, then it must've been bad.

I packed up my stuff and told her I was moving out.

Getting on the plane was like walking out of the apartment with the oven turned on full. It could all be up in flames by the time I returned. Valentina was up to something; so was Daniel. I didn't know which one I was more scared of losing.

There was the usual offensive procedure at the airport security check. I stood barefoot and spreadeagled whilst they patted me down, in no mood at all for invasions of this nature.

'Is this your bag, ma'am?' They indicated the old Russian case. I was instructed to open it, and a conference was called. 'Remove the wires from the violin, ma'am, and we'll let you through.'

They could not grasp my explanation of why the strings shouldn't be removed from the violin. It was quite literally beyond their understanding. I explained over and over that the bridge supporting the tension of the strings was counterbalanced on the inside of the violin by a soundpost, that the strings were pushing down, and that the soundpost was pushing up, and that the removal of the strings could cause the soundpost to split through the belly of the violin and destroy it. This was admittedly something of an exaggeration, not that it did me any good. Nope, all they saw were four garrottes and a woman itching to use them. I was going to miss my plane.

In the end, they let me through like it was some huge diplomatic favour, having checked my name on the Philharmonie website. 'In the future, ma'am, bring a letter confirming your engagement.' I got filthy looks from the other passengers for having kept the plane on the runway.

It became perishingly cold in the cabin towards the end of the flight. I didn't close my eyes for so much as a second. I kept thinking I'd forgotten something – the Shostakovich music, the violin, the bow, my dress, but it was Daniel I'd forgotten. Daniel and Valentina home alone in New York, beginning to smoulder, about to catch fire. There was something irresistible about the image of the two of them together. I couldn't get my mind off how lovely they would look. I almost wanted to see it.

I switched at Heathrow while it was still dark, and arrived in Cologne early the next morning, my face as grey as the overcast sky. The hotel didn't have a room ready at that hour. I had to sit in the drawing room and wait for a guest to check out.

A waitress brought me coffee and pastries. I didn't want coffee and pastries. I wanted to sleep. My body was crying out to lie flat. The rehearsal was scheduled for two, but I was still finishing the day before in my head. If I got my room by ten, I could sleep until twelve-thirty. Two and a half hours. I'd go to bed early that night. It was manageable; I'd manage. I generally did.

The rain that had been threatening since dawn finally started to fall. Cars hissed past on the wet street. A thin couple entered the room and sat on the sofa opposite. The woman lit a cigarette without seeking my permission. I made a show of wheezing on my inhaler, so the man lit one too. The woman's legs were hard and brown. The veins stood up like worms. The pair didn't say much to each other and when they did, the tone was unpleasant. Lots of reversed diphthongs and crashing consonants. They weren't German.

I closed my eyes and felt like I was lurching. I was back on the overnight flight. The cabin lights dimmed and we were preparing to land all over again. But the landing went on and on until it became unbearable. The plane tilted sharply, the engines shifted pitch. Something was wrong. We were going to crash.

Then I heard my name. *Eee vah tine.* It was more like *knyee vah teen*. My eyes flicked open and I was back in the drawing room. The pair on the couch were bickering away. I reached for the violin case. Still there. Had a member of staff called me? I glanced at the door. No one had entered the room.

The man turned his head and met my eye. There was nothing casual in his gaze. We stared at each other for a beat, then he looked away, and raised his cigarette to his lips. He smoked like a woman. I watched him assess his wife without affection. *Knyee vah teen*. It had been a female voice, hers.

She inclined her head slightly towards the violin case. So they *were* discussing me. Could Alexander have tipped them off? Could these be some of his very good friends? *She'll be arriving unaccompanied in Cologne on Thursday morning.* The woman had a look of Alexander, all right; same type of skull. But then, they all had a look of Alexander, every unfamiliar face that glanced at the old leather case. Was it the violin's destiny to pass from hand to hand? I still hadn't managed to get it insured.

But Alexander couldn't have known that I'd be in Cologne. Not even Zach knew where to find me. And if the pair on the couch were there to snatch the violin, they'd have done so the second my eyes were shut. I picked up the case and left the drawing room all the same. I'd had enough of their smoke and bad manners.

I sat tight in the foyer, the strap of the case hooked around my neck, the handle clamped in my hand. Several thousand people, it dawned on me, knew I'd be in Cologne. The entire orchestra with whom I was performing, plus the two thousand punters who'd purchased tickets. How extensive was Alexander's web? *I haff very good friends all over the world.* The thought simultaneously drained and alerted me. I monitored everyone who entered and left the hotel. I watched to see if they watched me. I was way beyond sleep.

At last they found me a room. I drew the curtains and got into the bed. My expectations were low. The curtains were golden-yellow and I wished that they weren't. They infused the room with sepia tones, made it into the past, made me into a ghost who'd been lingering there for years. The cathedral bells rang out the hour. Four more hours until the rehearsal, which left two and a half hours for sleep.

My eyes had been open for so long that they were set like a corpse. I lay face down on the pillow to press them shut. 'This is shit,' I told the pillow, just to hear my own voice. I was alone in a foreign city and had to keep my spirits up. 'This is shit,' I repeated, and I was not wrong. I missed Daniel uncontrollably then, like a twist in the gut. Next thing, I was on the phone.

I couldn't work out the time difference. Six hours, seven? I was beyond doing the math. Daniel didn't answer. The sensation of abandonment was vast. Was he sleeping? Sleeping with whom? 'Leave a message,' his voice mail instructed me, but I disobeyed. I slammed down the phone and bit my knee. A shudder of snot and tears; I bit my knee harder.

I unpacked Magdalena and set her under my chin. I propped up the Shostakovich music, though I didn't need it – that score was etched in my brain. I played and played until I felt recalibrated. I'd hate to be a pianist and have to perform on a different instrument every night. You can't keep a piano by your side for emergencies.

At a quarter to one I strapped Magdalena back into the case. I would sleep after the rehearsal.

The conductor's handsome young assistant was clearly unimpressed with me. 'You got here, Eva Teen,' he stated, and I smiled and said, Yes, Tyne, not Teen, and held out my hand, grateful to have at last connected with someone in this unfamiliar city. Sándor was startlingly attractive and I found it hard to look at him, as if he were the sun or something. He did not return my smile.

Instead he frowned and stubbed out his cigarette. 'You are nothing similar to your publicity photograph,' he observed. It was a criticism, albeit a fair one. I was nothing similar to my photograph that day.

'I haven't slept since Tuesday night, Sándor.'

It sounded lame, even to me. The dog ate it. The bus broke down. Either Sándor didn't understand or he didn't care. 'Follow me,' he said, and led me down flights of stairs. Down and down we descended; the hall was built at the level of the bed of the Rhine. I stopped him at the door to the stage.

'Before I go in, could you tell me how to pronounce the

conductor's name. My Hungarian isn't up to much.'

Sándor evidently didn't think anything about me was up to much. 'Maestro,' he said.

'Yeah, but his name, Sándor, there're about thirty consonants in it. How is it pronounced?'

'You must call him Maestro unless invited to do otherwise.'

Invite Ed to do otherwise. Sándor hadn't quite cracked the past tense. He opened the door onto the stage, where the orchestra was setting up. Eighty or so musicians. The sight of them was an onslaught.

Sándor directed me to the clearing beside the empty podium. The orchestra manager stationed a music stand before me. I stood behind the music stand and smiled at the group, and a few weakly smiled back. How peculiarly subdued the atmosphere was. The customary hum of chat was absent. I opened the case and took out my violin. Sándor folded his arms across his chest and nodded at it.

'Is this the Magdalena Stradivarius?'

I'd forgotten they'd booked me as a Strad. Sándor looked at the violin; I looked at him. His nose had been broken at some stage. Now was not the time for convoluted explications. 'Yes it is,' I said, and shoved it under my chin.

The rehearsal commenced without warning. I missed the signal that made the group swoop to their instruments and tune to A. I offered my hand to the concertmaster.

'Eva,' I told her.

'Kratisch,' she muttered, or a name like it. I needed to see it written down. She was tiny and grey-haired and quite sure of her ground.

The doors were pulled back and the Maestro stalked out. He was a very old man with a yellow complexion and bent back. A cigarette clung to his lip. He shook my hand without making eye contact and hauled himself onto the podium. Sándor stepped up and handed him his baton. The Maestro raised his hands into claws. The cellos and double basses started up their tones of dread, setting the floor vibrating. Oh Jesus, I was out of my depth.

I could barely take in the music, the rush of blood was so loud in my ears. My hands began shaking as I waited for my part to commence. The bow amplified the shake and it bounced along the string. *Dih-dih-dih-dih* went Magdalena on my opening note.

The Maestro bellowed.

'I'm so sorry,' I blustered. 'That's never happened before.'

Sándor relayed this message to the Maestro, whose scornful response Sándor decided I could interpret for myself. The orchestra kept their eyes on the floor.

The Maestro assumed the crouching-tiger position once more, and the cellos and basses recommenced the Nocturne. People assume it's the complicated staccato notes that are the hardest to play, but it's the long slow ones that'll bring you down, particularly when you're scared. My hand didn't shake the second time around, but I played timidly, and a soloist can't play timidly against a full symphony orchestra, not without being swallowed.

The Maestro bellowed something else, and the violinist behind Kratisch got up and walked offstage and climbed the steps to the back of the hall. We kept playing. The Maestro halted us about four minutes in and the violinist returned. A brief exchange ensued, which featured several eye-rolls in my direction. Neither of them looked pleased. The Maestro passed on an instruction to Sándor, who turned to me.

'Play better,' he said, and lit the Maestro another cigarette.

At three-thirty, the Maestro thrust his baton at Sándor and strode off. The orchestra manager climbed onstage and confiscated my music stand, though we hadn't yet covered the Burlesque. Sándor inserted the baton up his sleeve.

'You are Finnish Ed,' he told me.

'Finished,' I corrected him, but I was beneath listening to by then. I packed up my belongings in disgrace. My exit was met with a half-hearted clap, which I don't think was intended as ironic.

~

The blazing sunshine which greeted me when I emerged at street level was entirely disorientating. Weird things were afoot in my peripheral vision due to my lack of sleep. The twin spires of the Dom seemed more animal than mineral. I stopped off at a pharmacy and had a time of it trying to explain to the woman behind the counter that I wanted one of those things that shut out light when you were trying to sleep. I wasn't sure what they were called in English, let alone German. I tried every last term that entered my mind: blackout-mask, eye-mask, eye-shade, eye-thing, you know those *things* you get free from airlines so you can sleep?

No, the pharmacist didn't know. Her English was reasonably good, though my German had slipped a startling amount. I said the word 'jetlag' over and over, hoping it might be an international term, like AIDS or Coke. It was an international symptom, after all.

But jetlag meant nothing in Cologne, no matter how slowly or often I said it. The pharmacist offered me goggles, eye drops, a pair of shades. I bought the shades out of politeness. It seemed perverse that everything was hidden away in drawers behind the counter. Why couldn't they put their wares on display like everywhere else?

'Aspirin,' I said, and out came a box of aspirin.

I popped the blister pack and the pharmacist poured me a paper cup of water. We listened to me gulp. The gulp must've inspired her. 'Ah so,' she said, and produced an eye patch. I gave her the thumbs up, and indicated that I wanted two. They were the colour of skin.

I tried one on in front of the bathroom mirror back in the hotel room, and it did just the job. I ordered up room service and ate it in bed, watching cable through one eye. The patch was unusually satisfying. Attracta McGuirk had one exactly like it in primary school. She wore glasses so thick that her good eye swam. She'd angle it down at you in a manner that was alarming. Because she'd been held back so many years, she was a good foot taller than the rest of us.

Her physical strength ensured that no one ever called her names, not even behind her back. It was the vacancy of her face that was terrifying. The slackness of her mouth, the meatiness of her cheeks, the corned-beef biceps that were level with our heads. What Attracta didn't understand, she thumped, and she didn't understand much. There were random bouts of violence in the playground for which she was never punished. Nor was she resented, that was the odd thing. She was part of the deal, like spelling tests and maths. Wearing that eye patch made me feel inviolate. I strapped the second one on when I'd finished my schnitzel. The pressure sealed my eyelids shut.

Sleep was deep and black, but deteriorated into nightmares. A man was crouched like a spider in the corner. Zach came to drag me away. 'What about him?' I gasped. The man watched us with hollow eyes. 'Don't worry about him,' Zach soothed me. 'He's just eating the shadows.'

I woke up with my nightdress plastered to my skin. I peeled off the eye patches. Night had fallen in Cologne. 'Eating the shadows,' I scribbled on the hotel notepad. If I didn't leave the man to his task of eating the shadows, day would never break. The man had to eat all the shadows for that to happen.

I placed the note in front of the man's chair to remind myself not to be frightened of him if I woke again. I did wake again, almost immediately. I called Daniel. I wanted to tell him about my nightmare.

'Hello?' He sounded hassled.

'Hey Daniel, it's just me. Sorry, did I disturb you?'

'Mmm, don't worry about it.'

'I called earlier but you weren't home.' There was an echo on the line.

'I was out.'

'Oh right.' I waited for him to elucidate. He didn't. 'Out where?'

'Dinner.'

Who did you go with, I wanted to ask. 'Where did you go?' I asked instead.

Rustling in the background. Did he have company? 'Uh . . . nowhere. Some place on Fourteenth.'

'Oh.' *Oh*, whined the echo. There were hundreds of restaurants on Fourteenth. 'What kind of food?'

Another silence. A longer one this time. Way too long. Had he heard me? Had the line died? Should I repeat myself? Scream?

'What's that?' he eventually asked. So he had heard me. He just hadn't bothered answering.

'What kind of food was it?'

'Uh, continental.'

'Which continent?'

'What do you mean, which continent?'

'Jesus, I'm just trying to make conversation with you, Daniel. What kind of restaurant was it? Which continent?'

'Europe, of course. Eva, you sound weird.'

'What did you have?'

'What did I have? Salmon, I think. Yeah, salmon.'

'Any good?'

'Yeah.' Was he doing it on purpose? Were the uninformative responses calculated to antagonize? I would never have done it to him.

'So, are you all packed for your trip to Cologne?'

'Sweetheart, I wanted to talk to you about that. There's a problem.'

A plummet in the cavity of my chest. 'A problem?' I eventually managed.

'Yeah, a work thing.'

'You're not coming, are you?'

'No, baby, I can't make it.' The words didn't surprise me

174

one bit. 'I'm sorry, sweetheart.'

'You're not sorry.'

'Of course I'm sorry.'

'Don't lie. You never had any intention of coming.'

'Baby.'

'You shit.' *You shit*, came the tinny echo. Such venom in my voice.

'What's wrong with you, Eva?'

'What's wrong with *me*?'

'Sweetheart, let's not do this.'

'All right then, we won't.'

I sat in the darkness waiting for him to call back. *So much is expected of me*, I was all set to scream at him. *Have you no comprehension of the pressure I'm under?* I pressed the fabric of my nightdress to my face. The smell of my own skin was a comfort. Something, finally, that was familiar. I couldn't bear waiting for the phone to ring, so I took out Magdalena and played. I clipped on the mute and practised the opening bars of the Nocturne in the hope that my hand would not shake again the following day. *A B F, A B F.* There was a dry buzz in the violin. The humidity changes had upset it.

I ran the shower hot and placed Magdalena on a chair in the steam. I emptied glass after glass of water onto the carpet and stretched a soaked towel over the air-conditioning vent. Soon the carpet was scratchy dry again, the towel as stiff as a board. I pitched more water around, re-soaked the towel. Daniel did not ring.

I longed for the warm plump mass of Ming in my arms. I wanted to hold her close and listen to her purr. I dialled Valentina's number. If she answered, it meant she wasn't with Daniel. Valentina could put Ming on the line, and the purrs across the ocean would calm me down.

Nobody answered. Little Ming-Ming was in an empty apartment in the dark, listening to the phone ring. She really hated that sound. I started in on the top shelf of the minibar.

I lay there for hours, trying to find a cool patch on the sheets. The whiskey, I had reasoned, would help me sleep, but I was wrong. Electrical pulsations juddered through my reflexes. It was like being in bed with a monkey. I turned on the television and stared at a German rock band. I turned it off and sat by the window with the lights still out, listening to the cathedral bells toll the hours. After a time I started feeling limbless in the dark, neckless, colourless; a dolphin.

Dawn brought with it a chemical downshift. Once the curtains started glowing, I knew I was done for. I was in no state to face the day, let alone the performance that evening. Memories rose from nowhere of the time I caught a fever as a kid, and had to stay in bed for what felt like a year. The nausea of the hours spent staring at the drawn curtains, listening to the other kids playing outside. I discerned faces in the flowered fabric and the faces acquired reality over time. Each gained a personality, motives, bad intentions.

I picked up my violin and held it in my lap. 'My precious violin,' I kept telling it, striving to forge a relationship with it. I wanted something from it. Reassurance, a reference point. I wanted to feel my father in it.

I sat at the dressing table and played scales. The A minor over and over, until it seemed I was in a vacuum and the noise was in my head. Or something. It had gone wrong, the way words lose their meaning if repeated often enough. My fingers had no consistency. I swallowed and my ears popped.

At seven-thirty I had breakfast delivered. The sight of breakfast after a sleepless night provoked lavish tears of self-pity. I finished it off and wept. That's what did the trick in the end, I believe, the unrestrained wallowing on a full stomach. I shut my eyes and was gone.

I was woken by knocking. Daniel! I raced across the room and pulled open the door. No, not my baby, but the maid, all four foot ten of her, leaning on her cart like a barman. The cathedral bells sounded the hour. One p.m. I told the maid not to bother cleaning the room, but the lady was not for turning. Eventually we traded old towels for new, and she and her cart moved on.

I drew back the curtains and threw open the window. Sun beat down upon the pitched rooftops of Cologne. It had been close on twenty-four hours since I'd last left the hotel room. I stooped to pick up a piece of paper from the floor. 'Eating the shadows.' I dropped the note in fright. An intruder had entered the room as I'd slept. But wait, I was the intruder. It was about the man in the chair. Here he was now in daylight: my coat, slung over the backrest. The note was sinister, an artefact salvaged from a nightmare and dragged back to the waking world, the way I'd retrieved Magdalena.

The atmosphere in the concert hall was even worse than the day before. There'd obviously been words. The Maestro had requested an additional rehearsal at seven o'clock. The concert was due to begin at eight.

I showed up at five to seven with my Shostakovich music, but Sándor indicated that I was to sit in the stalls and wait. I got off the stage and took a seat. The Maestro came out and began with the Brahms symphony.

At seven-thirty, I was still sitting there watching them rehearse the Brahms. I couldn't believe it. I needed to warm up, get changed, prepare. So did the orchestra. They were still dressed in jumpers and jeans. Two ushers were huddled in agitation at the back of the hall – the audience was gathering outside. Sándor was in the seat next to me, studiously avoiding my eye. Something had gone wrong with the Maestro, he was moving very sluggishly. His hands travelled like a pendulum losing momentum, and the orchestra droned after him. The inertia was excruciating.

Eventually the Maestro's hands did come to a halt. He climbed none too limberly off the podium and shuffled away. Sándor jumped up and hurried after him. The orchestra sprang out of their seats and bottlenecked at the door. We hadn't touched the Shostakovich. I looked at the manager, who shrugged helplessly as he rushed past. It was a quarter to eight.

I locked myself into the dressing room. The concert hall staff had hung my poster on the wall by way of welcome, but Sándor was right, I was nothing similar to that photograph anymore. The disparity between my visualization of the performance and how it was panning out was humiliating. I took my green silk dress out of the wardrobe. It seemed kind of pathetic, bringing a dress like that. I was a girl who got lucky in a bar, no more. Playing a violin that was probably a fake too. It took one to know one. The orchestra could see it. So could the Maestro. I picked up the phone and called Zach.

'Hello Darkness my old friend,' he said. 'How's Cologne?'

'How did you know about that?'

'Who do you think recommended you for the job? So, how is it?'

'Zach, something weird is going on. There's a problem with the conductor.'

'The Maestro? I know.'

'How do you know?'

'Everyone knows. He's always been difficult. He's old-school.'

'Well, why didn't you warn me?'

'Because you didn't see fit to tell me you were going. Look on the bright side: you'll never take me for granted again.' That was true.

'We haven't rehearsed my concerto in full. I'm going out there without having played the final movement with this orchestra before.'

'Bummer,' he said, to annoy me. 'I guess you're just going to have to make the best of it.'

'Christ, Zach, what am I doing here?'

'Ah, Eva, what are any of us doing here?'

'No really, I feel like I'm melting or something. I'm so fucking tired.' There was a quiver in my voice.

'Eva, you don't need me to tell you how to use it.'

No, I didn't need Zach to tell me how to use it. A trumpet fanfare sounded over the intercom. It was three minutes to eight. 'For God's sake go,' he said.

The orchestra was banging around in the corridor, muttering to one another in clipped tones. I picked up Magdalena. A B F, A B F, I played until I was certain the shake was defeated. I could have played those notes at the age of five, yet my

179

own hand was no longer to be trusted. At least the dry buzz from last night was gone.

Five past eight. All quiet outside. The corridors were empty. The overture had begun. Time for a run-through of the Nocturne.

I took a deep breath and raised my bow, but stopped there, unable to remember what came after the A B F. The opening three notes had dissociated from the rest of the piece. The first bar of *The Four Seasons* was there. *Spring has come and joyously the birds greet it.* I hovered like an idiot with my bow still in the air, and I realized that it was all tangled up in my head, the Shostakovich and the Vivaldi. Vivovich, Shostavaldi. I needed my music. Where had I left my music? I looked desperately around the dressing room, but there was no sign of it. I ran out into the empty corridor, but that sheet was not to be found.

I was calm when the stage manager came for me at twenty past eight. I followed along behind him, through corridors stale with cigarette smoke and tension. We didn't exchange a word. The clearing behind the stage door had a desolate air; a train platform after the departure of the last train. The orchestra was onstage, the additional percussionists setting up behind them for an execution. The Maestro monitored the proceedings through the glass panel inset. Sándor stood to attention in the corner. The scene reminded me of Christmas, but in a forlorn way. Children on the outside looking in. We lined up behind each other like parachutists on a plane. I shivered, suddenly self-conscious of my backless dress.

The Maestro was muttering. At first I thought he was issuing instructions to Sándor, but in fact, the man was praying. The orchestra played concert pitch A. We heard it through the speakers. I tuned Magdalena to the piped sound. The Maestro glanced back at me, looking even more like Nosferatu in his tails. I couldn't read the expression on his darkened face. There might not have been an expression. His mind seemed elsewhere. He hissed something at Sándor, who promptly left.

There was a strange occurrence then. I wonder about it to this day. The Maestro was about to turn back to the door, but something caught his attention and he started. We locked eyes and a flash of white showed in his. He blinked uncomprehendingly as if he'd never seen me before, and as if in seeing me he had received a warning. His foreboding shot through my body. My throat dried up and I tightened my grip on Magdalena.

The Maestro, it was evident, had something to tell me. Something of import, something I would remember all my days. He took a deep breath; so did I. But of course, we shared no language. The Maestro looked around for Sándor, but Sándor had been dispatched. The Maestro was at a loss.

The stage manager leaned into his microphone. '*Bitte Konzertlicht.*' The house lights dimmed. The audience was waiting; the orchestra too. The Maestro jerked his head back to the door. A great, disquieted creature, he was. I shivered again and glanced over my shoulder, wondering if whatever had unnerved the conductor was still in the wings.

The Maestro gazed at the baton in his hand. I watched his fingers grip and release the handle. He swayed on his feet and his shoes creaked. The man was not at all well.

The stage manager pulled open the door and wished the Maestro good luck. '*Toi toi toi,*' he said.

'*Danke,*' replied the Maestro. The orchestra rose as he went forth. A swell of applause, which was muted by the seal on the door.

I stepped up to the glass panel. My heart was beating furiously, a loss of feeling in my legs. It's like standing in the sea, waiting backstage. Same kind of numbness, disorientated physicality. I placed myself close to the stage manager because I couldn't be alone. We watched the conductor take his bow, his composure wholly regained.

The Maestro turned, extended an arm towards the door. I nodded and the stage manager pulled it open for me. '*Toi toi toi,* Frau Tyne.'

'*Danke.*'

181

A pat on my bare shoulder as I took my first step. I glanced back. Sándor. He held up two sets of crossed fingers and looked fierce.

I lifted my face to the audience and was glad of the green silk dress. I crossed the stage to the Maestro's outstretched hand. His grip was icy. He pressed my fingers to the tight, dry skin of his lips. Kratisch rose and I kissed her cheek.

I turned and bowed to the auditorium, scanned the glittering sea of faces. The adrenalin rush was more potent than ever. It was more potent in that corner of the world because that corner was new. The heady rush that he might be in the audience, down at the back, in the shadow of the balcony, perhaps, head held low so as not to shock me, as nervous as I was, as excited; my father. My eyes did not alight on his face.

I nodded to the Maestro to indicate that I was ready. The tiger crouched, then pounced. The cellos and double basses sent tremors through the floor. The Maestro was back on form.

All eyes were fixed on me. All eyes, including my father's eyes. Especially my father's eyes, which to my poor mind have not left me since the moment he disappeared. He may not have been in the audience, but I played as if he were. I couldn't help it. It was a habit I had no desire to break. The day I broke it would be the day I finally conceded that he was gone.

I still don't believe my father is dead. They never showed us a corpse.

On the night of June 24th, 1995, my father, Mr William Tyne of Sandpiper, the Baily, County Dublin, disappeared in the dead of the night. That was the phrase used in the news reports, as if supernatural agents were suspected. 'William Tyne disappeared in the dead of the night. The Gardaí are treating the incident as suspicious.'

They weren't wrong. Long white wisps of vapour gather at dawn upon the hill, the dew rising and hovering above the land like a wraith. Strange and covert forces were at play the night my father left us, so strange and so covert that we've yet to achieve insight into them almost eight years later, despite the most relentless speculation imaginable. A person you love and trust goes to sleep as normal, but wakes a few hours later a changeling. He opens his eyes in the dark. Something has happened to his head or his heart. He lies beside my mother for a time, then slips out of bed and abandons his life for good. Just like that, without any preparations, at least, none that we could prove.

He didn't kiss my mother upon leaving – she'd have woken. He didn't come to my room to kiss me either. I too would've woken. There was no attempt at goodbye, which is partly why it's so difficult to believe that it was goodbye. William Tyne was never heard from again.

The story received more media attention than it would were my father an average man. There'd have been little interest in it were he, for instance, poor. But he was not poor, nor plain, nor dull. My father was glamorous, particularly by Irish standards. The word charisma was applied to him with such regularity that it became intrinsic to his conception of himself. My name is William Tyne, I am tall, I am charismatic, a positive expectation is generated when I enter a room. My mother gave the Gardaí her favourite photograph, and his handsome face was reproduced in all the papers.

At first the reporters dwelled on the obvious tragedy of the story – William Tyne had left behind a young wife and child. I was Eve, Aoife, Ava; fourteen, sixteen, eighteen. My mother, inevitably, was 'Grace Tyne, former airhostess,' as if categorizing her thus was a clue to my father's disappearance. Former airhostesses were women who'd masqueraded as airhostesses in order to bag themselves rich husbands. Once they'd bagged the rich husband, they jacked in the day job. They were not in fact airhostesses at all, but career wives. My mother wasn't blind to this contempt.

The tragic angle yielded quickly to the mysterious angle: Why would a man who had it all disappear? It didn't add up. Aspects of his wealth were related knowingly in newspaper columns to insinuate that money was at the root of the Tyne affair. Journalists sniffed around for signs of impending financial ruin. So did the Gardaí. How were his business affairs? Did he have enemies? What about the taxman, Mrs Tyne, any problems there? My father disappeared and about thirty strangers showed up in his place, so that we didn't quite grasp the full impact of his absence at first, except at night.

But no one unearthed anything. Which was read as proof that there was something, and that it was buried very deeply indeed. My mother was badgered for declarations that the marriage was on the rocks. 'William is a loving father and husband,' she was quoted as saying. A female Garda detective questioned me kindly. Did he say anything unusual, make any promises, give you a special present? No, no, and no. Think hard, she urged me, as if I hadn't been doing anything else all week. The riddle of the disappearance of William Tyne snowballed. Soon he wasn't classified as merely 'Missing,' he also came under the popular heading of 'Unsolved Mysteries.' What happened to Shergar? Who took all the country's money? Is William Tyne still alive, yes or no?

It was an unusually hot June in a quiet country, and not much else was going on in Ireland, bar the Troubles a million miles away, detonations we couldn't hear. Ladybirds and butterflies colonized the long lawn, which was rapidly becoming a meadow, in much the same way as my father was rapidly becoming another man. A new photograph appeared in the papers. We considered it for a long time, my mother and me. Neither of us had seen it before. My father on his yacht, with the Taoiseach's arm around him. My mother wasn't aware that he'd met the Taoiseach, and it was probably around then that she began losing hold of him, began questioning whether she'd ever really known him in the first place.

The picture struck the right note, or rather, the wrong note – two men of the world with their cigars and champagne, the island russet in the background, the sea sapphire, the sails taut in the breeze, the sun beating down. This wasn't the Ireland the rest of its citizens knew. Where was the rain, the drudgery, the bedraggled scenery? 'William Tyne in happier times,' read the caption, but the photograph said more. It said: This is no more a man who topped himself.

It was unfortunate that the two men were pictured laughing. Ireland was picking itself up after a cruel recession, and here were these jokers, living it up on a Sigma 38. Resentment was quick to surface. My father, the papers divulged in the third week, like many of the richest men in Ireland, barely had a tax liability due to the creative accounting of one Cathal O'Hare. By the time O'Hare was finished with the books, it was a miracle William Tyne managed to feed his family at all. 'No wonder,' one Sunday rag sneered, 'his young wife is so fashionably thin.'

Conspiracy theories thrived. Had he been kidnapped? There'd been several high profile abductions in the State's recent past, but no ransom note was forthcoming. Nor had an intruder entered the bedroom that night, my mother told the detective in charge. No one had dragged William Tyne kicking and screaming down the stairs. There wasn't any sign of a break-in. 'Could he have heard a noise outside and gone downstairs to investigate?' the detective asked. My mother shook her head. Were there a noise, she'd have heard it too. She was a lighter sleeper than William.

It was even fleetingly wondered if the Taoiseach was involved. 'Was he political, Mrs Tyne?' the detective persisted. The Gardaí were clutching at straws by then. My mother laughed scornfully and I wanted her to stop. I hated it when she made herself ugly. 'He barely even voted,' she sneered. The man cleared his throat. 'No, Mrs Tyne, I mean, was he *political*? Was he involved in the Republican movement?' She laughed that one off too. 'That man,' she informed the detective, 'knew far too well how to take care of himself.'

I found a new Internet listing on him the other day. My heart tripped over itself as the page downloaded. I thought it might be an entry from his new life, but it was just another regurgitation of the known facts. The words are so familiar, such a curse. In the dead of the night on June 24th, 1995, Mr William Tyne disappeared from his Dublin home wearing only his pyjamas.

An exact time has never been placed on the moment of his departure. It was a balmy night in June and the sky didn't fully darken. William Tyne took off into the navy night as if it were warm water. It bore his weight and carried him away, deposited him on distant shores. That's not what the article said, though. It just said he walked out.

In the crystal dish on the console table were the things he never left the house without. His wallet, his watch, his cigarettes. He left the house without them. He reset the burglar alarm and locked the front door, so that his young wife, Grace (former airhostess) and only daughter, Evelyn (16), would be safe. He posted the house keys through the letterbox, having first taken the precaution of relocating the doormat indoors in order to deaden the sound.

No note was left for the family.

It is surmised that Mr Tyne released the handbrake on the

jeep and pushed it along the driveway, since starting the engine alongside the house would undoubtedly have raised the alarm. It was a Range Rover with the engine of a tank. He had purchased it to pull his beloved yacht up and down the hill. His beloved yacht, the *Grace Eva*, was at the time berthed in the marina. It was frozen along with the rest of his assets. It became nobody's boat, certainly not Grace's or Eva's. I don't think the yacht club ever billed my mother for marina fees.

Grace Eva gravitated over time towards the least accessible corner, as club members pushed William to the backs of their minds. Slime grew on it, seagulls caked it in shit. The sails perished, the ropes withered. We couldn't sell it off since it wasn't legally ours. By the time my mother was granted title, water had seeped in. No one could get the engine to start. Poor *Grace Eva*. Poor, poor *Grace Eva*.

Once William Tyne was beyond the gateposts of Sandpiper, he started the engine and drove to the summit. He abandoned the jeep at the top of the hill, in the car park familiar to so many courting Dublin couples. Gardaí were unable to trace witnesses for that particular night, a Saturday, and are still appealing for any to come forward.

Mr Tyne climbed the low car park wall and cut a path across the moors. Gardaí followed a track of broken gorse and heather down to the cliff's edge, a two-hundred-yard walk. The track came to an end when the land did. Below, the waves crashed against rocks as restlessly as lions. It was a drop of one hundred and forty feet. The key to Mr Tyne's four-wheel drive was deposited at this point, secured beneath a large stone.

My father's accounts were frozen upon his disappearance. My mother was left with no income. Only bills came in the door. She was unable to access his money for seven years, which is the legal time it takes to pronounce a missing person dead. Everyone was talking about us, we both knew that. My mother announced we'd have to move to hatchet-land, and we kerb-crawled around the most deprived suburbs the northside of Dublin had to offer. There were some fairly grisly enclaves after more than a decade of recession and the heroin plague.

I stared out the window, silent and white-faced, strapped into the passenger seat of our executive Range Rover as she pointed out boarded-up high-rise corporation flats. 'That one looks empty. We could end up there.' Scorch-marks flared above the lintels. When the local kids started chasing us, hurling planks and stones, my mother panicked and tried to accelerate in too low a gear. As the kids gained on us, she screamed that she hated his fucking jeep as much as she hated him, that it would happily sell us down the fucking Swanee too.

'So we can stay then,' I stated, once I understood that the house wasn't hers to sell. The deeds were in my father's name.

She said no. At least, she didn't say no, she just shook her head. Various bills were spread across the kitchen table, and her head was in her hands. She'd been sitting there all morning. My father had handled the bills.

'Why not?' I persisted, knowing that I was pushing my luck. Silence was the only safe option when she was in this state. She looked up and trembled with rage, her face a hideous mask. Her skin was mauve, mascara pooled under her eyes. She must have read my disgust. I certainly read hers. The dislike between us was electric at that moment. She spat while she spoke.

'Do you think money grows on trees? Who is going to pay these bills?'

I'd no idea who'd pay the bills. I said that with a hand on hip, and she sprang out of the chair and slapped my face.

She phoned Mr O'Hare, or Mister No Hair, as Dad had called him. He was a humourless but diligent man. He showed up at the house the next day, wearing a buff anorak despite the heat. It turned out there was a savings account in my mother's name that she hadn't known about. O'Hare produced a navy account book and slid it across the table. One hundred and seventy-five thousand pounds was entered in the balance column. Twenty-five thousand pounds by seven. Twenty-five thousand pounds a year to live on until we got our hands on

188

his assets. My father had left enough money to tide us over until he was officially pronounced dead. He knew we'd never find his body. It was not in the sea.

Satanism was practised on the hill that summer. A donkey was slaughtered, horses blooded, cats strung up, an ugly time. Evil eyes were scratched onto the walls of derelict cottages and caves. Fingers were pointed at me. A girl who was party to it ended up in a psychiatric hospital for a spell. None of these events were related to my father, and yet they were all related. They were all part of a general climate of things turning sour. Eventually the story of his disappearance went quiet.

No items of clothing were missing from his wardrobe, not so much as a pair of shoes. His wallet was full of cash, and his credit cards and cheque books were never again used. But Ireland was rife with corruption at the time, businessmen behaving as if they were above the law – my father could've had an offshore account in a false name. Everyone else did on the hill. The man could've been siphoning money off for years beforehand. If he was anywhere near as crooked as his only child, it would have been no bother to him. Lying, cheating, dissembling, just to get what you want. I didn't lick it off the stones.

That's if I am still his only child. It hit me one day that he could actually have several. I could have a multitude of little half-brothers and half-sisters knocking around. Maybe his yacht club friends still bump into him on the international racing circuit. They say: Hi William, I mean, John, Robert, Tom. Miguel, Sasha, Jacques.

He could be anywhere by now, so that is where I look for him. Anywhere. Any audience, any city, any country, any year. I perform as if he's there, because he is always there. Somewhere down the back, flickering in my blind spot. He generates shapes in my peripheral vision that make my heart soar. Naturalized by now, speaking the language; unlike my mother, he had a knack for fitting in. Accompanied? A woman, a small boy in the seat beside him? No, he wouldn't do that to me. Dad, if you have another child by now, I don't want to hear it. I am the alpha baby, jealous of any pretenders.

I try to look receptive when I walk onstage. I hold my head high to indicate that I turned out all right. I wear my green dress, or my blue one or my red. It's important that my father note I inherited his style. I bear his name after all. But it's his charisma, mostly, I strive to duplicate. There are times when I don't recognize this woman who plays with such self-possession. She is something that I have faked. She is William Tyne's daughter, I suppose; his idea of her. I put her forward when I am performing so that he will approach me. I strive to make her taller than she is, more graceful, less unsure. I don't think other people have to try so hard in their lives. Or do they? Are we all living like this? So close to this mesh of nerves?

So I played my father another concerto, though he was never one for sitting still in a chair. He would make an exception for me, though, his firstborn. He would see the progress I have made. I like to think he's kept up with my progress, the way fathers do. Shostakovich's Violin Concerto No.1 this time around, a piece characterized by strife and violence. A discipline bordering on brutality is required to depress all four strings on the violin at once, a brutality all the more inimical for the precision of its application.

I worried about the soundpost crack, but I didn't hold back. I was briefly suffused with a sense of mission, broadcasting this codified search for a missing person. It seemed possible that this concerto, with its heightened emotional states, would be the one to forge the link. Shostakovich wrote it in Stalinist Russia in 1947. As this was a time of severe artistic repression and terror, it wasn't premiered until 1955, after Stalin's death. Due to the oppressive circumstances of its composition, the score is a compendium of hidden messages. Despair is thinly concealed in the hilarity of the Scherzo; the Nocturne is about darkness, not romance.

The piece is above all else a harrowing study of aloneness. More than four and a half minutes of unaccompanied solo violin in the Passacaglia, with a full symphony orchestra standing by in silence. This is a concerto that has to be seen as well as heard. Eighty musicians sitting with their heads down, and another two thousand spectators listening in the stalls. And one person dead in the centre, the sole source of movement and sound, the very personification of isolation. The Maestro crossed his hands and prayed beside me, or seemed to.

The orchestra kicked in on the first bar of the finale and we became a single unit again, one hundred and sixty arms wielding bows, brass, and beaters. We could've stormed a football pitch. We could've taken Cologne. I was out of breath by the time it was over. A blast of applause from the audience. Several people jumped to their feet, and for once they weren't clambering to be first at the bar. It was an ovation.

So Cologne was another place my father wasn't hiding. I was shocked, as I always was, to find I still harboured real hope he'd come looking for me. Any fool could've told me I'd never see him again. I couldn't face my mother, I understood starkly on the flight back to Heathrow the next morning. For years I'd daydreamed that I'd be the one to triumphantly return the prodigal husband. I'd parade him through the Arrivals Lounge to our mutual jubilation. There'd be a party on the long lawn which would go on for days.

I got as far as the Aer Lingus check-in bay, but couldn't make myself take the Dublin flight, especially now that Daniel had bailed out. I left terminal one for terminal three, and stood in line at the American Airlines sales-desk, consumed by ugly emotions. Shame, primarily. I had my return flight to New York brought forward by a day.

There'd been an incident with Sándor following the concert. I'd been drunk, emotional, and had asked him to help me find my hotel. I knew fine well where to find my hotel, but I wanted Sándor to show me. 'Show me, Sándor, please,' I'd wheedled. The father-hunger was bad.

I insisted that he get us a cab, what with the rain and my dress and shoes. Sándor obliged and informed me, as we sat in the backseat, that I had put in a magnificent performance. The standing ovation, he said, was my due.

I recalled his crossed fingers as I went onstage. 'Thank you,' I said, and patted his hand. He smiled and patted my hand back.

This gesture convinced me that we'd reached an understanding. The taxi accelerated through an amber light. The speed lent me courage. I leaned forward to kiss him, but the fucker recoiled, and in the searing mortification of the rebuff, I experienced an epiphany: I wouldn't have been a violinist had not my father disappeared.

This revelation was almost beyond me. It was nearly too big to take in. I needed to write it down before it slipped through my fingers, but I'd nothing to hand, no paper, no pen. I had to share it with someone immediately. Not Sándor, obviously – he was staring out the window as if I didn't exist. Zach or Valentina. I would ring them from the hotel. 'I nearly wasn't a violinist!' I would gasp. 'I almost didn't have to do this shit.'

They would understand the enormity. They would see I'd cracked a code. I didn't have to be this way: enslaved, indentured. I'd have made a fine architect, a journalist, an art historian. Something civic would've suited me down to the ground, or a position in the health sector. A parent, for God's sake. I could've been a parent, had I not been thrown into this attempt at a coping strategy, were I not on this international quest, this fruitless search.

But I puked as soon as I reached my hotel room, and was too ashamed to call anyone. I lay on the bathroom tiles in my backless dress and cried. The epiphany subsided as the hangover set in. I woke the next morning still on the payroll.

I put my credit card into an airport payphone and called home. The answering service picked up. My mother had already left the house to collect me at the airport. Of course she'd already left the house. My flight was due to land in Dublin in less than an hour.

She'd sit through streams of arrivals, all dressed up to meet Daniel. Who could say how long she'd give it before throwing in the towel? Hours, no doubt, gazing at the automatic doors sliding open and shut. Watching others being reunited with loved ones, and waiting for her turn to come. She'd fix her hair and reapply her lipstick, smooth out the crease in her skirt. The sinking familiarity as this vigil drags on. Eight years of it now, come June.

I spoke carefully and apologetically after the tone. 'Mum,' I said, 'I'm not coming home after all. I have to go back to New York. Sorry.'

That evening I disembarked from the plane in JFK feeling like I'd seen a war. Halfway through the flight, I'd realized I'd nowhere to stay. I called out Daniel's address to the taxi driver and sat grimly in the backseat, waiting for the Manhattan skyline to rise up on the horizon. I was never able to predict where it would appear. It was like the moon that way. I wasn't due back in the city for another day. I wondered how Daniel would take the surprise.

He didn't take it. That is, he wasn't there. Patrice came out to see what all the banging was about.

'Hey, tiger.' He looked at my cases on the ground. 'You guys back early from your sojourn, or something?'

'Yeah.' What had Daniel told him?

'That's a shame. Daniel was telling me he needed the break so bad. But he was saying you'd be gone till tomorrow. He only just left last night, after all . . .'

Daniel left last night? 'Right. I had to come back early.'

'Oh. Pity.'

'Yeah.' Patrice looked at my cases again. Why was I knocking at the door if I knew Daniel wasn't in? 'We had a fight, okay, Patrice?'

'Okay,' he said casually, like he was down with that.

'It's no big deal.'

'Of course not. I'll bet it was all his fault.'

I caught a taxi to Valentina's. Had the bastard, spotting an opportunity, decamped to hers? It was no longer safe to have her in his place lest Patrice ratted him out again. The traffic was light at that hour, but I was in no hurry to arrive.

The driver pulled up to the kerb on Ninth Street and switched off the engine. I paid him and we both got out of the car. I stood on the sidewalk, he crossed over to the deli on the corner. I wondered if the best thing was to go get a coffee too.

Delay the inevitable. My legs were shaky. So was my heart. The lights in Valentina's apartment were on. This is it, I said out loud, and let myself into her building. Lugged all my bags to the top, then loitered in the hallway to catch my breath.

I finally unlocked her door. Ming came trotting out to welcome me home, and threw herself on her back. I stepped over her and kept walking.

Nobody in the sitting room. Several candles on the coffee table, two wineglasses, empty dinner plates.

Draped over the phone seat, a man's coat.

Down at the other end, the bedroom door was shut. Voices. Valentina's maddening laugh, the bass drone of a man. I stormed through the apartment and banged on the door.

'Valentina? It's Eva. I'm back.'

A stunned silence, then a bedspring creak followed by the thump of feet hitting the floor. Ming shot down the corridor and howled. I banged again.

'Valentina, I know you're in there.'

I tried the handle. It was rigid. She didn't have a lock. Someone was holding it up. The two of us were standing there holding different ends of the same handle.

'I know you've got someone with you, Valentina. Why can't you just admit it?' I pushed my entire weight down on the handle. It didn't yield an inch. I kicked and hammered at the door like a maniac. All those nights of exhaustion and worry – they'd left me frayed.

'Open up. I know you're fucking him, Valentina. I know you've been fucking him right from the start. You're in there, Daniel, aren't you?'

'No.'

I released the handle and gaped at the door. The voice was a familiar one.

Ming took a run at me and attached herself to my chest like a brooch. I fell against the wall. My lungs had never shut down so quickly before.

The door was tentatively opened. Kryštof put his head

around. 'Oh Jesus, find her inhaler,' he shouted at Valentina. 'Search her violin case.'

Valentina came out of the bedroom in one of his T-shirts. 'Where's her case?' she cried, as if Kryštof knew everything. She fled to the living room on her bare feet.

Kryštof pulled Ming off and urged me to take deep breaths. Valentina returned with the inhaler and put it into his hands instead of mine. It was the inhaler I'd bitten a chip off. He snagged it on my lip. 'Look at me,' he kept saying, but I couldn't bear to. It was horrendous to confront his nakedness in the context of another woman.

'Get off me,' I hissed, and staggered to my feet. It wasn't an asthma attack, just the shock.

Back to the living room. Through the blur, I saw that it wasn't anything like Daniel's coat. I knocked it to the floor. Valentina was following after me with a glass of water. A glass of fucking water. Holding it out with her skinny trembling arm, as if that would make amends. How had I not recognized her pretty 'hello' on his intercom all those months ago? My God, it had been going on all those months ago. I told them I'd be back for Ming, picked up my cases and left.

I don't know why I cared so much about the taxi still being there. It was the least of my worries, all things considered. There were thousands of taxis in New York City, but I was desperate, for some reason, for my cab to be waiting. A desire to return to the ignorance of ten minutes before, maybe.

The kerb was bare. The sense of desertion was extreme. I dragged my luggage to First Avenue and hailed another cab. The really bad thing was that I'd have coped so much better had it been Daniel in there with her. I would have turned to Kryštof.

'Where to?' drawled the driver, and I didn't know. 'I don't know,' I told him, 'the Sunset Boulevard Hotel?' I said this with great uncertainty, as if it might be the wrong answer. But the driver had no opinion one way or another. He turned the cab around in that slow, bored way they have, and I was out on the rapids and undertows of the street again.

Zach wanted to see me first thing.

'What's with the glasses?' he asked when I walked into the rehearsal room. My big Cologne shades. They covered my wretched eyes. Most of my face too.

'Roy Orbison,' said Odile.

'Bono,' said Knut.

'Hangover,' said Konrad.

Valentina said nothing. She didn't so much as glance my way. Zach motioned me back towards the exit and we went out to the corridor. He walked me down to the fire escape.

'We've got a problem,' he said gravely.

I took my shades off. 'What sort of a problem?'

'Your violin. I've received a call.'

'Not the Entente again?'

'No, I'm afraid it's a little more serious than that.'

I pictured pall-bearing Russians. 'Who?'

'A lawyer.'

'What lawyer?'

'A lawyer representing an old Jewish couple.'

'I don't know any old Jewish couples.'

'It's not about you, Eva. It's about your violin. They say it's theirs.'

Zach, if anything, was more shocked than I. He had factored Magdalena into his future as comprehensively as I had. 'They claim it belonged to the woman's father,' he told me. 'It was stolen from him by the Nazis.'

'The *Nazis*?'

'For Christ's sake, keep your voice down.' People were milling around at the other end of the corridor.

'Jesus fucking Christ. The Nazis?'

Zach nodded. 'The woman attended your performance, and says she immediately recognized the tone of the violin. Then that review appeared in the *New York Times* a couple of days later, reporting that it was recently rediscovered . . .'

'That's bullshit. The woman only decided it was her violin once she heard it had just been found.'

'Her lawyer maintains she contacted him before the article appeared.'

'Well he would, wouldn't he? He's her lawyer.'

'The woman was eighteen when they took her father away. Old enough to remember the violin, I guess.'

'Come on, Zach, we both know that means nothing. Hearing is subjective.'

'Yes, we'll argue that.'

'Maybe I just play like her father. Has she considered that? Maybe he also played that Stravinsky concerto.'

'It's possible.'

'I mean, can you recognize the sound of a specific violin after, what, over sixty years?' I knew I'd recognize the sound of Magdalena anywhere. 'What is she, eighty? She's probably deaf.'

'Probably.'

'And senile.'

'Could be.'

'Were you talking to her, Zach?'

'No. Her lawyer.'

'What did he say?'

'He said we'd hear from him in writing soon.'

'He's only rattling our cage. Do you believe her story?'

'It's an incontrovertible fact that her father's violin was stolen by the Nazis. She's been searching for it ever since. I believe that she believes your violin is the same one. It's difficult, Eva. It's an emotional issue.'

'Has she proof? She'll need a well-documented claim, won't she? A receipt or something from before the war? A certificate, a proper description.'

'Receipts and documents get lost in wars.'

'Well then, we're all right, aren't we?'

Zach took off his glasses and started polishing them. I'd never seen him without them before. His features seemed to come off with the frames. He looked so defenceless, so unformed. 'The lawyer says she has a photograph.'

'Of my violin?'

'Yes, of her deceased father holding it. Taken in the 1930s. Before the war. Before he was sent to the death camp.'

Death camp. I stared at Zach. He kept his eyes on his glasses. The pain of imminent tears shot up my nose and I blinked them down. We listened to the group inside working on the Corelli. I took out my inhaler and examined it.

'Have you seen this photo?' I eventually asked.

'Not yet.'

'Get them to send us a copy.'

'It's already on its way.'

'I mean, how clear can a 1930s photograph be?'

'Exactly.'

'Violins all look the same in those photographs.'

'That's true.'

'Besides, it's not an incontrovertible fact that her father's violin was stolen by the Nazis. No Stradivarius violin went missing during the Second World War. I checked. She's misinformed.'

Zach kept cleaning his glasses. Nothing could be that dirty. 'Eva, her lawyer says that the violin isn't a Stradivarius as reported, but a del Gesù. We haven't released that information.'

That was the nail in the coffin. I railed against the inevitable all the same. 'We don't know that it's a del Gesù for sure. That Martel guy was a total chancer. You heard him – he was full of shit. The man isn't even registered.' My voice was pitched about an octave too high. I couldn't stand its shrillness.

'What about the man who sold the violin to you, Eva? The Russian?'

'Chechen. What about him?'

'Can you talk to him?'

'Who, Alexander?' I snorted. 'Two chances.' Zach didn't know what that meant. 'None and fuck-all,' I had to explain.

'Perhaps Alexander could help us. Perhaps he could cast light on your violin's chain of ownership.'

I laughed scornfully. I was turning into my mother. 'I don't think either of us wants to know how he came by it.'

'Fantastic,' Zach said. 'That's just fantastic.'

'I'm not worried about this,' I lied.

'Good for you.'

'I mean, the litigation will go on for maybe a year, and then I can appeal. That'll take another year. So I'll have the violin for at least two full years, even if they can prove it's theirs, right?'

'I guess that's one way of looking at it.'

'And in two years' time, I'll have built up my career. The publicity from this will probably help.'

Zach put his glasses and his face back on. 'It's not the kind of publicity you want, Eva, and it's certainly not the kind of publicity I want. The woman will swear in court that it's the same instrument. Her lawyer is sending us an affidavit to that effect, though we have to remember it's the testament of an old woman speaking about memories of her father when she was a girl. It won't stand up on its own, no matter how deep her conviction.'

I nodded. I knew how unreliable and seductive they were, memories of lost parents. I understood the lengths to which you'd go to feel close to a missing father. At that moment, more than anything, I wanted to be lying on my back in a meadow, gazing up at the sky through squinted eyes. My eyelashes would look as huge as jungle weeds. Somewhere on the grassy slopes of the Wicklow Mountains would be perfect. I hadn't been on a holiday in years.

'Nazis,' I repeated, shaking my head. 'Seriously, could it get any worse?'

Zach smiled mournfully. 'I know.' Then he offered a list of meaningless assurances. 'We'll get you the best lawyer.' 'We'll support you in any way that we can.' 'It's highly unlikely it's the same violin.' 'The burden of proof is on them.' The list ran out pretty quickly. 'Maybe she'll die, or something,' he shrugged, though I could tell he didn't like talking that way.

Hot skewers of pain shot up my nostrils again. I smiled one of those smiles that rapidly flips the wrong way around, then put my Cologne shades back on and left.

My cell rang as I wandered down Riverside Drive. *God calling* . . . I took a deep breath.

'So you're back,' Daniel stated.

'Yeah.' He waited for me to elaborate. I didn't.

'How'd it go?'

'Fine.' As if it was any of his business.

'So I ran into Patrice this morning. He said you came by my apartment last night.'

'Did he now?'

'Yes, he did. But I told him, no, Patrice, that can't be, Eva's in Dublin.'

'Yeah well, Patrice said to me that you'd cleared out of the city for the weekend. So I said, no Patrice, that can't be, Daniel's far too busy with work to go anywhere. So Patrice said, you know what, Eva? Daniel told me he was spending the weekend with you.'

'Right, and now you think I lied to you.'

'You did lie to me. Where were you this weekend, Daniel?'

'Dublin.'

I found myself unable to respond. I looked at my watch in an attempt to regain control of the situation. Three fifteen. I marched down the street as if I was in a hurry, tutting at the fools who got in my way.

'I was in Dublin, Eva, looking for you. I went to meet your plane, but you weren't on it. I sat in Arrivals for four hours. Flight after London flight came and went, and you weren't on any of them. Where the hell were you?'

I frowned at the traffic. I jogged across the street as soon as a gap appeared. 'I didn't go to Dublin.'

'Thanks. I gathered.'

'I came back to New York a day early.'

'While I flew to Dublin to surprise you.'

I stopped and pressed my forehead against the window of a college bookstore. I stared at their selection of academic texts. 'You flew to Dublin to surprise me?'

'That's what I said.'

I wheezed on my inhaler. 'Baby, that's terrible.'

'Yes it is.'

The sun was hot on the crown of my head. He'd been waiting in a plastic chair in the Arrivals Lounge of Dublin airport, slowly realizing, along with my mother who was sitting just a few feet away, that he'd been stood up. 'Daniel?'

'What?'

'Let's never do this again. Let's never get paranoid again. I can't bear it.'

'Sweetheart, I'm not the one who got paranoid.'

It was around about then that I decided to surrender. Love, I told myself, is an act of bravery and faith. I would be brave. I would have faith in Daniel. I couldn't keep battling, I told him over dinner that evening, and he nodded solemnly and seemed to know what I was trying to say (I had forgotten how beautiful he was, so vibrant, so vital, after those pallid winter-sick Europeans). I needed roots, I explained, someone to care for, someone to care for me. 'I'm so fed up,' I whispered, 'of being out in the cold.'

In a fit of optimism, he asked me to move in with him. He clasped my hand and kissed it, saying, 'Live with me, my Irlandesa. Let's be together, let's try.' The smell of his skin, the fascination of the body of another. Love surged through my veins like alcohol.

'Oh baby, of course I'll move in with you.'

I kissed his face a hundred times and smoothed his jet-black hair. We laughed at the madness of it and opened another bottle of wine. I seized his phone the second his back was turned. *Calls dialled: Princess.* And the time? Three fifteen that day. It was me. He'd called me. I was his Princess.

I moved in that very night. I checked out of the Sunset Boulevard and showed up on his doorstep, swinging a case in each hand. Magdalena in one case, Ming in the other. A cat and a violin. I inferred, from the expression on Daniel's face, that he understood his life had just gotten appreciably harder. Still he smiled and led us in with a show of welcome so radiant I thought of daffodils.

The Maestro, around the time that I was bedding down in Daniel's, was dying alone in his Budapest home. I did not give his departing soul a thought, not then. I hope it was peaceful, I hope there was no pain. His passing, it transpired, was not exactly unexpected. Seems he'd seen it coming all along. Seems they all had; Sándor, the Philharmonie staff, the whole sorry orchestra. Everyone, in fact, but me. No wonder there was such an atmosphere.

'After a short illness,' the report in the *New York Times* said. A detailed obituary appeared the following Sunday. The list of great orchestras and composers with whom he'd worked was formidable. Shostakovich had been a personal friend. 'With him dies a piece of the twentieth century,' the obituary concluded, and it did feel as if a piece of something had been lost. Nowhere did it say what killed him.

I keep thinking of the flash I saw in his eyes when he turned to me backstage. Its precise nature both evades and haunts me. It could have been the warning shot of an impending fatal stroke, or cancer cells switching off a part of the body. The brain shutting down might produce a flare in vision. Is that how it's going to be? Is that death? Is that what happened to my father on that warm night in June, making him get out of bed and walk away from his life for good? But the Maestro didn't walk away from his life. He sighed and faced it, went onstage, a little shakily.

I'm uncertain of how I feel about his last performance being with me. It's a privilege I didn't earn. Play better, he told me, and I did, which proves he was the conductor they said he was.

I'm convinced that something huge could be gathered from our encounter. But I just can't think. I can't see beyond my own hand. Which would be fine if I didn't understand that I was failing to see something, but I do. Acutely. I acutely understand that I do not understand what happened backstage that night.

Sometimes when I remember it, the flash of fear is not in the Maestro's eye, but my father's – the two faces meld in the dark and I am with him once more. Did fear detonate something in my father, something that changed him, made him not my father? I think of that photo of him on *Grace Eva* with the Taoiseach, and am confronted all over again with how little I knew of him.

There are times when I wonder if I even saw that white flash in the Maestro's eye at all. Might I have perhaps, through some act of transference, imagined it in his eye, when in actuality it was my own? Some information which flared up at the back of my mind and was just as quickly smothered. Something that I couldn't quite grasp, could only almost grasp. Something about transience, temporality, some revelation that this was it, this was all there was, here in the wings with an exhausted man, in an unfamiliar country, in an underground hall, itself a musical instrument, itself a jewel, with its floating staircases and amber glass ceiling. Waiting in tense silence at the depth of the bed of the Rhine, quite alone despite the two thousand strangers on the other side of the door, and the eighty musicians onstage. And this small piece of wood in your hand. This violin, which would outlive you, this ornate contraption of sprung wood and wire. Ridiculously fragile and not big enough to hide behind, and deeply peculiar if considered for too long. I held onto Magdalena tightly, but not tightly enough. My father would not be on the other side of that door, or any door. I would never lay eyes on him again.

The Maestro turned away and I shivered right down to my gut. It was unbearable, at his age, to still be doing this. Where would it end? But the Maestro was resigned to his lot and on he went. To the applause, the golden light, the fleeting grace. That is mettle, I thought, watching him take his bow. That is the mettle I lack.

The stage manager wished me luck and I was overly grateful. I found his steadiness inordinately comforting. '*Toi toi toi*,' he said, and I thanked him. He had seen this sort of thing before, seen us come and go, would restore order to the hall as soon as we were gone. And we were almost gone. Just another few hours. Just another few hours. Just another few hours to get through, and then we would be gone.

'The Magdalena del Gesù, now believed to have been one of the many treasures plundered by the Nazi's in the 1940's, disappeared for six decades, but has finally resurfaced in suspicious circumstances in the possession of young Irish violinist, Eva Tyne.' Thus read the newspaper article that Zach handed to me before rehearsals. I shook my head in disbelief.

'There is no Magdalena del Gesù, Zach. Don't you see how weird this is? I made it up. Magdalena was the first word that entered my head. I mean, Jesus, where did they get all this?'

'Better have your side ready. They're going to want to ask questions.'

'And what do they mean, "suspicious circumstances"? Where did that come from? Is someone feeding them this drivel? Are you talking to them, Zach? Did you tell them about Alexander?'

'Keep it down, people can hear you. Of course I didn't tell them about Alexander.'

'Well, someone told them.'

Zach showed me his palms to indicate he was equally foxed.

'I mean, could I just lose the violin? Is it like buying a stolen car? If they can prove it's the same violin, can they simply repossess it?'

Zach said he'd find out. I took back the paper and read over it again. Kryštof's photograph of me lying on the floor. 'Eva Tyne,' read the subtitle beneath it, 'owner of the famous Magdalena del Gesù, the title of which is now under dispute.' Since when was Magdalena famous?

'Don't let them upset you,' Zach said. 'These people can't even punctuate.'

~

In the *Daily News*, Magdalena had a full-blown history. Zach caught my eye as I was leaving and indicated that I should follow him. I had come to dread our visits to the fire escape.

'Manufactured in 1732 by Giuseppe Guarneri (or "del Gesù" as he became known for the IHS monogram on his labels) for Gian Gastone, the last male member of the ruling house of Medici. Sold to Napoleon's sister, Elisa Baciocchi in Lucca, where it would have been played by virtuoso violinist-composer Nicolò Paganini, in her service at the time. Acquired by the court of King Ludwig II of Bavaria in 1864. Seized by the Nazis in 1940, and not seen again until its recent reappearance in the hands of young Irish violinist Eva Tyne.'

Suddenly my name kept appearing alongside the word 'Nazi.'

'Can they do that?' I asked Zach, thrusting the newspaper back at him. 'Can they just go ahead and write that shit?' Dumb question. They already had.

Zach didn't know. 'Concert's sold out,' he said.

The *Post* carried a photograph of the Jewish lady's father. A dapper gent with a moustache dandling a violin on his knee. The article said he was thirty-five, but he looked more like fifty. He was dressed in a tuxedo and white bowtie. 'Leopold Hurowitz,' it said, 'with the Magdalena, formerly the Gastone, del Gesù, in 1937, shortly before it was seized by the Nazis.'

'There goes the Rosenbaum donation,' said Zach.

'Oh come on, it's a blurred photograph. That could be any violin. It proves nothing.'

'We're fucked. Still, there's some good news. We've been invited to go on a tour.' He took a fax out of his pocket. 'Philadelphia, Baltimore, Washington DC, and then on to the North Pacific, San Francisco, Portland –'

'Stop, Zach. I can't think about it now.'

'So think about it soon. I need a prompt decision, and if I don't say yes, we're screwed. What's all this about you not rehearsing with Valentina?'

'You ask her about that.'

I packed up Magdalena and left. It was like carting around a bomb.

'How much have you insured it for?' Daniel wanted to know that evening. He'd spotted the article while at work.

I muttered into the bag of Chinese takeout.

'I can't hear you, baby,' he shouted from the couch.

'Well, come into the kitchen and you might.'

'I can't hear you, baby. How much did you say?'

I poured his noodles onto a plate and put the plate on a tray. He was watching the Iraq coverage with the volume too high. 'It isn't insured yet, Daniel.'

'Don't shout at me. Why isn't it insured yet?'

'There're problems. I haven't gotten around to sorting them out because I'm up to my eyes, okay?'

'How is that okay? What if it's stolen?'

'Who the fuck is going to steal it?'

Well, my brain mused, Alexander for starters, or any one of his gimp mates. Then there's the Jewish couple, who reckon it's theirs anyway. After that, it's down to pretty much anybody who's read in the paper that a priceless del Gesù has been discovered, and to help our readers find her, here's a picture, she looks like this, and answers to the name of Eva.

'I want you to insure it for two million,' Daniel instructed me.

His tone was galling. Issuing commands without bothering to look up from the television screen. I emptied the contents of my carton onto a plate. 'I'm kind of busy at the moment, Daniel. I'm kind of playing a sell-out concert on Thursday.'

'Baby, this is important.'

'And Thursday isn't?'

'What? I don't get it. Why are you fighting me? I'm trying to help.'

'It's not helping, okay?'

'Jesus, take a pill.'

Ming sprang onto the counter, hooked a piece of Daniel's chicken onto her nail and flicked it between her teeth. I grabbed the little thief and picked the chicken from her jaw. She'd never done anything like that before. She minced out of the kitchen with her tail in the air, her nails click-clacking across the tiles like high heels.

'So I want you to insure the violin for two million, Eva. Tomorrow.'

I dropped the chewed chicken back into his noodles and brought the tray into the sitting room. 'I heard you the first time, Daniel. Here's your food.'

A horrible thing happened the morning after that. Wednesday at ten. We had only just started into the opening movement of 'Spring.' Valentina on first violin, me beside her. She sat; I stood. The group were playing so tightly that I could feel it in my teeth.

We reached the birdsong section. I stared at the girl as we played. She kept her eyes on her music. The transformation of Valentina; it was a marvel to behold. Without her violin, she was a beautiful young Monégasque, but when she picked it up, when she made those sounds and entered that almost ecstatic state, it took my breath away.

I recalled her bare brown legs under the T-shirt, and the lurid glare of Kryštof's nakedness, and it wounded me to the quick all over again. Our high-register runs and trills were so buoyant and exuberant and unrepresentative of how things were between us that outrage flared. I reached out and slapped her face.

There was a sound not unlike a piano being slammed shut as every instrument abruptly broke off. This was followed by a stunned silence. No one was more stunned than I. I had no prior knowledge that that slap was going to happen. It had never been my intention to hurt her.

Valentina put her fingertips to her reddening cheek and blinked at me, tears forming in her eyes. I doubt she'd ever been hit before. I'd never hit anyone before. Neither of us knew what to do next. Nobody in the group knew what to do next. There was no protocol for such an event amongst classical musicians.

'Eva, a word.'

I turned around. Zach. He instructed the group to take a ten-minute break. It took them a second to respond. Konrad came over and handed me my bow. It had skidded across the floor to his side.

I followed Zach out into the corridor, and we walked in silence to the fire doors. He leaned against one wall; I leaned against the other. Nobody emerged from the rehearsal room. Zach didn't say a word. Nor did I. I kept thinking of things to say, but none of them were any good. Each of us fixed our eyes on the other's shoes. My mother, I thought. This is how she felt that time she slapped me.

When the ten minutes were up, Zach asked whether I was ready to go back in. I nodded. He organized the group while I waited outside the door, listening to them muttering as they resumed their seats. Zach returned. 'They're all set.' In I went.

Valentina's cheek was red. Ghastly white on one side, livid red on the other. Nobody alluded to the incident. We carried on as if the interruption had been caused by a fire alarm or the like. 'From the beginning,' I said, and everyone turned back to the opening bar. 'A little less sprung this time,' I added, and there were murmurs of assent, as if I'd put my finger on it, as if the slap had come about because we'd been playing too tautly. They're treating me like a mental patient, I realized.

We played all four concertos through with a vigilance and edge that was new. The group sprang forward and scribbled on their music at my every comment. Nobody queried me or issued complaints. When we were done, they drummed their feet in appreciation, and I thanked them and wished them the best of luck for tomorrow. I left Valentina to lead them through the Corelli.

It was a warm breezy day in New York City and I felt like a schoolgirl bunking class. Hydrangeas were coming into bloom in doorside troughs, a full two months ahead of their Irish counterparts. I didn't much feel like going back to Daniel's place. I'll visit Estelle, I suddenly thought, and every part of me seized upon the essential rightness of this idea. Well, maybe a small part of me knew I was up to no good, but that part was used to being overruled. I rode a cab down to the East Village, stopping to buy a babka in the Ninth Street Bakery.

The door to Estelle's building was wedged open. The boys from Con-Ed were out with their monster truck and shiny tools. I pressed Estelle's buzzer and stood back.

'Ma'am, the power's down,' one of the electricians pointed out.

'I can see that, thanks.' I pushed the buzzer again.

'The intercom runs on electricity, ma'am. They can't hear you. Go on in.'

I climbed to the top floor making no effort to be quiet, but when I rounded the corner, Estelle wasn't stationed at her hallway post. Unusual. I knocked on her door and watched for the peephole to darken. I prepared an expression of warmth and happiness. But the peephole didn't darken. So I knocked once more. No joy. I knocked harder, then harder again. I slammed at the door with the flat of my palm and called out her name. 'Hello, Estelle, it's Eva. Hello? It's Eva!'

Kryštof's door opened at last.

He looked indefinably, afflictingly different, a laundered and pressed version of his old self. Someone had sewn his missing buttons back on, darned the holes in his socks. In his hands was a tea towel I had never seen before, and its connotations of contented domesticity were an affront. 'Eva,' he said in surprise, and I suddenly wished I'd stayed away.

'Hi, Kryštof. I came by to see Estelle.' I held up the babka, like a fool. 'I brought her a babka, but she doesn't seem to be in. Will you give it to her when she gets back?'

Kryštof caught his breath. 'Didn't Valentina tell you?'

'Tell me what?'

'Eva, I'm so sorry, but Estelle passed away a month ago.'

I took a step back in shock. 'What?'

'She had a heart attack.'

I glanced at her door. 'But she was fine.'

'I know. It was very sudden.'

'Jesus. God love her, I wish I'd known.'

Kryštof nodded. 'I thought I'd see you at the funeral.'

'I can't believe I missed Estelle's funeral. Christ, that's awful. The poor woman.' I looked at my cake.

'Listen, I've got mail for you. Come in.'

How tiny our old apartment looked. That two such sprawling lives had fitted into it seemed implausible. I didn't want to look around too closely. Didn't want to see anything that might hurt.

Kryštof disappeared to get my mail. I sat on the seat in the narrow hall so that the bedroom and kitchen were out of sight. But there it was, the evidence of Valentina that I didn't want to see. Girly cushions. I had lived in New York for four whole years and hadn't ever bought cushions. I wasn't there to buy cushions. I was there to graft.

Kryštof returned with a stack of letters and I was excessively profuse in my thanks.

'You're looking well,' I told him. Blue was always his colour.

'So are you, Eva. Success suits you.' He stood over me awkwardly, hands in the pockets of his jeans, so I flicked through the letters to distract myself. Junk mail, mostly. A few from the bank. I stopped flicking when accosted with the navy insignia of the hospital. Kryštof caught me staring at the envelope.

'Tea?' he offered. 'I think the gas is still working.'

'That'd be lovely, thanks. We can have this, I suppose, seeing as, well . . . Here.' I passed up the bakery bag.

'Saw your picture in the paper,' he called from the kitchen. 'The one taken in this apartment. Over there by the window, remember?'

'Of course I remember, Kryštof.'

'Congratulations on that excellent review in the *New York Times* a few weeks back. I felt very proud of you.'

'Thanks. How's the photography going?'

'Great. Really well.'

'Good stuff. You've earned it.' I tapped the hospital letter on my knee. Hadn't banked on hearing from them again.

'Best of luck with the Vivaldi tomorrow night.'

'You'll be there, will you?'

'No.'

'Oh, how come?' Kryštof attended my concerts whenever possible.

'I, uh. Valentina asked me not to.'

'Oh.'

'She said it'd make her nervous.'

'Oh, right.' She just didn't want him to see me with my new violin, I decided. 'You should go anyway, Kryštof. Sit down the end on the left and she'll never spot you. I'll leave a ticket in your name at the door.'

I ripped opened the hospital letter. 'Department of Obstetrics, Gynaecology & Reproductive Science,' it said. 'An appointment has been scheduled for February 12.'

The tears were instantaneous and I couldn't wipe them away quickly enough. Kryštof saw them when he returned with the tea. He put down both cups and took the letter out of my hand. 'You're pregnant?' he whispered in disbelief.

'Was,' I said, my voice thick. 'Kryštof, I had a miscarriage in January.'

It was possibly the first time in my life that I'd said that word. Definitely the first time I'd said it in relation to myself. Kryštof was quiet for so long that it crossed my mind that he didn't know the meaning of it in English, though his vocabulary had always been better than mine. I touched his hand. 'Do you know what that word means, love? Miscarriage?'

'It means we were going to have a baby.'

I nodded. Muscles contracted across my jaw, forehead, scalp. The strain was unbelievable. 'Yeah, angel, we were going to have a baby. But we lost it.'

He stared at me, the letter trembling in his hand. 'When did this happen?'

'The night I made my debut. You were out of town.'

'The night you had that asthma attack?'

'Kryštof, I didn't have an asthma attack that night. Do you think there's any aspirin in the cabinet?'

He didn't react for a second, then sort of started and went back to the kitchen. He returned with the aspirin and a glass of water, and sat on the ground at my feet. We'd never both been in this corner of the apartment at the same time before. Estelle would've listened in on our every word. I nodded in her direction and smiled through the blur of tears. 'You kind of miss her, don't you?'

But Kryštof couldn't think about Estelle. He kept shaking his head. 'Why didn't you tell me?'

'I don't know, angel. It was so quick. They gave me these painkillers and my hormones were all over the place. You were away and I just kept drinking. Everything went weird in my head. It all just, I don't know, went weird.'

This made no sense to him whatsoever, though I could see he was doing his best. He was trying as hard as he was able to get his head around this enormous, gaping omission on my part. 'Why didn't you tell me as soon as you knew you were pregnant?'

'I never knew I was pregnant. My period came and went as normal. The first I heard about it was when they told me I'd miscarried. I mean, if I'd known, of course I'd have told you, but I never knew.'

'Would you have had it?'

'Well, yeah.'

'Jesus Christ,' he said, then some stuff in Czech.

'I can't figure out how I got pregnant. We were careful, right? You were there.'

'Yes, we were always careful. That baby must've wanted to happen.'

'Don't say that.'

He rubbed his eyes so hard I thought they might burst. 'Fuck!' he shouted, and kicked the wall, leaving a black smear on the paint. 'I knew there was something wrong. I rang you so many times, but Valentina said you didn't want to talk to me. I should have opened that letter myself. Fuck!' He clutched his head and hunched over as if a bomb had exploded. Then he reached up and gripped my knee. 'Are you okay now?'

'Yeah. They just had to do this procedure. To, you know . . . finish things off.' Though Kryštof was still hunched over, it was clear from the shudder of his shoulders that he'd started to cry. A tear hit the floorboard, then another, and another. I stooped to kiss the back of his head.

He moaned and looked up at me. 'You should've told me, Eva. I'm not just some guy you picked up; I was that baby's father. It was my baby too.'

'I know.'

'You don't know. You treat me like I'm nothing. I could have helped you.'

'I didn't want to have a big conversation about it, Kryštof. I just wanted it to go away. I can't explain. I'm really sorry.'

'So then you met that man. What was his name?'

'Angel, don't do this.'

'Remind me of his name, Eva.'

'Daniel.'

'Ah yes, that's it. Daniel. Did you tell him?'

'No.'

Tears and snot were running down Kryštof's face. I didn't want to see him this way, and he knew it. 'All I ever wanted was to make you happy, Eva. All I ever wanted was to make you feel safe.'

'Angel, you did.'

'Then why did you dump me?'

'I didn't dump you.'

'You walked out, you packed your bags, you left.'

'It was only meant to be for a couple of days. If I hadn't gone out drinking or if you hadn't been away the whole weekend, then maybe we'd be together still.'

'I wasn't away the whole weekend. I came home early from Boston to be with you, but you'd disappeared. It's not my fault that we broke up, Eva.'

'Well, it's not mine.'

'Yes it is. That we are not together is entirely your fault.'

He immediately apologized. Said he didn't mean it. Said he understood things a little more now, that he was glad I'd told him, and that he was sorry, so sorry, I'd gone through it alone. 'It's okay,' I told him, and he said that it was not. He said that he'd failed me; I said I'd failed him. We let these words hang in the air. Kryštof wiped away the tears, blew his nose, pushed back his hair, and then we were calm for a while.

'Look at us,' he said.

'I know. This is shit.'

He laughed and said, 'Yes, this is shit.' He blew my fringe out of my eyes and kissed my nose.

We drank the tea, though it was cold by then. We didn't eat the babka, just looked at it. Kryštof said a few words about Estelle. Only eight people at the synagogue, counting him and Valentina. The other six were ancient and knew they were next. She'd no kids, no husband, no surviving siblings. No one had been up to her apartment since. She'd been living in it for fifty-two years.

Kryštof cleared his throat and said that he very much regretted the manner in which I'd found out about him and Valentina. I shrugged; my fault, barging in unexpectedly like that, having told the girl three days earlier that I was moving out. I didn't tell him I'd smacked her earlier. He put his head on my lap and cried. I cupped his lovely face in my hands.

We kissed on the mouth but it wasn't like before, so we stopped and held hands instead. I slipped off the seat to join him on the ground, and we huddled together under the coats. He said, 'Ming would love this,' and he wasn't wrong. She'd have been in her element.

I was about to invite him to come by and see her, but then remembered that she now lived at Daniel's. I didn't want to mention that name again. So I told Kryštof instead about how good she'd been, as good as a cat could be. He smiled and said he missed her still. I told him about how, in the shell-shocked days following the miscarriage, I'd clung onto her so tightly that she'd cried out in panic or pain, or both. Little steadfast Ming, doing her level best. Loving me as hard as she could, and it never being enough. Her fur was always wet and matted with my tears, her limbs were always cramped and too hot, but still she purred fiercely and kept us afloat.

I told him how I'd retched every time I cracked open an egg to find a bloodspot. So I'd given up eggs. I bit into an apple too hard and the apple seeds tumbling out made me reel. I burst into tears once at the sight of a budding flower. Standing there like a halfwit crying at a flower bud on the cash desk of a store on Madison Avenue. I'd hurried away with my purchases, apologizing. It was like being bruised all over, I tried to explain; it was like having no skin. Kryštof nodded attentively, his eyes on the floor. It occurred to me that I was attempting to describe a state that could only be understood by one who'd experienced it. The impenetrable abstractness of someone else's grief.

The hospital staff had asked me whether I wanted to see the baby. I said no, straight out. The prospect was terrifying. I mean, what were they going to show me? Kryštof wasn't sure either. 'Eight weeks into the human gestation period, the embryo becomes a foetus,' he said softly. This was a typical Kryštof formulation.

Another nurse asked me whether I wanted to give my baby a name, and that was the end of it. I hauled myself out of bed and left. I stood with my back to the hospital and was confronted with the essential wretchedness of the world, the fundamental bleakness. I felt everybody's suffering, as if it were viral, as if it were entering my lungs and attacking me. There was no defence to be mounted against it. It was an unusually pervasive kind of pain.

I took off uptown in search of oblivion, and threw myself into the arms of the first idiot I met. I hated New York then. What obscene vanity had driven me there in the first place? Why had I gone onstage after the pains had started? 'I got up on a stage during it,' I confessed to Kryštof. 'Do you see how sick that is? I got up on a stage, when it's possible that if I'd sat tight . . .'

'There was absolutely nothing you could've done to prevent it,' Kryštof insisted, but what did he know? I drank more in that one week than in an entire year put together, plunging into a January as deep and dark as a well. And then like a maniac pursuing that violin, telling myself whatever I wanted to hear, no matter how improbable, no matter how outrageous, just so as to avoid facing up to anything else.

Kryštof held me tightly and promised that he would always love me. I understood all over again how much I had lost, but held onto him as if he were mine. With his arms around me, it seemed we still had a chance. 'It could all have been so different,' he whispered.

The hall darkened as the hours passed. The electricity didn't return. This is going to take a day, I thought. This is going to take Kryštof and me a full day of sitting here in the gloom, and well into the night, before we've in some way absorbed what has happened. And that'll be just the first step. We'll need to think about it in our own time, then come back and spend more days trying to work it out. It could take a year. More. But it was peaceful, sitting there with him. It was an immense relief to at last in some way broach it, the lonely awfulness of that January night in the snow. There was even the possibility that at some point in the future, we might manage to put the whole thing behind us.

'Eva,' Kryštof said gently. We'd been lying in silence for so long that his voice was startling. I took my head off his chest and opened my eyes. Dark now, just about. 'Valentina's coming by at seven.'

'Oh,' I said. 'I'm so sorry. I'll go.'

I waited for him to say no, don't go, I'll cancel her, she'll understand, but he didn't say any of that. He said, 'She's going to be tired after a busy day,' and then he let go of my hand.

His life had moved on. I got it then. My pain was terrible, and he empathized deeply, but his life had moved on and he had other responsibilities now. I apologized again and blustered over my belongings. He handed me my post and let me out.

'Eva,' he said before I disappeared down the stairs. 'Are you still with him?'

'Who, Daniel?'

'Yes, Daniel, that is the name.'

'Yes, I'm still with Daniel.'

'Good,' he said curtly. 'I am pleased. It gives me comfort to know you didn't break my heart for some guy you met in a bar. It is a relief to be dumped for something that was serious. If you married him, I would feel even better. I want you to marry him, Eva.'

'I didn't dump you for him, Kryštof.'

'Oh but you did.'

The electricity shunted on, turning the hall a gaslight yellow. Kryštof winced at the brightness. He looked ghastly and drawn. I'm sure I looked worse. In the kitchen, his radio had come to life. The seven o'clock news bulletin. Valentina was a punctual creature. I had to get away.

'Okay, I admit it Kryštof. I fucked you over, all right? Is that what you want to hear? Are you happy now?' I hurried down the stairs so as to deny him a retort. He slammed the door behind me.

I'll never know why I caused it to end on a bitter note. My love for him was undiminished. I would have gone back to fix it, but Valentina was already ascending the stairs. I leaned over the banister and saw the honey hair, two floors down. I cut along the fourth-floor corridor and flattened myself into a doorway while she passed. I'll write him a letter, I decided. Yes I will, no I won't.

Valentina's steps were slow and lethargic. She sounded tired indeed. Kryštof would freak when he heard I'd slapped her. He wouldn't love me anymore. I strained my ears as she reached his door. She didn't have to knock; she had her own key. How thoroughly she had replaced me.

She shut the door behind her and I gulped. It was no more than I'd done to him, I had to accept. Substantially less, in fact. So this was how he felt in January when I walked out. Watching me go, believing I'd soon be in another man's arms, my mind no longer dwelling on him because Daniel was there, the way his mind was no longer dwelling on me because Valentina was there. That I had been so sickeningly cruel without even knowing it; that was a cold, hard shock. Such an ugly bite to it, the taste of my own medicine.

I brought the ugly taste back to Daniel's. He was sitting in front of the television, watching the Iraq coverage as usual. He muted it and turned around.

'Where were you?'

'Out.'

'I come home looking forward to seeing you and you're not here. I was lonely.'

'I'm not your mother, Daniel.' I looked around the living room. 'Where's Ming?' He turned the volume back up.

I called her name and she howled in response. I followed the sound to the bathroom door. She bolted out when I opened it. I went back to the living room and positioned myself between him and the television set. He watched the war through my legs.

221

'Why was Ming locked in the bathroom in the dark?'

'Oh, I thought she was quiet. I must have locked her in by accident.'

'So why are her food bowl and litter tray in there too?'

'Oh come on, Eva, I'm tired, I want to relax. Jesus Christ, I've had a tough day. I just want to be left in peace.'

So I left him in peace. I shut myself in the bedroom and sat with Ming on the bed. She purred furiously and pushed her head into my armpit. I kissed her and hugged her and promised she'd never be locked up again. Eventually she made a whorl of herself and fell asleep on my lap. I stared at myself in the mirror and saw that I was getting older, and not just older, but hideous.

I didn't wake when Daniel left for the office the next day at six or seven, or whenever the hell it was. He had been leaving earlier each morning, returning home later each night. Work, he said, was bad, he was under a lot of pressure. The long night's sleep had done me good, though. I looked all right again. I looked more like myself.

I made a bolt for Barneys straight after the dress rehearsal. I should've been admiring diamonds at the pre-concert dinner, but under the circumstances, I believe Zach welcomed my absence. Nobody wanted to be associated with a violin thief. I belted up to the fourth floor and paid a large sum for a pair of Miu Miu boots with go-faster stripes down the side. 'They'll be so cute on you,' the sales assistant enthused as I signed my name on the credit card receipt. 'They'd want to be,' I told her, 'at that price.'

The box the boots were packed in was bigger than Magdalena's case. Sturdier, too. I reckoned they'd look good together, my green silk dress with the tan kidskin. Most soloists get rigged out like bridesmaids for some reason.

Seven fifty-five and I left my dressing room to offer the group encouragement with the Corelli. 'Don't fuck it up, lads,' I said. Full house out front, many of them there to gawp at the Nazi violin, the Jewish couple and their lawyer not least amongst them.

Valentina was looking elegant in black chiffon. She only wore dresses when performing. Those long brown legs again, the delicacy of the backs of her knees. I looked at them and felt guilty. I'd shown up at Estelle's door primarily to see Kryštof. I'd gone to see Kryštof primarily to fuck him up, to fuck up whatever he had going with Valentina, although our encounter had quickly turned into something more personal than that. At least there was no slap-mark on her face.

But Valentina deliberately hadn't informed me of Estelle's funeral arrangements because naturally I'd have attended. Instead, she'd appropriated my place at Kryštof's side. And that was wrong. Estelle wouldn't have appreciated that. 'Who the hell is Barbie?' she'd have growled. So Valentina and I were quits.

'Nice dress, Valentina. You make it yourself, or what?' I hadn't spoken to her since catching her in bed with Kryštof. Had he mentioned I'd paid him a visit, I wondered? Had she told him I'd decked her?

'No, I bought it,' she answered cautiously, not wishing to be thumped again.

'You're getting great wear out of those shoes, aren't you?'

She shrugged. 'I like your boots. Fancy.'

'Tell me this: what language do you and Kryštof speak?'

She didn't seem to understand the question.

'I mean, how does it work, Valentina? English or French or German or what?'

'It depends.'

It depends. The cheek. I sniffed and went back to my dressing room.

Only we were far from quits. I realized that the second the door was closed. Valentina knew about the miscarriage, but left Kryštof in the dark. She'd stood by as he'd wondered why he'd so callously been dumped. All she had to say was, Kryštof, it wasn't an asthma attack, there was blood on Eva's dress. But Valentina kept her mouth shut. Because she knew if she opened it, he'd have rushed to my aid.

I stood in the centre of my dressing room and pushed it all from my mind. I contemplated my violin, my wings of wood and wire. Tenderwire, four strings of it across Magdalena's prow. Ordinary matter with extraordinary properties. I understood why men had devoted lifetimes striving to convert base metal into gold. Because they perceived more than base metal. So did I.

~

For most of his life Vivaldi taught orphan girls in the Pio Ospedale della Pietà, Venice. He was ordained a priest in March 1703, but was barred from saying mass some months later. Kept disappearing into the sacristy during sermons. In September of that same year, he was engaged as the music director of the Pietà, an institution for female orphans, bastards, and the just plain abandoned. A building full of girls nobody wanted – imagine the atmosphere, the tension. These girls didn't have so much as surnames. The young redheaded priest taught them how to play the violin.

The girls gave concerts in the great hall of the Ospedale, to which Venetian high society and visiting dignitaries swarmed. Hundreds of torches burned along the lagoon on the nights of these lavish and acclaimed services. Inside the great hall, cloths of gold caught the light of crystal chandeliers. The girls were seated behind a grille so as to be protected from the corrupting gaze of men. They played for a world from which they were concealed.

No composer before Vivaldi did more to establish the violin as a solo instrument. It was the time of Stradivari and Guarneri del Gesù. The three men died within eight years of each other; del Gesù in his forties, Vivaldi in his sixties, Stradivari made it to his nineties. Magdalena, it is likely, was produced during the golden period of these men's lifetimes. Vivaldi selected the most accomplished girl from the Pietà orchestra, and to her would go the soloist's part. It frightens me to think of how competitive those young women must have been. They had nothing to fight over but the violin and this young priest.

But occasionally Vivaldi had two first choices amongst the group, and then things got complicated. He responded by composing more complicated scores, and wrote nearly thirty concertos for two violins, thereby enabling his chosen girls to play together. These concertos explored the relationship between the two solo voices. Sometimes the violins were treated as a single, indivisible unit; other times they engaged in dialogue. A number of the concertos were pervaded by a sense of solitude and desolation so acute that the relationship between his two favourite girls must have been irredeemably broken.

Vivaldi evidently gained an insight into the dynamics between young women during his time at the Pietà. He clearly witnessed at first hand the intensity of the bonds uniting them, as well as the intensity of the pain suffered at the collapse of those bonds, to have distilled such remorse into the piece we played that night, the Concerto for Two Violins in A minor. Here we were, his two chosen girls, Valentina and me, playing our hearts out, fighting the same fights three hundred years down the line. Me in my boots, her with her delicate knees, and the animosity smouldering between us. I loathed Valentina with an intimacy characteristic of love. She loathed me in equal measure. I will have this larghetto played at my funeral, I decided. It is sad enough for me.

There was a tear spilling down her pretty cheek. A tear glistening for the whole place to see. I'd have slapped her again were we alone. 'What the fuck,' I hissed in her ear when the applause came, 'do you have to cry about?' A particle of glitter shimmered on her collarbone like a taunt.

I turned to the group, who had watched this exchange closely. We had never been so alert, so primed. I spoke one word, and that one word prepared us. It focused our energy into a searing column. 'Spring,' I said, and we went off.

Vivaldi, the musicologists tell us, very probably had asthma too. The chronic illness of which he complained throughout his life was either asthma or angina. He was buried in an unmarked pauper's grave. I wonder what his girls made of that. Did they fight to tend it? Did they bring him flowers? Or could they even find it? Was his grave as neglected as his work? His music lay forgotten in a monastery archive for nearly two centuries after his death.

Zach was triumphant at the post-concert party. 'There's serious talk of a European tour,' he told me. 'That's a German concert promoter over there. And the guy by the window is a Sony producer. And that lady . . .'

His voice trailed off as my face dropped. A man in a black suit was striding across the room, so tall that his head was visible above the crowd. He cut through it like a shark fin through water and pulled up in front of us.

'Hello, Jane,' he said happily. 'I mean, Eva.'

'Alexander,' I tried to say, but nothing came out. It was the first I'd seen of him since that snowy day in Tompkins Square Park.

Zach looked to me for an introduction, then to our new arrival, who presented his hand.

'Hello, I am Alexander. You will know my name.'

Zach grimaced as his hand was crushed. Alexander turned back to me.

'It took me a while to find you, Jane. I am here for my missing money.'

Zach froze. 'Get him out of here.'

Alexander clapped the shoulder of this amusing fellow in a tuxedo. 'I am going nowhere without my missing money, yes?' Two of the sponsors had already turned around.

I leaned into Zach. 'Could you excuse us for a moment?' Alexander had chosen his moment with care.

'Take it outside.'

'Can't you just give us a moment alone? He's not going to leave until I talk to him.'

Zach assessed Alexander's resolve, and didn't find it wanting. 'Okay,' he conceded, 'but keep it down.' He joined the pair of onlooking sponsors and guided them towards the drinks table.

Alexander smiled fondly and wagged his finger. 'You tried to cheat me, Jane. I sit down to count the money and find I am seventy thousand dollars missing. Seventy thousand US dollars! Is a lot, yes?'

'It was a mistake, Alexander. I found the extra envelope of cash as soon as I got home. I had it there for you the whole time, but I'd no way of contacting you, so, well, I've kept it for you.' Indeed I had not. I'd given sixty grand back to Daniel, and frittered away the rest.

'It's gone up to one hundred thousand, Jane.' No smiles now.

'What?'

'One hundred thousand or there'll be trouble.'

'You're having me on. I'm being sued, Alexander. People are claiming that the violin was stolen from them years ago and that they can prove it. It'll be repossessed and I'm going to lose everything, and now you crash the party demanding a hundred grand?'

Alexander sighed. 'This is not my problem, Jane. Pay me, or else.'

'Or else what?'

He wiggled his missing finger in my face. Or rather didn't wiggle it, seeing as there was no finger. He just sort of flexed the stump.

'I'm not scared of you,' I lied.

He was delighted with that, he really was. He threw back his head to laugh. 'The fighting Irish, ha!' Half the room turned around. 'So yes, I will be waiting in Tompkins Square Park for my missing money next Sunday, two p.m. Same bench as last time. Bye-bye.' He turned on his heel and strode away.

Zach reappeared by my side. 'So he's the one who sold you the violin.'

I nodded.

'And he told you he was Chechen?'

'Yep.'

'He was obviously trying to gauge the depths of your ignorance.'

'What are you saying?'

'Eva, that man isn't Chechen. Or Russian.'

I stared at Zach, my heart pounding as if he'd unmasked Alexander as the devil himself. There were rumours that Paganini was in league with satanic forces. That's how he

228

played the violin so well. No ordinary human possessed such capacities. So they refused to bury him in consecrated ground. He owned a del Gesù too.

Nightmares again that night, really bad ones. Alexander was back, all seven foot of him, a swastika stitched to his arm. He could barely insert his length into the room. He slumped forward and slithered across the floor like a snake, seeking out Magdalena with his vulgar forked tongue.

I woke up in the dark, gasping for my inhaler, and stumbled out to the living room. Ming wove figures of eight through my ankles, begging to be held, but I was not in a holding mood. I threw open the leather case and brought the violin back to the bedroom, slipped it under the bed and slept over it. Alexander would have to get past me first. Daniel's feet started padding and he muttered something Spanish in his sleep. It sounded like a threat.

At ten a.m., I was woken by my cell phone. Zach. The Jewish lady's lawyer had messengered the affidavit over to him that morning.

'Oh Jesus,' I said. 'Read it out.'

The shuffling of papers. 'Okay. A bit about her father, Mr Leopold Hurowitz, a child prodigy who made his debut in 1912 in Paris at the age of ten. "Warsaw banker Mr Jakob Zilberstein purchased the Gastone del Gesù in 1922 for the young Polish virtuoso, who went on to perform on it as soloist with the most prestigious orchestras in Europe, under the batons of conductors of the calibre of Weingartner, Furtwängler, and von Karajan, the latter a member of the Nazi party. The Gastone del Gesù was confiscated by the Nazis in 1940. Mr Hurowitz died in the Treblinka Concentration Camp in 1943, followed soon afterwards by his beloved wife, Ester."'

'Okay, here we go: "In January 2003, Mrs Weintraub, née Hurowitz, saw a photograph of the Gastone del Gesù in an advertisement for the New Amsterdam Chamber Orchestra. She recognized it instantly as the property of her late father, and contacted her lawyer immediately. Mr and Mrs Weintraub attended Ms Eva Tyne's performance the following week, which confirmed beyond all doubt Mrs Weintraub's conviction that this was her father's violin. Two days after the performance, the *New York Times* reprinted the photograph, erroneously identifying the instrument as "the recently rediscovered Magdalena Stradivarius." Mrs Weintraub subsequently –"'

'Wait, go back. It says she recognized her father's violin in my publicity photograph?'

'Yeah. "Mrs Weintraub, née Hurowitz, saw a photograph of the Gastone del Gesù in an advertisement for the New Amsterdam Chamber Orchestra. She recognized it instantly."'

'That's a legally binding document, right?'

'Yes, it's an affidavit. It's confirmed by oath.'

'And she's signed it and all that?'

'Uh huh, a little wobbly signature. Something Weintraub. Looks like Frieda.'

'Zach, listen to me: That publicity photograph was taken by Kryštof last summer, way before I got Magdalena. That's my old violin in the photograph. It's the old French one, the Vuillaume, the one that now belongs to David Rivers. It's not the Magdalena at all. Or the Gastone. Mrs Weintraub is recognizing the wrong violin.'

I held my breath and listened to Zach working out the implications. The inaccuracy of the first part of their testimony eroded an already under-documented claim. It may well have been the same violin, but it didn't look like the Weintraubs would be able to prove it.

'We have them,' said Zach, and I shrieked.

Daniel had left a note on the countertop, inviting me to lunch at a place in Midtown, a few blocks across from his office.

Ming was curled up in the violin case. I couldn't wait to tell him my wonderful news.

I wore my new white linen summer dress. The full skirt twisted and swirled around my bare legs, and I billowed along the street like a galleon. It was the first outdoor-dining day of the year, and the restaurant had corralled off a row of tables on the sidewalk. Daniel was already seated, dressed in his perennial business attire. He'd removed his suit jacket and rolled up his shirtsleeves, but he still looked like Secret Service. He put a hand to his chest to check that his tie was in place.

I waved to him, but he didn't spot me at that distance. He scanned the street with a scowl to indicate that he was in control of the situation, though I knew his eyesight to be so poor that he could discern little. He was scowling at nothing, letting it know that he was watching it, that it was not to mess with him, that he was the man.

He stood up when I approached and kissed me on the lips. I touched his cheek, marvelled anew at his vivid beauty. 'Don't, baby,' he protested. My Daniel sounded dispirited. I couldn't bear that the pressure at work had done this to him, and on a day so lovely. 'Hey, it's practically the weekend,' I told him, 'be happy.' Daniel smiled at me like I could never understand.

The waitress brought two glasses of water and I ordered a salad with blue cheese and white grapes. He called for steak and three side dishes. Daniel always demanded more than he could consume. He was a small boy that way, greedy.

The sun bounced back at me from the bottom of the water glass and detonated a burst of joy in my brain. I couldn't keep from smiling. The glass was like a swimming pool, a miniature crystal swimming pool set on the table before us. The freedom of water, this vessel of captured sunlight – suddenly I felt gloriously, childishly high. We could've been in the south of France, the pair of us. We could've been two giants looking down on a pool in the south of France.

I sat back the better to take it all in. The starched linen tablecloth, the glinting silverware, the explosions of sunlight in the glass, the beautiful man before me with the tiger stripes in his eyes. The brilliance of everything, the heat on my face, the exhilaration of the onset of a better season – I grasped Daniel's fingers and pulled him into a kiss.

The wind rose and lifted the tablecloth. My napkin was swept from my knee. The porcelain vase overturned and burbled water. A crash behind us as one of the potted standard bay trees toppled. This surge in the energy of things – our kiss had initiated it. I laughed. Daniel didn't. 'Christ,' he muttered as his tie flipped over his shoulder. A fly landed on the tablecloth, insets of peacock-blue lacquer on its glossy black back. I had never perceived beauty in a fly before.

'Did you get your violin insured?'

'Yeah, of course. I took care of it this morning.'

He stroked my hand. 'How much is it worth?'

'It's not for sale. Daniel, I love you so much, you make me so happy. Let's just go.'

'Go where?'

'Let's go to France. The Riviera, Cannes, the Côte d'Azur. Let's just pack up this weekend and do it.' I knew I was talking nonsense. I didn't care.

'Yeah,' he said, in a way that meant no.

'Your job is killing you. Nobody should have to live like this. Is it really worth it? We could sell up here and buy a house in Peru, and still have enough left over to live well for the rest of our lives. We'll work on your uncle's horse ranch, how about that? We'll breed show jumpers for export to the States and Europe. Or we could set up a music school and teach local kids how to play. I'll get a suntan and be as brown as you. Why have you gone so quiet?'

'I was just thinking about how we never got around to visiting your beautiful Eyrie.'

'Air ah.'

He smiled. 'I know.' He raised my fingers to his lips. 'You're a very special person, Eva. I want you to always remember that.'

I took back my hand. I didn't like his words. It was the kind of thing you said to someone you wouldn't see again. It was the kind of thing my father should have told me before walking out.

The waitress brought our order and we ate in silence, a silence so telling I was fighting tears by the end of it. After thirty minutes or so, Daniel left to return to work. He wouldn't allow me to walk him to the office. We hugged goodbye on a street corner and somehow our sternums collided. That had never happened before. I caught the subway back to his apartment, having altogether forgotten to tell him my good news about the Weintraub lawsuit.

Patrice smirked as we passed on the stairs ('Cute dress, girl-friend'). A fuming cat howled at me when I got in the door. There was a turd in the violin case, a hard dry cat turd. Ming's dirty protest. Her litter tray hadn't been cleaned out in two days.

I couldn't face dealing with it, so just shut the lid. I ran-sacked Daniel's bedside drawer. No more credit card receipts. His passport was there, however. The big fuck-off presence of an American passport, full of unspecified threats about the constitutional rights of its citizens, as if they were more pre-cious than regular human beings. The eagle glared unseeingly at nothing, just like Daniel.

I flicked to the visa page and read the latest entry. 11 April. Buenos Aires, it said, not Dublin.

I flew to Dublin to surprise you, Eva.

Only you didn't.

And I fell for it.

I packed up my belongings. I didn't have to think about it, just rolled up my sleeves and got to work. There wasn't much since I'd only been there five days. One suitcase, one violin case, one Miu Miu box in a Barneys bag. I stacked them by the door and took down Ming's carry case. 'That's it,' I told her. 'We're out of here.'

As if on cue, my cell rang. It was him. 'We need to talk,' I said, as though I'd made the call.

'Where are you?'

'Your apartment. We need to talk about your passport.'

'What about my passport?'

'We need to talk about why it says you went to Buenos Aires last weekend when you told me you'd gone to Dublin.'

'Okay.' Calm as you like. Seems he'd been expecting it. 'I'll meet you in an hour.' He named a restaurant on West Sixty-second Street, and told me he'd be there at four.

At ten past four, I entered the restaurant, but was informed by the host that Mr Jackson had yet to arrive. I took a seat at the bar and ordered a pomegranate margarita.

At twenty past four, I called Daniel's cell. 'Where are you?' It wasn't like him to be late.

'Don't move, sweetheart – something came up here. I'll be there in ten, promise.' I signalled for another margarita.

At twenty to five, I tried him again. He didn't answer this time. That pissed me off, knowing he was ignoring my name flashing on the screen display. *Princess calling . . . Princess calling . . .* Princess, he'd decided, could wait.

I dialled his work number. Never call me at work, he'd said. A woman picked up.

'Daniel Jackson doesn't work here anymore.'

'Since when?'

'His employment was terminated two weeks ago.'

'*Terminated?*'

She didn't respond.

'Did something happen?'

She said she couldn't discuss it for legal reasons.

'But I'm his girlfriend,' I pleaded, as if that made any odds. She said she was very sorry, but that I should really speak to Daniel.

'Oh God, please tell me,' I implored her, 'please tell me what's going on. Oh sweet Jesus, I need to know what's happening.'

I must have sounded pitiful, because she took pity on me. 'He's being charged with embezzlement,' she whispered, then hung up.

I sat there for a few seconds with my hand over my mouth. It was my father who instantly came to mind. The secrecy, the lying. Something terrible was about to unfold.

I ran out to hail a cab. The host ran out after me. I hadn't paid for my drinks. 'I'm so sorry,' I told him. 'I've just had a shock.'

I took out my last few tens but knew I'd need cash for a cab, so I had to go back inside and do the palaver with the credit card machine. As I waited for the receipt to print, I suddenly saw the plot. Sending me to a restaurant fifty blocks uptown: throwing a stick for a dog, then absconding while the dog runs to retrieve it. Daniel was diverting me from his apartment.

Why?

So that he could pick up his stuff. So that he would have a head start. By the time I came on the scene, he'd have disappeared.

Disappeared. It was happening again.

I raced after him anyway. I told myself there was a chance. If I can just find him, I thought, I'll be able to change his mind.

I ran down to Columbus Circle. Rush hour, every last cab taken. I rang Daniel's cell again, and again he didn't pick up. This time I left a message. 'Don't do this,' I urged him. 'I know about the job. Nothing is as bad as it seems right now. If you can just hold on for a bit, things will work out, I promise.' Then my battery died.

I stood in the middle of the traffic lanes, waving at the cabs that swerved around me. There was nothing I could do. There was literally nothing that I could do. It was so bad as to be inconceivable. Daniel had probably been watching the door of his building, and run in the moment I'd run out. I'd run out over an hour and a half ago. You could cover a lot of ground in an hour and a half. The time for freaking out was long past. I freaked out all the same.

Eventually a cab stopped. 'Thank you,' I gulped at the driver. Five fifteen, read his dashboard clock. I was all but shaking by then. We took off and I wheezed on my inhaler. It was so good to be in the cab. Calamity was ahead, but in the meantime I had this journey, this period during which my hands were tied.

'Why are we stopped?' I asked the driver.

237

'Crash.'

'No!'

'Yes.'

I actually laughed. Nothing for it so, but to let it happen. I slumped into the seat. All over this city there were agents of fate, and then there were the puppets. I was one of the puppets. I was dangled by others on the ends of strings. Any impression of autonomy was an illusion.

I monitored my protracted progress on the grid-map pinned to the taxi partition as we made our way along Fifty-seventh. I was right there in the middle of the map, but it was nothing like the street outside. I looked at the street, and it was about as abstract as the map. I couldn't respond to it. I had disengaged. It was the weirdest feeling in the world, after the months of fraught activity and scheming, to accept that free will was gone. I was just this little point in space travelling towards that little point in space. And Daniel was another little point in space, moving away. I was powerless to stop him. Whatever awaited me in his apartment was a fait accompli.

There was a message from the mayor of NYC warning me not to smoke. But did the mayor of NYC still have jurisdiction over me? I couldn't feel his authority. I was no longer a constituent of NYC; I was a plaything of fate. Different committee. There was a box of Marlboros on the dashboard and I asked the driver to give me one. He eyeballed me in the rear view mirror and I eyeballed him back. We sized each other up in silence. Then he held out the carton. I took a cigarette and stuck it between my lips. The driver stuck one between his.

We drove through a set of lights like that, the cigarettes jutting out of our mouths like bomb-fuses. The driver rummaged in his glove compartment. His hand came up, and he flicked open an old army lighter. I leaned into the flame and lit my cigarette, and thanked him through an exhalation of smoke. He nodded and lit his own.

We proceeded crosstown at a grandly slow pace. I'd have gotten there faster by walking. But playthings of fate didn't get out and walk. Not unless they were made to. I sat back and let the traffic decide when I would get to Daniel's. The traffic decided that I'd be seriously late.

Carnegie Hall passed by on the right-hand side. I rolled down the window and flicked my cigarette butt at it. I huffed on my Ventolin (running low). We turned onto the vista of Fifth. A rust-coloured moon had crested the skyline, though it was still bright out. Dust in the air: Tomorrow would be fine. It would be another fine day in New York City. So what? Who cared? Not me. I shut my eyes. The cab was roomy and comfortable. Time passed. I was calm.

At five past six, the taxi pulled onto Daniel's corner, and the city reasserted itself around me with a roar. I became aware of a siren that might have been blaring for some time. New York was a place to be evacuated at speed. I paid the driver and steeled my nerves, let myself into the building and began the steep climb to Daniel's door.

Patrice was not lurking around. That was the first bad sign. The salon was closed, but the lights were still on. It flashed into my mind that something terrible had happened, that they'd all rushed out in haste. But no, it was Friday evening. Patrice always took them for a staff drink at this time.

Not until I reached the top of the stairs did the other prospect dawn on me – that Daniel, unknowable, inaccessible Daniel, might have despaired. He might have taken his own life. *You're a very special person, Eva. I want you to always remember that.*

Everything about the building immediately corroborated this possibility. The numb silence, the more powerful than usual smell of gas, the absence of Patrice. I faltered at Daniel's door, thinking, I can walk away, this is not something I need to see. I can call the cops and get them to go in first.

I knocked. Not a sound. No movement in the sliver of light beneath the door. I wanted to run away, but I wasn't my father. I took a deep breath and turned the key.

Daniel would have favoured a violent death. In my heightened state of fear, I was sure I heard a rope creak. 'Baby?' Ming blinked at me from the sofa. She was purring quietly, submissively, the way she did when getting her injections: Please stop, I'm being good, don't hurt me anymore.

I scooped her up and held her tightly. She was a big solid cat. We crept towards the bedroom. I'd left the door open, but it had since been shut. I knocked. 'Sweetheart? Are you in there? Daniel?'

Nothing. I pushed down the handle.

The bedroom was empty. So was the wardrobe. So was the bedside drawer.

A phone pierced the silence and I jumped. Ming sprang out of my arms to dive for cover. I recognized the ringtone. Daniel's cell. For a very stupid moment, I thought he was back. But no, there was his phone in the fruit bowl. I seized it.

'Hello? Daniel?'

Spanish. A man, shouting.

'I don't understand you!' I shouted back.

An abrupt silence, then more Spanish.

'I don't speak Spanish!' I roared and hung up. Thirty-two missed calls, the screen display indicated.

The place had been looted, plundered like a tomb. I ran around the apartment, turning on all the lights, opening all the doors, screaming Daniel's name, until I found myself back in the living room.

He was gone.

As was another thing.

My violin case. I sank down on my knees.

I was still on my knees gaping at the case's absence when I realized an asthma attack was underway. I scrambled across to my bag for my inhaler. Two sprays and it was empty, but that was okay, that was fine. I knew not to panic. I had started taking extra precautions. Had to, with the state of my lungs of late. I'd committed to always carrying a spare.

I kept this spare where I'd have access to it no matter where in the world I was, whether day or night. I'd pointed it out to Daniel. I'd said, Hey Daniel, switch off the TV a minute and let me show you this. If I ever get an asthma attack and you can't find an inhaler, this is where to look. There'll always be a spare Ventolin right here, in the rosin compartment of my violin case . . .

Things were pretty serious by then. I emptied my bag onto the floor and picked up my phone. Battery dead. I crawled onto the landing and was hit by the wall of gas. On the top stair I collapsed.

Ming came out to hazard a look at the big bad world. She

stuck a gentle paw in my face and mewed, then tiptoed hesitantly down the stairs.

All sorts of things passed through my mind.

That the original betrayal, that of my father's disappearance, had in no way prepared me for subsequent betrayals.

That Ming had just escaped and would be run over on the street.

That I should've gone into that church that time, lit a penny candle while I had the chance.

That I'd never have gotten over Kryštof anyway. I wished I'd picked a name for our baby.

That my father didn't disappear; he'd jumped off the cliff. It was suicide, it was despair. I could search all I liked.

Footsteps below. I opened my eyes. Someone had entered the building.

'Hello, pretty kitten. I'm sure you shouldn't be down here.'

Patrice must've heard me gasping for breath, because he booted up the stairs and grabbed me. He had an inhaler to hand. Of course Patrice had an inhaler to hand. Should've known a weak chest when I saw one. He administered some Ventolin to me, and then to himself, and we both gulped air in relief.

The attack subsided, but I felt not the slightest compulsion to get up. I'd had it with this city, I'd battled long enough. So we lay there at the top of the stairs, Patrice and I in each other's arms, me listening to his heartbeat, him stroking my hair, and he talked and talked as he waited for me to collect myself. Anything that entered his head, out it popped, no matter how silly, no matter how trivial, just to keep a patter going and counteract what had almost happened. His mother this, his sister that, his ex-wife the other (Patrice was married? Patrice was straight?), his receptionist Tina, who in the end he'd had to fire.

'Tina?' I whispered.

'I know, I feel so bad.'

'You called me by that name once.'

'Oh hey, sorry, girlfriend. You're way cuter than her.'

Ming had returned by then. She climbed onto Patrice's lap and demanded that her belly be rubbed. He was so kind to us. I had given up on the subsistence of kindness in that building. He insisted I keep his inhaler, said he'd a whole bunch downstairs.

I told him I always kept a spare in my violin case, but that my violin case was, well, gone. Patrice nodded his head vigorously at that – yeah, he'd seen Daniel leaving with it about a half-hour after I'd left. He thought that was weird, Daniel leaving with my violin. I turned around and looked into his face.

'Were there other women, Patrice, coming up here when I wasn't around?'

'Are you kidding me? Why would he need other women when he had a girl like you?'

After a while, he helped me to my feet and I thanked him and went back into the apartment. Unsettling, being there, knowing it was no longer Daniel's place. No point in even trashing it.

The cell phone was ringing. That Spanish guy again, repeating the same phrase over and over, as if I would miraculously comprehend. 'Fuck off,' I told him, and hung up. Daniel had once described to me how they could pinpoint you by satellite once you were carrying a cell phone. He really got off on that kind of stuff. He said they could even programme a nuclear missile to target your exact location. Or the phone's location, rather. That's why he'd left it behind. So that I couldn't track him down. So that I couldn't blow him off the face of the earth.

I placed his phone on the kitchen floor and smashed it with the heel of my shoe. I stamped on it until it splintered into shards. A note was stuck to the fridge door by a magnet. I'd never seen his handwriting before, and it lacked grace.

'I'M SORRY MY IRLANDESA,' it read in block capitals. 'CLAIM IT OFF INSURANCE. DANIEL.'

DANIEL.

NAILED.

'You fuck,' I told the note. 'It isn't insured. I lied.'

243

Celebra il Vilanel . . .

The peasant celebrates . . .

from
L'Autunno, Autumn
Le Quattro Stagioni, The Four Seasons
—Vivaldi

A couple of days' grace in Sandpiper, then the first nocturnal storm knocks us off course. An almighty barrage of them after that, striding full blast off the Irish Sea like Colossus. A wind that'd put the fear of God into you, wind that might well lift the roof. The rain spits against the windowpane like hailstones; sleep is impossible in these conditions. Anguished cries arise in the intermittent lulls – cats screaming? Foxes? Is it the right time of year? The lighthouse starkly illuminates the terrible scene like lightning, revealing . . . Well, that's just it. Revealing nothing.

On the night of the first storm I raced downstairs, shoved my feet into my father's shoes, stumbled outside and rattled the bolt to the stable door. Now I don't leave the house anymore. I watch the garden from my bedroom window, spellbound by this turbulent panorama; the tree canopies swaying like sea-grass, the bay peaked like a mountain range, the stable door slamming time and time again against the house. Or not slamming, as the case may be. I can hear it, but I can't prove it. The stable is screened from my window by trees.

And then in the morning, serene as Bach. A lemony haze over the long lawn as the dew burns off. The garden flush with a million tiny motions; butterfly wings, the dispersal of pollen, petals yielding to the sun. The storms are not finished, though. They bide their time out at sea, returning when darkness returns. I don't know what's happening while my eyes are closed.

Preliminary matutinal investigations disclosed the following:
    Phone-line down, electricity not.
    The wisteria trained against our boundary wall now broken.

As if somebody scaled the wall. Jumped down. Approached the house.

A widespread desecration of my mother's flowers. The last of the camellia blossoms, sprinkled across the lawn. Peonies, alliums, rhododendrons, the roses – stems snapped, buds broken off. The fleshy petals of late tulips bent back on themselves like fingernails. Could this be solely the work of the wind? Something says no.

A tree branch alien to our garden in the centre of the lawn. Dead in the centre. The wind? The wind doesn't favour symmetry. Something still says no.

A footprint, a man's footprint. Oh God, a whole set, crossing the dewy lawn to the stable and back. Back to the house – my heart, the terror – where is he now? I look around wildly. But wait, they're my own prints, made whilst hurrying out to the stable in my father's shoes during the night.

I beat back nettles with the handle of the kitchen brush. There is solace in the work. I am much rewarded for my efforts, uncovering evidence of anti-social activity in the tunnel onto the beach. Spliffs, beer cans, a mouldering condom. By the gate, a circle of scorched stones.

The padlock, which at a glance appears locked, falls apart in my hands. The gate screeches open of its own accord, and I sense the very definite presence of the dead. A smuggler, a shipwrecked sailor, the ghost of my father. It is always chilly in the tunnel.

I step out onto the blindingly bright beach and kick back the ridge of high-tide seaweed. Small flies rise out of it, and a mighty smell. Upon closer inspection, the evidence of anti-social activity in the tunnel is old. The work of last summer's teenagers, is all.

Bray Head still there, though some latitudes south of where expected.

The stable? Tricky one. Untouched, as far as I can discern. The contents of the stable, also untouched.

My mother: quite oblivious to it all. 'What storm?' she says.

'What noises?' This, from the light sleeper. Is she on pills? Will she share them?

Not a conclusive list, I agree. Taken as a whole, all it confirms is my paranoia. Until we get to:

The aforementioned man's shoes, discovered and borrowed by me in the middle of the night, now gone. From *inside* the door.

The skin on the back of my neck tingles. Someone is up to no good.

At seven Irish time on a pleasant Sunday evening, Alexander's deadline elapsed. A crescent of yachts was scattered across the sound, the dwarf birches trembled green amongst the heather. Did the pallbearers deal him another black eye, I wonder? Did he lose another digit? Gain another stump? No doubt the real story of how he lost that finger is mundane.

It would take Alexander longer than this to track me down though, surely. Not that he won't track me down, just that it would take him longer than this. Nor would he dither about in a herbaceous border. It won't be flower stems he breaks. When Alexander is on my doorstep, I'll know.

Ming. Poor Ming-Ming, in her cage in the wall of cages. We drive out to visit her each day, Mum and I. 'Oh look at her little face,' Mum exclaimed when first she saw it. 'Oh look at her exquisite little face. Wouldn't that just break your heart?'

Ming can't understand why I don't seem to care about her anymore. Wasn't she brave and loyal? Didn't she love me so fiercely that her small heart nearly burst? When had she ever given less than her best? And yet I leave her behind in this loveless place day after day. The unfortunate creature has to endure the quarantine for a full six months because I forgot to pack her vaccination cert.

What possessed me to inflict this on her? I could've dropped her off at Kryštof's. I won't get the same cat back. She looks old, all of a sudden. The fur around her chin is turning beardy

249

and grey. She might well die before her release date. It's been a horrible year for her as well. And her years are cat years. Seven horrible years. She peers in tight-lipped horror into the other cages, the way my grandmother peered at the other patients when she was taken to the hospice to die.

Phone lines restored. A call to Zach. He hasn't yet spotted my absence. He launches into a progress report on the Weintraubs. They've dropped the case.

'That's great,' I say.

'You don't sound like you think it's great.'

'No, I do, really. Just, I don't know.'

'What?'

'I don't know. Nothing. I keep thinking about the Maestro, that's all.'

'Yeah, it's so sad. At his age.'

'Zach, I was there when the first stroke hit him. He was standing beside me and he sort of reared up, and I immediately knew something had happened in his brain.'

Silence, much silence. It is a delicate matter. I look out the window and think of our voices soaring across the heavens. Finally Zach speaks, slowly and kindly, as if addressing a child.

'Eva, the Maestro didn't have a stroke. It was suicide.'

I slam down the phone as fast as I can. But not fast enough. Something has escaped into the room.

The weird weather continues, no longer confined to night. Bright hot sun, then heavy purple clouds, followed by rain, sheets of it. A clap of thunder, another. Then the bright hot sun again, the rain steaming off the ground. The sky is moving too fast. The sea won't commit to one colour.

I take myself down to the local hardware to replace the rusting padlocks. I recognize the boy behind the counter from my class in primary school, though he's not a boy anymore. I pretend not to know him and he pretends not to know me, as if we've changed so much that the adult is no longer discernible from the child, when the absolute converse is blatantly the case. We are so like our fumbling childhood selves, it is comical.

His name is Declan. He looks good. He was a good-looking kid. He discusses my security options knowledgeably, as if he is a real grown-up. I listen to him, nodding, as if I am a real grown-up too. I frown over the choices, then go with his recommendation, coming out of his shop with two fine locks. One for the tunnel gate, one for the stable door. These are attractive objects, heavy and tactile. I open and close them both a number of times, admiring and enjoying the precision of the click.

I present a set of keys to my mother for the tunnel gate, but not the stable. She is not interested in the contents of the stable, she maintains.

There's a general air of disrepair in the house. Things are growing in the drains, the guttering. The cherry blossom shuddered off its flowers in a shower of warm snow. The pale pink petals quickly turned orange-brown and filled up the drains, the guttering. I make another call to Zach.

'Things hurt,' I blurt, I don't know why. It wasn't what I intended saying. In fact, now that I have him on the line, I've no idea why I called him in the first place.

He knows after the Maestro thing not to crack a joke. 'What do you mean?'

'I don't know. Ordinary people sitting in a room, they look like they're doing nothing, but what if they're in pain?'

'I'm sure they're not in pain.'

'But how do you *know*? How can you *tell*?'

'Is this about the Maestro?'

'No. Maybe.'

'Where are you, Eva? What's that sound? No one's seen you in ages.'

'I'm in my garden.'

'What garden?'

'At home. I was swimming earlier. It was freezing.'

'You're in Ireland.' A statement, not a question.

'Yes. I've moved back.'

'Jesus fucking –'

I put the phone down on him again, then continue on my rounds, rattling window latches, checking locks. You can never be too careful.

My mother is asleep in a deck chair, her mouth wide open as if dead. Daniel. If he had an ugly name, would I think of him as much?

We built a monument to my father in the immediate wake of his disappearance. I tried to tell Daniel about it once, on one of those waterlogged moments when he said, 'What's wrong?' and I replied, 'Nothing,' and he took me at my word. One morning, about ten days after my father went missing, I awoke to the sound of dragging.

I crept into my parents' bedroom. Empty, bed unmade. Back out to the landing to lean over the banister. My mother was hauling my father's escritoire along the corridor, his paper-weight and pen caddy still on top of it.

'Grab the other end,' she said when she saw me. We carried it out through the French doors, the contents of the drawers rolling around inside. The glass paperweight slid off and exploded on the steps. The pens scattered everywhere.

It was a warm breezy morning and I blinked at what had taken place while I'd slept. She had to have been on the go since six. The lawn was full of my father's possessions. I can't explain how startling it was to see these familiar domestic items laid out on grass. Things I'd grown up around – his reclining chair, now under the crab apple tree, his standard lamp by the fuchsia, his occasional table and revolving globe book-ending the blue hydrangea. It was as if the roof had been lifted off the house, or the carpet replaced with grass. We set down the escritoire by the holly bush and stood back. I mean it: I cannot explain how odd these objects looked in the full

252

glare of the sun. Almost as odd as Sandpiper looked without them.

'Get dressed,' said my mother, and I went upstairs and pulled on a T-shirt and jeans. 'Here.' She handed me a bottle when I came out. 'Put that on.' Sunscreen. 'And tie back your hair.' I hitched it into a ponytail. You'd think we were off to a picnic.

The removals continued for maybe another two hours. He'd accumulated so much stuff.

Books, mainly antiquarian. We lugged them out in stacks and boxed them.

His coin and medal collection. She thought that was sad. A grown man collecting coins and medals was sad. Out they went with a jangle.

His stuffed animals. They'd always given her the creeps. We released them back into their natural habitat.

His records. All Elvis, except for the Mario Lanza. You couldn't say a word against Elvis, though I could tell she wanted to. Not because she disliked Elvis, but because they were my father's.

His yachting photographs. We unhitched them from the wall, exposing pale rectangles.

The family holiday snap on the mantelpiece. The three of us smiling in the Barbadian sun. 'Oh come on,' I said, 'can't we at least keep this?'

My mother regarded the photo, and I detected a momentary softening. Then she took back the frame, and into the box with it.

The last thing to exit was the contents of his wardrobe. His clothes, hangers still intact, followed by a bin-bag of shoes. She dumped them onto his recliner. Fortunately, my father disappeared during a dry spell. It was the only convenient thing about his departure. We sat down at the kitchen table and ate cornflakes in silence.

'Right,' my mother said decisively, as if the next step had only then become clear. 'We need to empty the stable.'

253

So we dragged the contents of the stable into the garage. The stable hadn't been used during our tenure of Sandpiper, not by a pony anyway. It was full of rubbish – newspapers, magazines, my old cot and pram, a broken lawnmower, a Belfast sink. The sink, used by the previous owners as a feeding trough, was too heavy for us to shift, which is why it's there still. I insisted on sweeping the place out before loading it up again. The corrugated perspex roof too – I ran the brush along it and all kinds of dry matter rained down. My mother would've been happier had the dry matter been left intact. It would've garnered her more satisfaction.

I snapped a desiccated wasp nest off the wall and desiccated wasps tumbled out. I'd have hosed the place down given the chance; I wasn't. I stood in the doorway when finished, coughing and surveying the glinting objects on the lawn. They still looked so bizarre.

'They aren't all going to fit in the stable,' I pointed out.

My mother threw me a look: They would be made to fit.

We started with the big things. The recliner, the escritoire, the suitcases, the boxed-up books. These formed the bottom layer. The irregularly shaped items went next. There was an abundance of those. A rifle, cameras, editing equipment, a drawing board. Solitary pursuits of every nature. At the top, we placed the heads, the dusty stuffed animals. The hare looked on in alarm, the fox snarled defensively. The heron, being tall, had to lie for all eternity on her side.

We regarded the monument from the doorway. We had not, in fairness, done much of a job – already it inclined dangerously forward. Although we had stacked it, it seemed like something my father had constructed himself. A shell he'd discarded, a husk. I wondered after the contents of the suitcases, the escritoire drawers. They must've contained clues as to what had gone wrong in his head. My mother had buried them the deepest. It'd take another afternoon's work to unearth them again.

I cleared my throat. 'It's going to fall.'

She shrugged. Let it.

'Did he keep a diary?'

'Don't you think I thought of that?'

'What about his papers?'

'What about them?'

'There must've been something there.'

'There wasn't. I checked.' She reached for the door.

'What about that shirt?' I nodded at the old white cotton shirt on her back. She used it for gardening. 'That's his too.'

My mother tore off the shirt, balled it up, and threw it at the heap. It caught on the leg of the drawing board. 'Happy now?'

Ecstatic. She slammed the door and padlocked the bolt before the whole thing came tumbling down. And that was the end of it, I didn't have a key.

My last hour in New York, and the Aer Lingus ground stewards are a comforting sight in their turquoise green. Standing in the sales-desk line is a patriotic experience. Here amongst the other nationalities, these passengers stand out as Irish. I couldn't pick them out individually on the street, but as a collective they are familiar. If you took away the airline signs, I'd still gravitate towards my own – we are the pinkest. I feel all the better just for seeing them, us. I purchase a one-way ticket home.

I call my mother before checking in. It is a garbled conversation that achieves nothing but mutual distress. 'I'm coming home,' I announce brightly, and Ming howls like a creature possessed. 'Do you want anything in the Duty Free?'

By the time I replace the receiver, Ming is emitting a noise like a record being played too slowly. Her projection is impressive, as good as Magdalena. People are doing double-takes on the carry-case. 'Rosemary's Baby,' says a man. I haul her over to the seats and place the case on my knee. 'Please stop,' I beg the little caged face. I could never be a mother.

Eye contact is a mistake. Once Ming sees she has my attention, she redoubles her efforts. The noise blasts out of the box

255

like heat. I put the box on the ground and bite my knuckle. I am unable to deal with a cat.

I arrive in Dublin and am relieved of my possessed cat at customs. I am almost glad to see her go. Hysteria pitch had carried over to the other side of the Atlantic. I'd never known her to smell like that before. The relief of her absence is immediately replaced by guilt. She is all on her own now. In a small nose-and-paw-proof container on her own. Who will console her? How will I cope without her?

I come through the Arrivals Gate feeling way too light. I have just the suitcase and the Barneys bag. No cat, no violin case. My mother is waiting for me behind the barrier, and I realize then that I couldn't have faced the Arrivals Hall without her.

We converge on the exit to my left. I hug her, surprised at how small she is. I keep expecting her to be taller than me, I keep expecting her to feel the way she felt when I was ten. 'They took away my cat,' I tell her, like that says it. Then I start to cry.

I cry all the way home, worse than Ming. My mother knows better than to ask any questions. I go straight to bed and sleep until lunchtime. When I wake, I ask her for the key to the stable. In fact, I don't ask. I just say, 'I need the key to the stable.' She hands it over, no stonewalling.

I swing open the stable door and regard the full aspect of the monument for the first time in nearly eight years. During my absence, it had assumed towering proportions in my head, but when I unlock the door it shrinks down again, the way my mother did in the airport.

There has been a minor subsidence – the coin collection, for the most part, is on the floor – but not the major collapse we'd anticipated. A few strands of honeysuckle have crept in through a crack and are already in bloom, though the parent plant is not. It is a different climate in the stable, a different country.

I step forward and add my contribution to the Republic of

Dad. I lay it there like a flower on his grave as if to say, Hey, guess what, I'm a chip off the old block. I'm as hopeless as you are, I've run away too. Here you go. I shove it in alongside the reclining heron: the Barneys bag. The Miu Miu box is inside. I add it to the monument as a symbol of my folly.

Then I close the door. Padlock the bolt. Face the house. From the kitchen window, my mother pretends not to be watching.

Two million. There it is on the Internet. The amount Daniel is accused of embezzling. The amount he instructed me to insure the violin for. It says he's done a runner. He's a wanted man, all right.

Difficulty detaching Ming from my shoulder this afternoon. No sooner is one claw unhooked than the other catches hold. No sooner is that paw unhitched than the first one is reattached. All four limbs splay and paddle as I bundle her back into the cage. She is as ungainly as a set of bagpipes, and just as tough on the ear.

'She's quite a character,' the attendant concedes as the paw shoots out through the prison bars, catching the hem of my T-shirt. We start the alternate nail-unhitching routine again. Definitely not cut out to be a mother. She'll be released in time for the Halloween bangers. Not even New York will have prepared her for that.

The man's shoes are back.

I hear noises again in the night, so downstairs I go. I steal along the corridor in the dark, listening, creeping, listening, creeping. Into the kitchen, and there they are by the back door, clearly visible in the moonlight. Thank God I've brought my inhaler.

The light shunts on blindingly. My mother, in her nightdress, appears by the fridge like a ghost. 'What are you doing out of bed?'

'Look!' I gasp, pointing at the shoes.

She sighs wearily. It's not quite the reaction I'm expecting. 'They're mine.'

I blink at the shoes. 'What?'

'They're mine. I leave them by the door to deter thieves. I don't want people knowing I'm alone in the house.'

Oh. 'Oh.'

'Go back to bed.' She turns toward the door.

'Mum?'

'What?'

'Where's the note?' It has occurred to me that at this hour, at our age, barriers might be down.

She turns back from the door, squinting. The light is hurting her eyes too. 'What note?' As if she has to ask.

'The note Dad left the night he disappeared.'

'There was no note.'

'He must've left something.'

'He didn't.'

She's lying, I know it. She's been lying all this time. It's supposed to be an attempt to protect me, I understand, but it's got to stop. My frustration is tempered by the awkwardness of the situation. Her in her nightdress, me in mine, four white feet on the cold tiled floor. She shivers, the fridge groans, I'm making erratic gestures with my hands. 'Mum, I had hoped, you know . . . I'm an adult now. It's clear Dad's never coming back, so why don't you just tell me?'

I had plundered every drawer, every shoebox, every cupboard for his note. I'd found their love letters, their Valentine cards, their most intimate keepsakes, but no note. I believed he'd written one. I couldn't believe he hadn't.

She looks hard at me and fear rises. She's about to spring something on me, something I don't want to hear. Some information she's bottled up for years. *They eventually found his body. The sea had destroyed his face. I couldn't find a way to tell you.*

'Go back to bed,' she says instead.

'Tell me.'

'Jesus, tell you what? I know no more than you know. There was no note. He didn't bother leaving one.'

She turns out the light, leaving me standing beside the man's shoes in darkness. For the first time in my life, it occurs to me that she might be telling the truth. This thought is so ground-breaking that I have to stand there for some time. I huff on my inhaler. *My mother might actually be telling the truth*. She might actually have been telling the truth all along. She might actually know no more than I know.

The summer wears on. I peer into rock pools in search of lost treasure. The sea anemones retract into glossy cherries when the tide goes out. I can't remember whether they sting or not, so I prod at them with stalks of seaweed. I knock limpets off with stones. I overturn rocks in pursuit of crabs. Something is being triggered in me, some old longing. I move sleeping bees off bridle-paths so they won't be stepped on, though I know they're not sleeping really; they're dying. Many bees fall asleep in inappropriate places at this time of the year. It's a worry.

A loud bang then. I turn to look in the direction of the island. A flare has been set off. Trouble at sea.

The postman rings the bell, and there's much ado at the door. My mother belts up the stairs to my bedroom. She sets a box in my lap and stands back, waiting for me to open it. US stamps. I recognize the grace of the handwriting and tear the package open. My silk and chiffon concert dresses are inside, enfolded in tissue paper. Valentina has taken pains.

The rest of my belongings are to follow surface mail, her note says. She is moving to Paris with Kryštof in November. If I want either of their old apartments, I just have to say. They'll be travelling around India first. I miss you, her note also says. 'I miss you, Eva, and I am deeply sorry about how things turned out.' I read over this bit time and time again, feeling it keenly, the loss of my best friend.

My mother enthuses as I lay the dresses on the bed. She is

nearly as taken with them as she is with Ming. I pull the green one out of my suitcase and add it to the pile. We decide, after much debate, to take the plunge and hand-wash them. I'd always wondered whether the incessant dry-cleaning was actually necessary, but I didn't want to take a chance. 'They're silk,' my mother keeps saying, holding up the labels and making me read them in case I don't believe her. 'See? They say 100 per cent silk. Our dresses were silk when I was a girl and nobody bothered with dry-cleaning then.'

They are tiny when wet. They ball up like kittens on the palm of my hand. I wash them one by one and rinse them in the bath. It is another warm day. They dry quickly on the line. I suppose they're destined for the stable, too. Not yet, though. Tomorrow. I will fold them back up in Valentina's tissue paper and lay them on the monument tomorrow.

The green one I leave for last. It looks almost botanical, a specimen the garden has grown. I watch it dance lightly, compulsive as a ghost, bewitched by the girl I used to be. Sometimes I miss my father so much, but what's worse is that now I miss myself.

I know it's all over when my mother says she wants me to meet a friend of hers. 'I'm a widow,' she tells me. 'You'll like him.' I won't.

'You're not a widow,' I counter.

Gerard is fine, he's inoffensive. I don't care enough to have an opinion one way or the other. Fifty-something, sports jacket, opens doors, pulls out chairs. It strikes me as a bit late in the day for the formal restaurant, the careful manners – he's been sleeping under our roof for months, possibly years. I'm on familiar terms with his shoes.

We shake hands in the car park, and my mother and I drive home without discussion. The matter doesn't require further discussion. It's been discussed in full without me.

The pair of us glare at the BBC Proms through poor reception. An eloquent rendition of *The Lark Ascending* by a beautiful young Englishwoman. 'She plays a fine new violin made by Claude Martel and Son of New York,' the commentator tells us over the applause. So Claude wasn't a total chancer. Magdalena could be a genuine del Gesù after all.

My mother frowns at me in suspicion. 'What's funny?'

The estate agents arrive to nail up their colours. Sandpiper is for sale. A second board is propped against the gatepost.

AUCTION OF THE ENTIRE CONTENTS
(ON THE PREMISES)
'SANDPIPER'
ANTIQUES/COLLECTIBLES, ETC., ETC.

Cars slow down as they pass to read it. 'Take anything you want,' my mother tells me, and I am irritated out of all proportion.

'Take it?' I query her. 'Take it *where*?'

A silver Mercedes was parked on our gravel for a full day. The auctioneer climbed out and sniffed the air, territorial, bloody-minded; he's been anticipating this carve-up for some time. His assistant shut the passenger door with such diffidence it hardly made a sound. The auctioneer snapped something and the two of them approached. They approached, they approached, I felt a bolt of pure dread. My mother click-clacked down the corridor and admitted them before I could tackle her to the floor. The auctioneer was brash and overbearing, his assistant could barely spit out a *hello*. It took them eight years, but they have finally penetrated our defences.

In a fortnight, every dog and devil will trudge through the door to size up our belongings. Despoiled, our home will be. The auctioneer and his lackey spent the afternoon in the stable, dismantling my father's monument into lots.

I stand at the kitchen window and stare at the garden. It is a lawn made for ascending. Sometimes I'm scared my father's bones will inch their way through the tunnel, strung together with seaweed. The endeavour of tracking him in my imagination will never be over. He has no clear lines anymore. I add a little more silver to his hair every year. His birthday came and went last Friday. I held my breath all day. I am holding it still. A fist of nerves in my stomach. When my father treks up the long lawn, it will be to strangers. My mother and I are almost gone.

She comes in from the garden, fresh cut roses on her arm. 'It's really quiet out there,' she says, 'really still.'

'Yeah.' It is. I know what she means. I know exactly what she means.

She brings the flowers to the console table, Lot 216, and inserts them into the Victorian jug, Lot 219, handle damaged. I listen to her snipping away at the stems. It will never be like this again. My mother is humming to herself gently, as if nothing is amiss.

I stand there holding onto the kitchen sink. I cannot feel my legs, I'm clinging on so tightly. The bay is a soft glorious haze. Ships on the horizon, a plane crossing the sky. The lighthouses along the coastline are calling out to one another across the waves, as if they just don't get that they will always be separated.

The long lawn is as inviting as ever. The rosebushes and hydrangeas are at their peak. Further down, but getting closer with every passing day, is the gorse, and the gorse, and the gorse.

Zach on the blower. The Carnegie Hall performance is in two and a half months, with the tour scheduled to commence directly after it. He needs to finalize contracts.

'Zach,' I sigh.

'Knock it off, Eva. Am I to replace you, or what?'

I am taken aback by this question, I really am. More than I have a right to be. 'Try Valentina.' Has she told him she's moving to Paris?

'Valentina could never cut it as a soloist, you know that.'

I know that. I tell him I'll call him in a couple of days. There's some stuff I need to sort out, I say.

~

Magdalena came to me last night. I woke up petrified because I was no longer alone in the room. I sat up in bed and there she was, kneeling before the window. Magdalena praying for me, praying for my sins. A red halo glowed above her head.

She was young, she was lovely, she had a smooth majestic bulk. Elegant, yet huge as a Roman statue, a Juno. Even on bended knee, she towered above me. If she sensed that I was watching her, she betrayed no awareness, so immersed was she in her supplications. It was almost a trance, an ecstasy. I dared not interrupt. Something sanctified was underway. Magdalena was interceding on my behalf. Her petitions demanded every resource she possessed. Has it come to this? I wondered. This young woman praying for my soul? Wasn't it supposed to be the other way around? Had I not been appointed to watch over her?

The glowing red halo became the digital numbers of my alarm clock, and I realized that Magdalena was not in the room, not really. The space before the window was bare. I lay back down. I still sensed that some good had been done. It wasn't until morning that I remembered Magdalena was not a woman, exactly. And that she was not exactly gone.

I laughed on the overnight flight from Kennedy airport back to Dublin. Surely I was not a woman in any position to laugh? I don't know about that. I had drifted off to the drone of engines, but came to laughing. I enjoyed this laugh as best I could, because I knew it'd only be funny for about three seconds, and that I may as well get the most out of them. Almost immediately, I started to cry.

The tears passed smoothly and I was inexplicably content once more. I didn't feel like myself. I felt like weather. I felt like a sky in which weather happens. Expressions tumbled across my face like clouds and sun, but they weren't properly developed emotions. They didn't penetrate further than my skin. Is that, I wonder, what it's like being Daniel?

I pulled myself into a sitting position and looked around. The movie was over, the cabin lights had been dimmed. After the meal, the mother across the aisle had wrestled her children into pyjamas and read them a bedtime story; now she and her children were fast asleep. I turned to the window. It was dark outside and I faced my reflection. We were over the Atlantic. Where was Daniel? The Pacific?

Hours earlier, the presence of malice in his apartment had been overwhelming. It had descended like a drop in temperature. NAILED, my eyes saw, and the ruthlessness conjured by that word was so corporeal that I sensed him standing right behind me. I gasped and whirled around. My ordeal was not over yet.

I stuffed Ming into her carry-case and grabbed the suitcase and Barneys bag. I was out of that building like a greyhound from a trap. Speed was key. I was scared to even stand on the kerb for long enough to hail a cab. I ran along Thirteenth, bumping little Ming against my leg. She howled, oh she howled. She never let up.

The taxi I climbed into took off downtown.

'Are we not taking the Midtown Tunnel?'

'No,' grunted the driver. 'Traffic's too bad.'

We left Manhattan via the Williamsburg Bridge. A JFK road sign flashed past, but the driver didn't take the exit indicated. He drove like it was a computer game, lurching between lanes until I wanted to puke. Each time a gap opened in an adjacent lane, he lunged into it, only to lunge back out again seconds later. I opened up the Miu Miu box and performed surgery on the contents. This procedure was accompanied by cat screams.

I raced through the airport building to the Aer Lingus sales-desk line. Ming was going off like an alarm. The security check left me shaking. Siddown, stand up, spread your legs, remove your shoes. An elderly lady undergoing the same ordeal was blushing terribly. The catch on her bra set the metal detector off, as did the fastener on the waistband of her slacks. She kept glancing over her shoulder, trying to locate her travelling companion, but no one came to her rescue.

Eventually they were done with us. I collected the Barneys bag from the X-ray machine chute and ran for the plane. In that bag was something that'd set no scanner off. Five hours earlier, I'd discovered the words 'Buenos Aires' on Daniel's passport. This evidence was so condemning that I packed my bags. I put Magdalena into the Miu Miu box because Ming had shat in the violin case. I put the Miu Miu box into the Barneys bag, and that's when he phoned. 'Meet me on Sixty-second Street in an hour,' he said.

I opened the box in the back of the cab and got to work on the violin. Nothing could delay our evacuation of the United States, lest Daniel catch up and nail us. I unwound the strings and yanked them out of the holes in the pegs, pocketed the bridge and tailpiece. It was like ripping out teeth, tearing toenails off with pliers. My violin was a numb, blunt, featureless thing when I was finished with it.

I discarded the strings in the back of the taxi and packed what was left in the box. Magdalena left America exactly as she'd entered it – bundled up, unannounced, and on the run. 'Like mice!' Alexander had bellowed. 'Stradivarius violence sneaking across Europe like mice!' I woke up laughing, though it still wasn't funny. Daniel had made off with the violin case. The old black leather violin case which, as soon as he deemed it a safe distance, he'd break open to discover that it did indeed belie the value of its contents. Nothing was inside. Well, almost nothing. A hard dry cat turd and my chipped inhaler.

I take the train into town to visit the old haunts. Expanses of sky everywhere – Dublin looks like a bomb has hit it. Nothing's been knocked down, though. No bomb has hit Dublin. I'm used to high-rise elevations, that's all. Used to New York. I miss it, sort of.

I get back on the Dart. Kids are sitting on a wall somewhere between Kilbarrack and Howth Junction, lined up to wave at the train. Small kids, six-year-olds. The row of skinny white shins makes me smile. We are past before I manage to wave back.

An old man lowers himself into the seat opposite. He's got to be in his eighties at least. He places a gift-wrapped box on the empty seat to his right, and reaches for it a second later, evidently worried that he's forgotten to bring it. He settles back into his seat upon its rediscovery, then starts again, reaches for the box again, settles back again.

This routine proves infectious. I find myself reaching for the case at my feet. Still there; I settle back. It is the finest violin case the merchants of Dublin had for sale. We will soon be on our way once more, Ming, Magdalena, and I, with the considerable proceeds of my share of Sandpiper. Claude seemed delighted to hear my voice. 'Okay, okay,' he affirmed, 'we do a full restoration soon. My boy, he will be so pleased.'

I close my eyes and sway to the rock of the tracks. All is well, for now. The train driver addresses us over the intercom in a powerful Dublin accent: 'Passengers are reminded that it is illegal to smoke on the Dart.'

'We can't hear you, son,' the old man calls.

Acknowledgements

A big thanks to the two violinists, Michael d'Arcy and Catherine Leonard, who were so generous with their time and knowledge throughout.

Further thanks to music director Nicholas McGegan, violin-maker Michiel de Hoog, Cornelius Keil & Christiane Linnartz of the Cologne Philharmonie, Karen Gilligan & The Miscarriage Association of Ireland, Cormac Brady, John Buckley, Maureen & James Doherty, James Finlan, Aoife Fitzpatrick, Marianne Gunn O'Connor, Mia Kilroy, Pat & Melanie McCaughey, Elizabeth MacDonald, Tina Pohlman, Justin Quinn, and to The Arts Council of Ireland, An Chomhairle Ealaíon, for their financial support.

A very special thanks to my editor at Faber and Faber, Angus Cargill, for the intelligence and insight he brought.